ONLY YOU

S. WILLIAMS

First published in 2020 by Bloodhound Books.

www.bloodhoundbooks.com

Print ISBN 978-1-913419-85-1

For Gill and Peter.

'I do not wish my heart to beat
Why should it beat?
It beats with neither my desire nor permission.'
Cathy

BLEA FELL HOUSE, NEW YEAR'S EVE, 1998

BELLA'S LAST DAY: DAWN

I wake up to the ticking of my bedside clock in the dark bedroom, and for the briefest of seconds I think everything is all right. I'm warm under the blanket and can feel the cold air of the room beyond.

And then I remember, and I know that everything is *not* all right, and nothing will be all right ever again. The breath catches in my chest; stuck. A flash of fear lightnings through me, pure and burning.

And then I remember what I've decided to do.

I need to get through the day, make it to the night, and see it through to the end.

Then everything will be all right.

Then everything can just stop.

I breathe, sucking in the cold air, and get out of bed.

1

PRESENT DAY

'Sorry, love, you can't smoke in here.'

The voice is harsh, the tone rough like a wooden floor that's been scrubbed after a fight.

Athene blinks, turns away from looking out at the brutal landscape beyond the café's window, and focuses on the woman speaking to her. Outside, the light has nearly been wiped from the sky, leaving the valley coloured in shades of green and black. The ancient analogue radio sitting on the counter is tuned to some local station, the signal fading in and out: the music barely there one second, then islanding itself out of white static the next.

'I'm sorry?' Athene raises her eyebrows.

The waitress – the *owner*, because there's no way the micro-café could support an extra wage, or possibly any – nods at Athene's table meaningfully. Athene looks down at the Lucky Strike soft pack of cigarettes, with a solitary unlit smoke sitting on the table's plastic surface, and the brass Zippo lighter. The pack has only been opened in one corner, the foil carefully sectioned and torn. There is also a small cup of espresso.

'No smoking, sorry,' the woman repeats. 'If you want to smoke, you'll need to go outside.'

Athene smiles apologetically, reading the woman's name tag pinned to her stained T-shirt, and reaches for the cup of coffee. Her hand is steady.

'No, it's okay, Mary. I don't need to go outside. I don't smoke.'

Athene takes a sip of her drink, staring at the black liquid, then lets her gaze wander back up to the woman. 'Is this your café?'

The woman's eyes linger on the pack of cigarettes on the table for a beat, her face a nest of confusion, then shrugs. She leans against the serving counter, letting it take the weight of her a little. Giving her feet a rest. She looks around the building slowly, and nods.

'Yep. Why, do you want to buy it?' she quips, but there is no humour there.

Athene picks up the cigarette and slides it back into the pack. The way Mary had looked around the café was the way a prisoner looked about their cell.

'Is it worth anything?' Athene says.

The woman smiles grimly.

'Not unless you want to work all the hours God gave you for no pay, take shit from the tourists – no offence – and then die here, in this valley, still owing on the mortgage.'

The look of Mary's face says it all: self-loathing, betrayal, loss.

Athene puts the pack of cigarettes, along with the Zippo, in the backpack by her chair. Outside, the early evening begins to fill with pre-rain, the drops of moisture making little ticking sounds as they hit the window pane of the café. The day has become noticeably darker, the light receding back across the valley.

'You make it sound so tempting, but I think I'll pass.' Athene gives a sympathetic grimace.

'Don't blame you,' Mary says.

Athene was not surprised the café was empty if this was the way she spoke to her customers.

She nods and drains the last of her coffee. The radio flares its static snow for a moment, drowning out the song, then falls silent. Both women look at it.

'Storm coming.' Mary's voice sounds suddenly very intimate in the stillness. Athene is the only patron. When she cocks her head, questioning, Mary nods first at the radio, then at the disappearing day beyond the window. Black swirls of rain are sifting from the clouds further down the valley. The green and the grey of the rugged landscape seem unnaturally bright in the thick muddy air. 'You can always tell. The signal goes to pot.'

Athene looks out at the valley. The café is situated high up, near the head, looking down over the dale. The landscape is a strange mixture of small pocket-fields, limestone outcrops, and moorland; like it is a junction between three different worlds. Athene feels butterflies in her stomach and a lightness in her head as the air becomes ionised. The heavy clouds look like they are hiding lightning. She takes a shallow breath then turns back to Mary.

'Right, well I'd better get going then. I'm actually looking for a holiday cottage I rented. My satnav brought me here and then just cut off. I guess the signal is pretty bad round here for that too?'

'Absolutely atrocious.' Mary shakes her head. 'We're still in the dark ages.'

Athene stands and shrugs her Parka on over her jeans and baggy jumper. Her rainbow-dyed hair is tied back with a headscarf, strands of colours slipping out. The dip-dye is new, so the colours are vibrant; almost shockingly so in the strip lighting of the café.

'Never mind, I'm sure I'll be able to find it. How much do I owe you?'

Athene swings the backpack over her shoulder, and reaches into her jeans for change, looking enquiringly at the woman.

'Just three quid, love,' Mary says.

Athene smiles and places a five-pound note on the table. 'Cheers, then,' she says and begins to walk towards the door. Outside, the rain seems to be unsure whether to fall, or just stay suspended in the air.

'What was with the cigarette, by the way?' Mary asks, as Athene reaches the door. The voice is almost accusatory, as if the question is about something else.

Which of course it is, Athene thinks. She turns and looks at Mary.

'I'm sorry?'

'What's the deal with laying one out on the table, if you don't smoke?'

There is faint suspicion on her lined face like someone has made a joke at her expense. *Suspicion and*, Athene thinks, *a memory-sadness.*

'Nothing.' She shrugs. 'I smoked once, and it's a little ritual I do.' She smiles brightly. 'It kind of keeps me connected to the past, you know?'

If Mary knew, she doesn't say; just stares at Athene. After a pause, Athene shrugs again.

'Well, bye, then.' She turns back to the door.

'What's it called?'

Athene's hand pauses as she reaches for the door handle. In the glass panel she can see her face reflected back, pale and ghostly. She can see the stickers on the glass, telling the tourists that dogs are welcome, as are muddy boots. She can see the crumbs of rain – the water mixed with the dust that was on the panes – sludging down the window. And beyond, in the car park, she can see her car, alone in the lot.

Athene turns.

'I'm sorry?'

'I know all the cottages in the valley.' Mary grimaces. 'Due to living here forever. Maybe I can direct you. Which one are you renting?'

Athene looks at Mary: the woman must be around thirty-five, but half of them have been spent in hard work and sustained depression and anger, giving her skin a colour not dissimilar to beaten eggs. Pale yellow under the light, with streaks of broken-road veins just beneath the surface. Athene can see that she would have been beautiful, once, back when she was young.

Of course she would, Athene thinks. She smiles widely.

'Really? Great! I've got the name written down on my phone. Hang on.'

Athene fishes out her android from the massive pocket in her Parka and swipes at the screen; uses her thumb to scroll down, then nods as she finds what she wants.

'Yes, here we are. Blea Fell House.' Athene looks up from her phone. 'Do you know where it is?'

The woman stares at Athene. The sound of the rain is not quite metronomic, but not quite random either. The café is a prefab structure, and the noise made by the weather is shockingly loud in the silence between the two women. Mary slowly shakes her head.

'No, sorry. I can't say I've ever heard of that one.'

It is clear that Mary is lying. Her skin has become slack. Slacker. She looks afraid. Athene gazes at her, interested.

No, not afraid. *Haunted* would be a better term. She looks like someone walked over her grave. Walked over, paused, then came back for a proper look. Maybe a bit of a poke too. Mary's hand, hanging down loose by her side, seems to have an electrical current running through it.

'Are you all right, Mary?' Athene, concerned, takes a few steps towards her. Mary actually takes a step back, then gives a small start when the radio spits out a gob of static.

'Why are you renting a cottage?' Mary asks, ignoring the question. 'Is it for the walking? Only you don't seem the walking type...' Mary glances down at Athene's footwear, a pair of battered converse basketball boots.

Athene nods.

'You're right. My mum rented it for me to finish my masters. A month of solitude with a laptop and no distractions!' Athene smiles and pats her bag.

Mary looks at her oddly for a moment, then sighs. 'What's your name, love?'

'Athene,' says the girl. 'Like the bird.'

'Well, Athene.' Mary carefully enunciates the girl's name. 'Why don't you come and have another cup of coffee on me. The weather's filthy out there, but it might clear in a few minutes. The clouds can rip through this valley something rotten. And now I think about it I *have* heard of Blea Fell House.'

'Really? Great!' Athene walks back towards the woman. Mary shakes her head. The haunted look has gone. *Or maybe not gone*, Athene thinks.

Maybe buried.

'I don't think so... not for you, anyhow.' Mary walks around the counter and takes two cups off the shelf above her. She turns and puts them on the long service table. Athene supposes the idea was that it was meant to look like an American diner. She watches as Mary fills them with black coffee from the percolator. Athene suspects the coffee has been there all day: that it will be bitter and burnt.

That's okay.

She likes bitter and burnt.

'Why not?' She sits down at the counter stool.

Mary looks at her, as if trying to slip under her skin with her eyes. 'You're not from around here, are you?'

Athene shakes her head. 'Southerner, I'm afraid. City girl. I'm used to my weather being broken up by tall buildings. Not...' She turns and points at the day beyond the window. 'Thrown at me by Heathcliff in a bad mood.'

Mary laughs. The laugh is somehow hollow; empty-husked.

'You should see it in winter! All the roads in the dale get covered in snow at the beginning of December, and the whole valley is an ice-trap.'

'No way!' Athene takes a sip of the coffee and tastes charred wood. She was right: bitter and burnt.

'Totally. The gritters come, but the roads just freeze over again. Something to do with the microclimate here.'

The overhead fluorescent lights flicker, and there is an electric buzz as the mercury vapour is reignited.

'Bloody power.' Mary looks at the lights as they kick back in. 'It's like the radio signal. Always dropping. I keep a generator in the shed, the service is so unreliable.'

'Wow, it's like living in the olden days! I wouldn't like to be here alone; all I have is a tiny torch and even that's got flat batteries.' Athene pats her Parka. She thinks it's something someone from a southern city might say. Mary doesn't comment, just takes a sip of her coffee and looks out at the worsening day. Athene wonders if the mention of Heathcliff was a little too much.

After a pause she says, 'You thought you might have heard of Blea Fell House, after all?'

Mary stays looking outside. *Or maybe not outside*, Athene

thinks. Maybe at something else entirely, that only she could see.

'*That was the latest from Kanye, and after the news, you need to get grungy, grab your skateboard and hippy skirt, because we're going to be winding it back all the way to the nineties.*'

Mary and Athene both look at the radio. The sound of the DJ's voice has a faraway quality, the top and bottom frequencies lost in the static. Then the signal blizzards, drowning out whatever news there was about to be. Athene turns back to find Mary staring at her. Although the skin on her face looks like it has been butchered by time, her eyes look worse. Up close, Athene can see spider web veins, criss-crossing the yellow-white. The eyes themselves look dry, like all the moisture has been used up.

'I'm surprised someone your age has even heard of Heathcliff. What's your masters in: English?' Mary says.

Athene shakes her head.

'No, Psychology. I'm looking at Post Traumatic Stress Disorder, and its effects on the subject in society.'

Athene looks at Mary expectantly, and there is a pause while the older woman processes.

'What, like when the soldiers come back from Iraq or whatever?'

'Like that, yes,' Athene says, then points at the window. 'Look, I'd love to chat, but the weather really does look rotten. Did you say you thought you might...?'

Athene waves her mobile, with the address of the holiday property on its screen.

'Blea Fell House, yes,' Mary says. 'Well the thing is, love, I think someone's scammed you.'

Athene creases her eyes. 'How do you mean?'

'Blea Fell House. The reason I didn't remember it straight away is that it isn't a holiday house.'

'What?' Athene says, looking confused. 'But I've got a booking confirmation!'

Mary shakes her head. 'Did you do it through a travel agent?'

'It was my mum. My mum found it.' Athene shrugs one shoulder. 'I don't know where she got it from. What site, I mean. It popped up when she was looking for places.'

'Sounds about right,' Mary says firmly. 'We get a lot of people turning up to the holiday homes, only to find someone else has booked it as well.'

'But you're saying this isn't even a holiday home?'

'It's not even a *home* home. Blea Fell House was abandoned years ago. All it is now is an overgrown wreck.'

Athene stares at Mary, who nods again.

'Sorry,' she adds.

Which is when the static storm ends and the DJ fades back in again.

'*Right, let's kick off our nineties night with Britney, and "Hit Me Baby One More Time"*.'

As the synth line starts, Athene looks at Mary, with her egg-skin and her haunted eyes and the broken way she holds her body, like a secret.

Nineties night, Athene thinks.

How absolutely fucking appropriate is that?

2

EXTRACT FROM BELLA'S DIARY

BLEA FELL HOUSE: SUMMER, 1998

sometimes I think my body is a ship: something
that gets tossed on the sea of life.
and sometimes I don't think it's my body
at all.
sometimes I think I'm like the pinball machine
in the pub; like the ball that flies around,
rebounding off rails and lighting up pins,
until everything is lights and sound and tilt
tilt tilt.
16 today, and I already feel world-sleepy.
x

3

Mary watches as Athene looks at her in consternation.

'A wreck?' says the young woman, aghast. Outside the weather has upped its stakes, rattling the windows in short gusts, trying to find a grip on the building. The radio-tide of static and music washes in and out. Mary nods.

'Completely. Hasn't been lived in since just before the end of the last century. Sorry to be the bearer of bad news, love, but I reckon you've been shafted.'

'Athene, please. Call me Athene. If you're going to give me bad news I'd rather you use my name. But we received an email and everything!' Athene reaches down and rummages in her backpack, picking through the contents with quick hands until, eventually, she pulls out a well-thumbed collection of printed A4 sheets, carelessly stapled together in the top corner.

'See?'

As she puts them on the counter, Mary can see a printed picture of the house, Blea Fell, on the cover sheet. Not the house as she imagines it looks now, all broken and hollow, burnt and crumbled; but as it looked then.

Back in the days when it was occupied.

Back in the Bella-days.

Mary feels a tightness in her chest as the barbed wire of memory grips. The image brings back thoughts and feelings that she locked away years ago. She feels that if she were to touch the picture, it wouldn't be paper and ink she felt, but stone and ivy.

Just looking at it makes her heart ache.

Shaking her head slightly, she scans the contents. As well as the picture, there is a short welcome section explaining the dos and don'ts of the property, followed by a paragraph listing local amenities, and things of interest to do in the area.

'Looks very professional,' Mary says, flicking through. There is a slight wind-moan creeping around the corners of the café. 'They've really done a number, haven't they?' She looks a little closer, squinting. 'They've even listed my café!'

'Are you sure you haven't made a mistake? Mum and I paid a lot of money; we've rented for the whole month. Maybe you're thinking of a different house?' Athene's voice is hopeful, like verbalising the idea might make it real.

Mary shakes her head. Next on the sheets came a brief description of the history of the house. Mary holds her breath and looks at it closely but it is harmless; merely giving information about the architecture and design of the property and the juniper wood in the field opposite. Mary skims through the rest.

'Sorry, Athene,' she says, pushing the papers across the counter. 'This is definitely Blea Fell. I knew it back in the day, when it looked like this. I don't think it even has a whole roof anymore. I wonder where they got the picture from?' She taps the sheets. 'You see that there's no contact number, or email or whatever, on this? For the pretend owners, I mean. In case of emergencies? Just the local police and hospital. Nothing connecting it to whoever sent it to you.'

'Are you sure?' Athene flicks rapidly through the document. After a moment, Mary sees her shoulders slump slightly.

'Fuck, you're right.' She looks quickly up at Mary, an apology stamped on her face. 'Whoops! Sorry. It's just that–'

Mary shakes her head, smiling. 'No need. I swear like a trooper when no one's around. Running a café is practically swearing 101.'

Mary sees that Athene isn't really paying attention; she's re-flicking through the paperwork, checking to see if she's missed anything. Mary takes a moment to study her. She guesses she's about twenty, but it's so hard to tell these days. The difference between teenager and adult has blurred so much. Kids seem to stay young forever, hitting eighteen and then putting everything on cruise control, not even growing up when they get kids of their own. Mary doesn't blame them. Growing up is bollocks. Growing up is like being dead only without the rest; giving up on all the fun that youth can bring, and just keeping the pain.

Mary looks down at the picture of the house again.

Although sometimes, she thinks, *youth isn't fun at all, and growing up is the only way of escaping it.*

She looks at the picture a moment longer, then blinks the thought away and turns to look out at the day beyond the window. It is now near dark, with the glass acting as a gloom-mirror, reflecting the two women as ghosts, sitting in a ghost café.

Seeing the image, Mary feels a shiver down her neck, as if someone has trickled a handful of cold earth onto her. For a second she wonders if any of this is real. The girl, and the café, and the rain. The track on the radio, from so long ago. Maybe she is still there? Still young. Still with a future. Still going to leave and never come back.

She looks at the ghost-her in the glass, and blinks.

Or maybe not.

Mary bites her lip, and paints a smile on her face. She looks at Athene. The girl can't be more than fifteen years younger than her, but she looks like she's from another age.

'Look, it's way too late to travel back down south. I don't suppose...?' Athene looks out at the night.

Mary feels a sudden stab of panic. For a moment she thinks the girl might ask if she can stay with her.

'Do you know of a B&B or something? Somewhere I can bunk down?'

'A B&B?'

Athene nods. 'Or maybe a hotel near, or something? The weather's really shitty. I think I need to find somewhere to stay around here or I'll end up in a ditch or something. Maybe sort out this stuff in the morning, yeah?' She looks down at the brochure. 'This hotel it mentions in the amenities section. The Craven Head. *Good food and clean sheets.* Is it real, or just there for show as well?'

Mary looks at her for a moment, then looks away. 'The hotel in the village. Yes, it's real. More of a pub, really; but I imagine they'd be closed now. The season's ended and–'

'You don't have a number for them, do you? It's not listed here,' Athene pleads. 'I really don't want to drive far in this.' She indicates the rain lashing down outside.

Mary swallows and nods. 'Of course. I could phone them from here and see if they have any rooms if you want.'

'Are you sure?' Athene's face lightens a little. 'I might have more chance of getting in if it comes from you.'

'Well, I do know the manager.' Mary smiles, but her smile is tight.

Athene smiles back, then looks down at the sheets of paper in her hand. 'Mum booked by credit card, so we should get our money back.'

Mary thinks that Athene must be one of those people who

say their thoughts aloud, processing in real time. A heart-on-her-sleeve kind of girl. That was not what Mary did. Not anymore. Not for a long time.

'I can probably even get you local rates.'

'That's, um...' Athene clears her throat, creating a pause. 'Really kind of you.'

Athene gives her a quizzical look, and Mary suddenly wonders if the girl thought she was hitting on her. Mary imagines herself through the girl's eyes: some worn out woman who might have been pretty once, but now resembles the grey cloths she uses to wipe up the grease left by other people. She feels a twist of disgust in her gut and quickly says, 'No problem. I won't come with you cos I've got a ton of things to do around here. Okay if I draw you a map?'

Athene nods and looks away, toward the door. Mary feels like she's made some terrible social taboo. She hopes it is just imagination: that it's all in her head, and the girl didn't misinterpret her suggestion. She reaches under the counter and finds a biro and an old order pad.

'Great.'

She begins to draw a map of how to get to the village.

'The roads get a little dangerous round here, you see? The mist can come down, and the signposts are for comedy, so a person can get lost before they know it.'

Mary knows she's gabbling, but can't help herself. She wants the girl to see that she's normal; a caring person helping out a stranger in need. The picture of Blea Fell has knocked her off-kilter.

'Sure, and with no satnav... I really appreciate it, Mary.'

Athene leans forward to look at the map Mary is drawing, turning her body so the two women are side by side. The radio is static, gentle like falling snow; and the rain has settled into a steady pour. When Mary has finished she points out the route, starting with a block in the top corner.

'This is the café, yeah?' Athene nods, the escaped strands of her hair like seaweed. Mary wonders how long it takes to dye it so many different colours. 'Okay. So you go back down the dale until you get to the crossroads, and then you turn right under the railway bridge. About a mile further on, it's left, and then after that it should be simple. You'll see the lights from the village as you come around the corner, then it's just a case of heading for them.'

'And the hotel?'

'Pub, really; the Craven Head.' Mary nods, and writes down a number. 'It's the only pub in the village, so there's no confusion.' She pauses, then quickly writes another number underneath. 'And this is my number, in case it all goes horribly wrong and you get lost and need me.'

'Which would make me an idiot, as I've got your wonderful map.' Athene smiles.

'You know what I mean,' Mary says, feeling slightly awkward.

Athene packs away the information about the bogus holiday cottage and picks up the map. 'And you'll phone them?' she asks, her eyes wide.

'Absolutely. As soon as you go I'm closing up, and I'll give them a bell. Ask for Jamie when you get there; he's the manager. Although manager might be a bit of a posh word. Bartender-cum-owner-cum-chef might be a better word. But like I said, it's clean and cheap, and will give you somewhere to sort yourself out. Phone your mum and stuff.'

'I really appreciate it, Mary.'

Athene swings the backpack up over her shoulder and walks to the door. She looks at the rain beyond the pane for a beat, then turns and smiles. 'Even in the rain it's beautiful here, isn't it? You're very lucky.' And then, before Mary can answer, she swings the door open and makes a dash for her car.

Mary watches as the young woman gets in. There is a pause while she types something on her phone – probably a message to her mum telling her the bad news – then starts the vehicle, and drives out of the car park. Mary watches as the tail lights recede, away and down toward the village at the base of the valley. Even once the car has disappeared, Mary stays watching. Looking at the last spot she could see the lights.

After a long minute, she looks down at her hand, wondering if she imagined it. Imagined the touch of Athene's finger on her skin as the girl picked up the map Mary had drawn. Mary takes in a slow breath. Even if she *had* ghost-stroked her, it would surely have been an accident? A casual, unmeant, brush of skin-on-skin as she reached for the map. Unmeant and unmeaning.

Mary shakes her head.

'Stupid cow,' she reprimands herself.

In the clicking of the overhead lights and the tip-tapping of the rain, Mary reaches for the telephone, to call the pub.

4

😈 Working so far
Staying @ CH
M freaked by cigarette
Mentioned H
x

Athene read back the message she'd typed on her phone, the rain tip-tapping on the windscreen, then touched the send icon.

She glanced at the woman watching her from the door of the café, turned the key in the ignition, then eased out of the car park and onto the road.

5

MOKE PRIMARY SCHOOL: MOUSE'S FINAL YEAR 1992

Mouse stayed quiet, under the chair in the corner of the one-room school. The stove was burning merrily, snug against the wall that was adjacent to the playground. The flames were made criss-cross by the permanent metal guard that caged it, keeping it safe from the inquisitive hands of the children. Outside the school's windows the sleet was ripping up the dark day, but Mouse was all cosy under her chair, watching the other children, painting them into stories with her eyes. She watched Lucy play with the plasticine and Honey hitting David with the snapped-off leg of a doll. Normally they'd be made to have play-time outside but Miss Crumb had decided the weather was too dire. In the corner of the room, by himself, Jamie methodically attached a cog to his Meccano structure, building something that nobody cared about. Occasionally one of the children would look at Jamie and snigger, but nobody ever looked at Mouse, because she had learnt to make herself invisible. She had learnt to make herself smaller and smaller, until she could hardly be seen at all. When the bell rang, and everybody went back to their desks for the lesson, Mouse stayed quiet under the chair, watching and watching.

6

THE CRAVEN HEAD

'How did you sleep?'

Jamie tries hard to keep his eyes fixed on Athene's face as she sits at the breakfast table, when what he really wants to do is look at her breasts. More than wants to. Even though he is looking at the woman's face, in his peripheral vision he can see them, or the shape of them, beneath the jumper.

The hint of them.

He licks his lips.

'Great, thanks. The bed was really comfy.'

'And the rain didn't keep you up?'

Jamie raises his eyebrows, the order pad held in one hand, a pen poised in the other. The girl shakes her head, causing her multicoloured hair to rainbow across her face. She uses a finger to tuck it back behind her ear. Jamie keeps his gaze firmly on her eyes; does not even allow himself to flick to the ear. The ear, in his experience, can lead to the neck, after which there was no fucking chance.

'Didn't hear a thing.' Athene gestures at her surroundings. 'These walls must be really thick!'

'Built in the sixteenth century from local stone.' A touch of pride colours Jamie's voice. 'Been in the family for two generations. The walls are over a foot in width. Have you chosen what you would like for your breakfast?' He risks a quick scope while the girl scans the menu.

'Right, yes, it all looks lovely. I'll have bacon, please, with tea, and hot rolls on the side.'

Athene smiles and returns the laminated menu.

Jamie grins and slots it between his side and his arm as he finishes writing down the order. 'Great; the bacon is local, and the bread is baked in the next village, so you know everything is fresh. I'll be back in a bit with the tea.'

Jamie smiles at her and walks away from the dining area, through the arch, across the lobby and into the kitchen. As he begins putting the breakfast together, he lets his mind wander over the girl's body. When she had arrived the previous night she had been soaked. He'd already laid out a towel for her in the bedroom and made sure there was hot water in the tank in case she wanted a bath. She was the only guest, now the season had ended, and he was grateful for the business. In the winter, apart from the week of the fair, the whole valley turned into a corpse.

He'd waited by the little reception desk. It had been nearly an hour after Mary had phoned, and he was beginning to think the girl was a no-show. He wouldn't have blamed her. If it had been him, and someone had stiffed him out of his holiday cottage, he'd have wanted to fuck off and stay in the Travelodge near the motorway: somewhere clean and modern where he could regroup and re-plan. Jamie was a big fan of Travelodges. Nobody bothered with your business in those places. Everyone stayed anonymous.

No. Wouldn't have blamed her... but would have been pissed off. Heating the emersion wasn't cheap. And he'd changed his top because, well, you never knew in this game. Sometimes people coming on holiday wanted to include the landlord in their experience.

When she'd finally come through the door, soaked, however, he knew he had no chance. She was younger than him, not that that always mattered, but he could tell: this time it completely mattered. The clothes she wore, and the hair. The way she held herself and the fact that she looked straight into his eyes.

No chance. Completely out of his league.

Still, the sticky way her sodden top clung to her cleavage when she'd taken her jumper off... that was a freebie, wasn't it? That was a Brucie-bonus for him.

Jamie had welcomed her and taken her coat, and only ogled her breasts when he was mainly certain she wouldn't notice. He learnt a long time ago to think *mainly certain*, as opposed to *completely*.

Because there *was* no completely. Women always seemed to know. Even when their backs were turned, and he was checking out the rear view, he could see a stiffening of the posture. A pulling up of the jeans or a smoothing down of the skirt.

Jamie sighs and takes the pre-cooked bargain price bacon out of the fridge, and puts it into the microwave. As the bacon starts its slow spin he opens the freezer and removes a couple of part-baked rolls and pops them into the oven on a baking tray.

Fresh today, he smirks to himself.

While he's waiting for the bread to cook he thinks some more about his new guest.

He's not quite sure what it is, but there is something a little off about her. He absently scratches his balls through the deadening material of his jeans, and flicks on the kettle.

Jamie thinks about what Mary had told him on the phone the previous night, about the girl being stiffed out of some cottage rental. Maybe what was off was the fact that the girl was going to rent a cottage at the time when everybody else *stopped* renting them.

But then, if she was up here to finish her essay, or whatever they did for a masters, then just when everyone else left would be *exactly* the time, wouldn't it? And it would be half the price, out of season.

Jamie pours the boiling water into a little teapot-for-one and sets it on a tray. He adds a tiny milk jug, butter dish, a couple of sachets of sugar, and a small wicker basket for the rolls, then leans against the prep table, absently stroking the scar on his face. It stretches from his left eye, and up into his hairline. It is razor-thin and hasn't itched for years, but he still strokes it.

Jamie lets his hand drop.

Maybe it's that she just acts so young? She couldn't be more than ten years younger than him – fifteen tops – but she still held herself like she'd just got out of school. When she'd first come in, out of the rain, she'd ripped off her scarf and shaken her head like a dog, spraying water everywhere, and pissing herself with laughter.

Jamie has a sudden porn-flash image on the wall of his mind; of the girl in a school uniform, dog collar attached around her neck, skin all flushed and shiny, shaking pearly thick liquid off herself. He blinks it away and leans down, opening the oven and taking out the rolls. He places them in the little basket, along with a teaspoon and knife for the butter.

How did I stop being young? he thinks as he takes the bacon out of the microwave and puts it on a plate. When did he stop being young? After the wedding? After the fight? Or just when he'd left school, and started working for his dad in the pub.

Maybe he'd *never* been young. He'd started helping out when he was eleven; pot-boying, and washing up. Cleaning the rooms on a Saturday. He'd enjoyed it. Drinking the dregs of all the pints before he washed the glasses. Nicking little bits of money from the rooms – never enough to arouse suspicion – and using it to buy sweets to show off at school. Not that it ever did any good.

And sometimes not only money. By the time he was in his teens he was nicking other stuff.

Underwear. Toiletries. Anything that might have touched a naked body.

He'd had his first sexual encounter at thirteen, when a guest had caught him doing something he shouldn't have been doing in her bathroom. Rather than tell his father, she had shut the door, stood in front of him, grabbed his shaking hand and pushed it down the front of her skirt. Jamie had been petrified. She had smelt of old-woman and dead-flowers and had whispered threats and swear words in his ear as she made him rub her. Faster and faster, with more and more violence in her words, more and more stench on her breath. Afterwards, he had run to his room at the back of the pub and wept into his pillow. A little after that he had revisited the moment; the feeling, the sheer wrongness of it, and found himself aroused.

After *that*, he suspected, he had no fucking chance of having a normal relationship. He'd found himself becoming more and more isolated at school, if that were even possible. He hadn't been able to look at any of the girls in his class, in his year, without thinking about what was under their clothes. What they did to themselves when they were alone. What they'd do to *him* if they found him in their bathroom doing something he shouldn't.

Jamie picked up the tray and took the breakfast back through to the girl. With each step his face slowly changed, his mask stitching back into the resemblance of ordinariness, until the smile he displayed as he re-entered the dining area looked almost completely genuine.

7

MARY'S HOUSE

She can see Bella talking, her head close to Trent's ear, but she can't hear what she says.

The music is too loud, and she is too drunk. Or maybe it's the drugs. Or what Bella whispered in her ear as they danced.

The car is slipping and slewing on the snow and ice, but Trent isn't slowing down, he's photograph-still, driving one-handed, the other wrapped around Bella. Trent's been in a Heathcliff-mood all night. From when he picked them up, through the fair, to the disco in the Craven Head and this mad drive home.

'Trent, for fuck's sake slow down!' is what she wants to say, but the words come out of her mouth like syrup. They seem to coalesce in the air, and slip down her front like they're too heavy. She smiles.

Outside the stars are frozen in the black sky. She feels like everything outside of her head is made up. That the stars are painted on the car window. She is having trouble focusing on her thoughts.

'Where are we going?' she mumbles, fumbling out a cigarette from her coat pocket.

Bella turns round in the bench seat to grin at her. 'Straight To Hell!'

She grins back. She was right. The Clash was pulsing out of the speakers, with Joe Strummer saying there was no need for her. That they were indeed going straight to hell.

And then Bella turns back round, shouts something, and grabs the steering wheel, knocking Trent sideways. She feels the car sliding on the ice. There is no screeching brakes and no screaming. Just the silent and unstoppable movement of a tonne of steel and bodies skating across the icy road.

She has just enough time to wonder why Trent isn't braking before the car hits a patch of road where the ice has melted and flips over, and then she can't think anymore.

Mary wakes up screaming Bella's name, screaming the scream she hadn't screamed then, when she watched Bella die. Mary looks around wildly, covered in sweat, with her heart pounding, until eventually she realises where she is. Sighing shakily, she lies back on her sodden sheets and looks at the ceiling.

'Bella,' is all she whispers. No one answers. The ceiling is bumpy, like someone decided to pebble-dash the inside. As she looks at it, letting her heart settle, she thinks of Bella, and of Trent.

And then she thinks about what the girl, Athene, said to her in the café. About how the weather here reminded her of Heathcliff.

'Trent,' Mary whispers.

8

BELLA'S LAST DAY: BREAKFAST 9AM

'Morning, Mum.'

Sheila paused from attempting to stroke the Esse stove into life and turned to look at her daughter as she entered the kitchen. Bella was wearing her normal uniform of ripped shapeless jeans and thick socks; baggy black French-necked jumper over a white grandfather shirt. The jumper had large holes where the cotton had become unthreaded. Perched on the back of her home-chopped horror-doll hair was a black beret. The girl walked to the scarred kitchen table and sat down, scraping the chair back over the slate floor. Sheila winced slightly. The noise smeared across her brain, sandpapering pain into her hangover.

'Morning, Bella,' she said, smiling vaguely, and turning back to the stove. Her jaw tensed as she concentrated, trying to coax a flame out of the smouldering embers with little scraps of wood and strips of paper. She would normally have banked the fire last night, but the argument with her husband had resulted in her storming off to bed, leaving him with the responsibility of shutting down the house.

And the house required shutting down properly otherwise it

would bite you in the morning. If you didn't pay attention to it last thing at night, it would punch you in the face first thing when you woke up. The place seemed to have a will and weft of its own. If the fire wasn't going then it became the temperature of a tomb; even in summer.

'Sleep well, darling?' Sheila smiled with satisfaction as a twist of the newspaper she had delicately placed a moment earlier caught alight.

'You know. Dead days and all that.' Bella pulled out a soft pack of Luckys from the sleeve of her jumper and tapped it against her palm. A cigarette slid out of the corner where she had torn off a portion of the foil. She'd seen a documentary about James Dean once, on the antique black and white telly she had in her bedroom, and that was how *he* did it. Tapping the pack against his palm so the cigarette came half out, then pulling it the rest of the way with his lips, and firing it up with a Zippo.

'At least it's quiet. Have you seen outside?' Sheila reached in her apron for her own cigarettes: menthol and in a hard cardboard box; not like her daughter's. God forbid they should smoke the same brand. Not that Sheila smoked at all anymore; she still liked to feel one between her fingers. Between her lips. Especially at this time of year. Between Christmas and new year. The dead days.

Sheila heard the click of the lighter as Bella flicked the lid of her Zippo, spun the wheel, and lit her cigarette. Gritting her teeth, Sheila placed wood on the embryonic flames. Bella didn't answer her question about having seen outside, but then Sheila didn't expect her to. Getting an unsolicited 'good morning' out of her sixteen-year-old daughter had practically made her day. Communication was mainly a one-way street these days. Sheila closed her eyes, feeling the burden of guilt pressing against the inside of her skull; making migraine-fish swim on the insides of her eyelids. After a moment, she opened them again, constructing her features into a semblance of cheeriness.

'You should have a look; it really snowed heavily last night, then froze at dawn. There's a hoar frost on the trees you wouldn't believe!'

Bella shrugged her stick-shoulders slightly, dragging on her Lucky. Sheila saw that her daughter's black painted nails were bitten and ragged.

She wondered, with a tiny scratch of sadness, if she had heard her crying into her pillow last night.

She debated whether to say anything. Tell her that, whatever happens, she loves her.

'Why don't you play with your sister, while I make you some breakfast?' is what she said instead. 'Now I've got the stove going I can get some coffee on.'

Bella nodded, took a drag of her fag, and placed it carefully in the ashtray her father had 'liberated', as he put it, from the local pub. Then, with a fluid movement, she stood and walked over to the playpen in the corner of the room. Inside, sat on a rough patchwork rug, was her baby sister.

'Hello, *Thing*,' Bella said softly, kneeling and sticking her fingers through the coloured bars.

'I wish you wouldn't call her that,' Sheila said, pouring water into the percolator and putting it on the stove hob. 'She's got a perfectly good name.'

'Yes, *Thing*, you have.' Bella smiled, wiggling her fingers. The baby crawled forward and grabbed hold of the dancing digits, smiling like it was the most amazing thing ever. 'And it's *Thing*, isn't it?'

Sheila bit back a retort, controlling herself. Just the fact that Bella was in the same room as her was front-page news these days, and she didn't want to spoil it. She sat down on the wooden stool next to the stove and watched her daughter.

Daughters. Watched her playing with her sister. Since the birth of the baby, Sheila was acutely aware that she wasn't paying enough attention to Bella.

Wasn't following who she was hanging out with. Wasn't following how she was doing at school. Over the last six months, it was clear that Bella was changing. Sixteen years old; it wasn't surprising. What was worrying Sheila, when she had enough strength to be worried, was what she was changing into.

'*Thing's* nappy needs sorting out,' Bella said, giving a final waggle of her fingers, then standing. The baby gave a chirrup of disappointment as she pulled away. 'And don't ask me to do it, because it's disgusting.' Bella walked back to the table and sat down, tucking one leg under her as she seated herself on the refectory bench. She picked up her cigarette.

Sheila poured the coffee, and brought it over to her daughter. She saw that the sleeves of her tramp-jumper overran her wrists, to reach halfway down her hands, the fingerless gloves just poking out beyond. She was painfully, rawly, aware that she hadn't seen her daughter's arms for several months. Even in the summer she had worn long sleeves. Dark colours.

In the front of her mind, Sheila put it down to the music Bella listened to. All the bands she liked seemed to dress like they'd raided a beatnik party or a period drama. Either that or stolen clothes from the homeless.

In the back of her mind she thought it might be about hiding, rather than showing. Once again she felt a stab of guilt.

'Here you go, love,' she said, putting the cup of coffee down. Bella nodded her thanks.

Sheila sat down opposite her. 'New Year's Eve!' she said with false brightness, willing her daughter to make eye contact. 'Are you going out with Mouse tonight? To the fair?'

'Maybe. I'm not sure yet.'

Bella's response was flat, and Sheila could see the blood

pulsing in a vein at the side of her neck. She tried to think of a way of drawing her out; getting under the veneer that she had so carefully built around herself, along with her clothes and her make-up and her music.

'Or you could have her round here, if you like,' Sheila persisted. 'Or anyone. Are you still friends with that boy?'

Bella finally looked at her. Sheila saw that she had grey eye kohl on her lower lids, smudged like the models in the sixties used to do. Strangely, it made her look older and younger at the same time. After several intense moments, Sheila looked away.

'I wish you wouldn't smoke in front of the baby,' she said, putting her own unlit cigarette back in its packet.

'Why not?'

'It's bad for her health.'

Bella stayed looking at her, unblinking. Sheila thought her whole body became tighter in the stillness. Harder. More like a statue than a girl.

'Bad for her health? You're bloody kidding me, right?' was all she finally said.

Sheila looked at her in confusion, but deep down inside herself, she felt the magma of panic moving; the pressure building.

Before she could say anything Bella let out a short stream of smoke from her lungs. 'I'm going upstairs; thanks for the coffee.'

And that was it. Gone. Bella stubbed out her cigarette, picked up her drink, the packet of smokes and the lighter, and walked out.

'Well, will you be in for lunch?' Sheila said to her retreating back.

'Not sure. Probably not. I'll see you at tea though.'

And then the wooden door shut, and she was gone. Sheila listened to the light tread of her going up the stairs to her room. Waited the few moments until the meticulously retro record player began playing out the meticulously retro first song, about boys who never grow up, or girls who always stay sad.

Sheila thought about her life stretching out in front of her, getting thinner and thinner, and tighter and tighter, until one day it might actually snap. Absently, she pulled her cigarette back out of its packet in her pinny, and put it in her mouth, staring into the stove fire. The sound of her baby pulled her out of her thoughts. The infant was clearly uncomfortable in her soiled nappy and the increasing warmth of the room.

'Well, *Thing*,' Sheila said, mimicking the name her daughter had coined, standing and holding her arms towards her. The baby immediately smiled and fell over. 'That went well.'

9

BOW COTTAGE: MARY

'Hi, it's Athene.'

Mary holds the phone to her ear and feels the click in her brain; a switch allowing a little extra current through at the sound of the girl's voice. The scream she woke up with is still in the corner of her mind, behind the cobwebs of her dream. 'I was in your café last night? You sent me to the hotel?'

'Sure, yes, I remember. Athene, like the bird; hi. How was it? Did you manage to find the place okay?'

'Yeah, it's great! I got a little lost on the way – these roads are brutal – but no sweat. The manager or whatever, Jamie, is really nice. And the decor is mental! It's like something out of a film!'

Mary smiles. She's fairly sure the pub – hotel was stretching it – hadn't been decorated this century; or possibly a lot longer before. She hadn't been in for a long time, but she remembered that wood panelling featured heavily, along with dark paisley carpets that would forever hold the smell of cigarettes and old men in its swirls.

'But not a film with a lot of budget,' she says.

'Fair point, but the wifi is top-drawer,' Athene says. There is a slight pause, then: 'Look, I just wanted to thank you for helping me out last night. I was in a real mess when I found out about the rental, and you really sorted me out.'

'No problem. It was a shitty night; there was no way you were going to drive home then. Are you heading south today?'

Mary mentally kicks herself. She can hear the slight tension in her voice, which is ridiculous. The girl is almost young enough to be her daughter. If she had a daughter.

'Actually the guy, Jamie, he's given me a really good deal on staying here for the week, until I sort myself out, so I'm thinking of hanging for a few days. I've spoken to Mum, and she's agreed to sub me until the refund from the scam cottage comes through.'

'You'll get it back then?' Mary says brightly. 'That's good.' She looks out at the day. After the storm of last night, the world seems scrubbed clean. The remnants of her dream are still clinging to her, but Athene's warm voice is burning it away, cleaning her mind.

'One of the joys of credit cards; the insurance covers it.'

'Countered by the debt and subsequent life spiralling out of control,' Mary says.

Athene's laughter down the phone is fresh and warm. 'No need to tell *me*; I'm still technically a student, but it sounds like *you* speak from experience.'

'Self-employed businesswoman; debt is my S-O.' Mary hadn't meant to say so much; talk to Athene as if they know each other. The student doesn't need to know anything about her life. Mary quickly tries to normalise the conversation. 'Anyhow, it was nice of you to ring, and I'm glad it's all sorted out with the cottage.'

'Oh, no, that's not sorted out at all.' Athene's voice changes; the lightness there a moment ago, gone.

Mary feels a knot forming in her stomach. Or maybe it was

there all along, and she's only just feeling it. 'I'm sorry? I thought you said–'

'The money's sorted, sure, or at least will be once the credit card pays up. What I mean is the cottage itself.'

The day, so bright a few moments ago, seems to fade to grey.

'What do you mean? What about the cottage?'

'Look, don't worry about it.' Athene's voice becomes more cautious. Mary wonders if she thinks she has offended her. Overshared, or whatever it was called these days. 'I was clearing my pockets out from last night and found your map with this number on it. I saw it and remembered how tired you looked. I was so grateful you took pity on me. I wanted to say thank you for helping a girl out, that's all. I didn't mean to bang on.'

There is a pause on the line, like Athene is going to say something else.

Rather than leave the silence hanging, Mary says, 'I'm pleased you rang, and if you're staying in the area you're more than welcome to pop up to the café. I do a mean apple pie, complete with cheese.'

Mary pushes the phone harder against her ear, and bites her lip before she can say anything else. *I sound like a fucking schoolgirl*, she thinks, dismayed.

'Cheese?' Athene sounds amused. 'With pie?'

'Local custom. For local people,' Mary says, quoting an old TV programme.

Fuckfuckfuck, you sound like a mentalist!

'Um, well, thanks for the offer, I might just do that.' Athene laughs. 'There's only so long you can theorise the *trauma of being* before you go batshit crazy!'

'Great! Anytime. Hope you have a good day, Athene.' Mary keeps her voice light, even though she is using the girl's first name.

'You too, Mary. Later.'

Athene hangs up, and Mary is left with the phone to her ear, staring out at the day. Slowly, she takes the device away, and holds it in front of her, staring at it quizzically. Outside, beyond her window, she can hear birds singing. She looks at the phone, and tries to think back to last night. To the storm, and the window, and the girl so close to her that Mary could smell her skin as she drew the map. Her skin had smelt of Christmas oranges.

Did she?

Without even thinking, did she?

And this is my number, in case it all goes horribly wrong and you get lost and need me.

That's what she'd said, with the music and the static, and the shock of seeing Blea Fell.

This is my number.

And the faintest of touches.

In case you need me.

A ghost of a stroke on the side of her hand.

'I must have,' she whispers, looking at the smartphone in her hand. She thought, in her head, that she had given Athene the telephone number to the café. Mary had been there another hour after the girl had driven away. Clearing up the detritus of the working day; even though the main tourist season was over, hardcore fell cyclists still made day trips and liked to treat themselves to a carb-laden all-day breakfast when they'd finished. But she clearly hadn't. She'd given out her mobile number. Given out her mobile number like she wanted to be reached, wherever she was. Whatever time.

Mary shakes her head.

Everyone gives out their mobile number, she thinks, staring thoughtfully out of the window. *It's just a common thing to do. Nobody even uses landlines anymore. Nothing weird about it.*

Mary lets the stream of reassuring thoughts settle into her.

She thinks back to the conversation, to see if she said, or even hinted at, something she shouldn't.

Satisfied, she gets herself together, and leaves her house, locking the door behind her, ready to open up the café. She is about to get in her car when she pauses. She feels the trickle of earth down her neck, like the night before. She looks around, trying to determine what is wrong.

It takes her a few moments to realise what it is.

All the birds have stopped singing.

Mary peers into the woods that surround her cottage, but although the day is bright, it is not bright enough to penetrate into the gloom beneath the canopy.

'Hello?' she shouts, her voice slightly higher than she would have liked. 'Is anyone there?'

She waits, ears straining, but no one answers.

Of course *no one answers*, she thinks. *Because there's no one there.*

Hurriedly, she gets in the car and pushes down the lock. As she starts the engine, a flock of starlings burst out of the trees and take to the sky.

'Jesus fucking Christ,' Mary mutters as she drives carefully up the track towards the main road. 'I'm too old to be frightened of the bloody woods.'

10

BETTLE WOODS: MARY'S HOUSE

TEXT TO ATHENE'S PHONE

👻 She's just left
At one point she was looking right at me
Seems so sad
And scared
I'm not sure it's her

11

BLEA FELL HOUSE: JULY, 1992

'It's impressive, I'll give you that.'

Bella and her parents stood on the scrub of moorland just outside the walled boundary of Blea Fell House. On the scrub moorland, curlews were nesting in the undergrowth, and the air was full of the lazy weight of summer.

'It certainly is! The main part of the house is sixteenth century!'

The estate agent, Colin, seemed to astonish himself with this news, pointing in a vague direction across the moor, as if some monks might suddenly appear, and ask for them back.

'Which one's the prayer room?' Bella asked, staring in awe at the house. To her eyes, the building seemed to be a mixture between *Wuthering Heights* and *The Addams Family*.

Colin looked at her, smiling. He knew that if he could get the daughter on side, then the parents would have no chance. He pointed to the squat stone turret at the far front corner. Bella squinted her eyes, following the line of his finger.

'See it? Perfect for a princess with a spinning wheel, or a budding writer, wouldn't you say?'

Bella studied it. The stone was clearly different than the rest of the house. Rougher, more like rock than something shaped by human hands. More like the landscape.

Colin watched the girl obliquely. He took in the ponytail, and the quiet way she was cataloguing every detail of the building with her eager eyes. He reckoned that she already pictured herself looking out of the turret's window, across the moor, with the gorse and the ancient juniper wood. Maybe she imagined a fire crackling and a book of poetry on her paisley skirt and silk blouse. He smiled, reading her as a done deal.

He winked at her happily, then turned his attention to the mother, who had her arm linked through her husband's.

Colin gave her his full-wattage smile. 'And there's plenty of room for a nursery, Mrs Moss, if you were thinking of growing your family!'

'Oh, no, one is quite enough, thank you.'

The tone of her voice had enough of a harsh edge to it for Colin to pick up the warning signs. The girl either didn't, or chose not to, notice, and wandered a little way ahead, carefully crossing the cattle grid and onto the track that curved around the front of the house. The husband sighed and removed his arm from his wife's, and walked off to examine the wooden garage by the side of the cattle grid.

New start, thought Colin, observing the hardening of the wife's mouth. *Something in the past, affair maybe, and this is a new beginning. Still in the tricky phase, but making an effort.* Mentally, he changed gear and raised his voice a little so both of them could hear.

'The walls of the property are over two feet thick! If either of you is the bookish type and thought about perhaps converting one of the rooms into a study, I can guarantee peace and quiet!'

The husband seemed to perk up at this and paused in his examination of the garage to look at the house. The building was another hundred feet up the track from the cattle grid, but Bella had already reached the front of it and was peering through the tiny windows.

'Why is there a gate *and* a cattle grid?' asked Mr Moss.

Colin looked at the man to see if he was joking. Moss was dry and bitter looking. His skin was tight around his face, as if it had been shrink-wrapped onto his skull. His eyes were cruel.

City pillock, Colin thought. 'Good question,' he said brightly. 'If you look beyond the house, you'll see a barn?'

Mr Moss peered up the track and nodded. 'Well, one side is a byre, or cowshed, and the other is stables. The barn is two storey, so above the stables is a space for storing hay. The cows the farmer kept would roam out on the moor, then come back to the barn for milking. The cattle grid stopped them wandering back up before their time, as it were, whilst allowing vehicles through. When they did need to come back, the gate could be opened and... *voila*!'

Colin made an open-hand gesture, like a magician. He glanced sideways at the woman as he did so, to see how his French had gone down; he often found that the ladies liked a little sophistication. She didn't even look like she'd heard him; she was staring at her husband's back. Colin was shocked to see the look of sheer hatred on her face.

What did you do? Colin thought, following her gaze and looking at the husband. *What did you do to deserve a look like that?*

'So if you were thinking of keeping horses, you're all set up.' He walked forward and opened the gate, ushering the family through. Mrs Moss had stopped staring at her husband, and was looking at her daughter, who was staring over the low wall at the juniper forest in the rough field in front of the house.

'Is there even any electricity?' Mr Moss said as they walked up the track. The track was comprised of hard dirt, with a layer of lime chalk sitting on it, and as they stamped up it, swirls of dust were kicked up, and hung in the hot air.

'Oh, yes, Mr Moss. No oil or gas, I'm afraid, but there is electric! And telephone.'

Mr Moss looked around dubiously. 'I don't see any poles.'

'Buried. The wind coming off the moor would make telegraph poles a dangerous proposition, so when they ran the electric through they did the telephone too. It continues past your property on to the next farm.'

Colin held his breath, but nobody pulled him up. He had found that, when it worked, calling the property *theirs*, as if they already owned it, helped cement the image of themselves in it, making the sale easier.

'And do they have through-access?' the husband asked, joining his daughter, and peering over the low wall at the stunted trees.

'Technically,' Colin conceded, 'but they never need it. The place they live in hasn't been a farm for years either, and the only livestock they keep are chickens and cats.' Colin smiled at the mother. 'In fact, Mrs Moss, they have a daughter around about your girl's age, I would guess. She goes to the primary school in the village.'

'Oh, really? That is interesting.' Mrs Moss looked at her daughter. There was a strange expression on her face. *Only child,* he thought. *Maybe struggles to make friends.*

'Yes, it's a really good school. Very big on the basics. I went there myself, in fact.'

'Didn't fancy straying too far then,' said Mr Moss, walking round to the side of the house. It was clear he was sneering.

Colin felt a flash of anger, but thought of the possible commission from the sale. He nodded and grinned, as if the man had just paid him a compliment. 'Absolutely. Why move away when you already live in the most beautiful part of England, right?'

Mr Moss gave him a hard stare, suspecting he was being laughed at, but Colin kept his wide-eyed country-boy thick-as-shit face open.

'How do you heat it, with no gas or oil? Is it all run off the electric?' Mrs Moss asked quickly. Bella, the daughter, grabbed her mother's hand and walked across the path and looked through the mullioned window again. Colin followed them and stood by Mrs Moss, at the side of the house, next to the little porch that served as the entrance.

'Both the heating and hot water run off an Esse stove.' He nodded at their look of confusion. 'A bit like an Aga, only more robust,' he elaborated. 'Shackleton, the explorer, had one on his expedition to the Arctic, that's how good they work! Very efficient.'

Colin reached into his pocket and pulled out a key. He handed it to Mr Moss. The man hesitated a moment, then took it and unlocked the porch door.

Make them feel like it's already theirs, Colin thought smugly, as the husband pushed the door open.

The girl, Bella, slipped between her parents and raced into the house through the porch. She had only disappeared for a few seconds before they heard a squeal of delight.

'Mum! You've got to come and look at this. It's bigger than our entire flat!'

'Sounds like your daughter has found the farmhouse kitchen.' Colin smiled.

Mrs Moss smiled back and followed her daughter into the house.

Mr Moss waited until she had gone, then turned to the estate agent.

'It seems very...' He paused, as if not quite sure of the word he wanted. He pointed at the surrounding moor. At the twisted collection of juniper trees at the front, like props in a forties horror film. 'Isolated,' he settled on, eventually.

'As much or as little as you want, Mr Moss,' Colin said promptly. 'There are farms and cottages scattered about the moor, and in the wood, but if you don't want company, they know to respect that. On the other hand, if you wish to be social, you'll find a good spread of people.'

The husband made a non-committal noise, halfway between a grunt and a laugh. 'Bet it's a fucking bitch in the winter,' is all he said.

'I suppose it depends what you're used to,' Colin replied coolly, shocked at the use of language. 'You can pretty much guarantee a white Christmas, I will say that. Where is it you're from? Down south, I'm guessing?'

'South west,' muttered the man, after a moment.

Colin grinned. 'Then definitely I think you'll find the winter's a little colder than you're used to. But the beauty of this building, Mr Moss, is that with the Esse and the walk-in larder, it could snow the whole season and you'd be right as rain. You'd be snowed in with only yourselves for company, but you'd be snug as bugs.'

Colin felt a slug of ice turn in his stomach as he watched a smile form on the father's face, like a rat coming out of a hole.

12

THE CRAVEN HEAD

MARY: 9AM

I *'m only going to go in to check that she's all right, to make sure she has got herself sorted out.*

Mary grimaces.

Right.

Mary taps out a nervous staccato on the steering wheel of her rusty Nissan Micra, staring at the pub. She'd spent a long time awake last night thinking about Athene. It was driving her crazy. The girl was like a scratch in her mind; she didn't understand it. And then the dream...

Mary shudders and focuses on the pub.

Other than Jamie coming out for a smoke, and a couple of shifty teenagers – breakfast staff or cleaners, she supposed – she hadn't seen anyone.

What the fuck am I doing here?

Absently, Mary bites her nails.

And if the mention of Blea Hall was like a punch to the head, then seeing the photo was an explosion in her heart. The photo, of how the house was before the fire; *before* the fire... and then Athene had mentioned Heathcliff...

'Fuckbunnies.' Mary rubs at the plastic steering wheel with

her thumbs, staring at the entrance to the pub, willing Athene to come out. She doesn't. Mary swears again, thinking.

It wasn't just that the girl had brought memories of the past. There was something about Athene herself; something unnerving.

There was a stillness about her. A sadness, deep under the skin, like the words in a stick of rock. And Mary wasn't kidding herself. She recognised it because a word ran through her too. If she were to cut herself open, she knew what the word would say, all the way to her centre.

Guilty.

Mary blinks and shakes her head slightly, dislodging the past. She concentrates her thoughts on Athene.

She was the sort of girl someone could become obsessed with, and Mary was too old to become obsessed.

But then when Athene had phoned her this morning, the itch just got worse.

'Fuck it.'

Mary gets out of the car, the door creaking as she pushes it open. She stands by the vehicle, unsure what to do. She takes a quick look about.

The village is quiet today. Unsurprising; the season over and the place closing down, tick by tock. The two cafés other than hers had shut, and wouldn't open again until March. The trees that line the beck are losing their leaves to the wind, sending them swirling through the air; slips of letters addressed to the winter to come.

She rarely comes into the village, preferring to do most of her shopping online, rather than visit the little grocery store. The store is, like in all villages, a meeting hub for the social members of the village; a place where they can gossip, and make their pronouncements of what's occurring in the area.

Mary can't stand the scrutiny. Even after all this time.

Because, she thinks bitterly, time in a village doesn't mean anything. If you're still alive, then everything in your life is fair game; there's no moving on. The only way to escape village gossip is to either move out of the area, or be dead.

And sometimes even death isn't enough.

Mary feels her throat contract, like it wants to stop her heart from running away.

'Fuck it,' she repeats.

Mary pushes herself off the car and strides purposely to the pub. Before she can change her mind, she opens the door and walks inside.

As soon as she is in, the memories hit her. Of her and Bella and Trent, in the games room at the back of the pub, playing pinball. Smoking and drinking and laughing. The landlord knew that she and Bella were underage, but it didn't seem to matter. With it being a hotel there were always younger people in there, and as long as they didn't actually order any drinks he could deny all knowledge, even though his son was in their year.

Mary felt a shiver just being in the building.

And then later, when Trent was gone. Her and Bella and–

'Mary!'

Jamie walks toward her from the saloon bar, a grin plastered on his face.

Although Jamie hadn't been part of it, hadn't been in their circle, he had always been *there.* Either working for his dad in the bar, or skulking in the corridor at school. Somehow he had always been around, just on the periphery. Bella had always found him a bit creepy. Mary had thought he was sad. She thought he was the kind of boy who didn't know how to talk, but knew a great deal about how to watch.

She glances at his scar.

And sometimes, how to do more than watch.

Mary looks at him, stitching a smile onto her face. 'Jamie, hi! How's it going?'

Jamie shrugs, his eyes flicking to her breasts, then to the corner of the room, then to her face.

'You know; end of the season and all that. Thanks for the extra guest though!' The grin hasn't left his face. Mary wonders if he practices it in the mirror. She feels her own smile sitting on her face like a slug.

'No problem. I was in the village, and I thought I'd pop in to see how she was. It was a real piss-down last night, wasn't it?'

Weak, she thinks. *How fucking weak does that sound?*

'Right!' Jamie performs the flick again; Mary is grateful for the baggy jumper she had thrown on that morning. 'Sure, she arrived fine. Quite late though; she must have taken a wrong turn somewhere.' Jamie's grin widens. 'She was absolutely sodden when she came in!'

Mary thinks of Athene, soaked; and of Jamie's special flick, and gives another little internal shudder. 'Right, well, happy to help.'

She pauses, taking a shallow breath as she mentally winds herself up, then says casually, 'Is she about, by any chance? Only she was asking me about something earlier, on the phone, and I've had a thought.'

'Sorry.' Jamie cocks his head slightly. 'You just missed her.'

Mary tries not to let the disappointment show on her face. 'Oh, right. She phoned me about half an hour ago, so I thought she'd still be here. Well, no worries.'

'She hasn't taken her stuff yet though, so I'm sure she'll be back.' Jamie looks at her, an odd expression on his face. 'In fact, I've offered her a deal, so I think she might book in for the week. You could stay if you like?'

'I'm sorry?' Mary looks at him, unsure what she had heard.

'Wait for her. We could have a cup of tea or something.'

'Oh! I see. No, you're all right, Jamie; thanks anyway. It wasn't that important.'

'No problem.' Jamie's voice, although still friendly, has become slightly harder. A little bitter, even. 'Do you want me to give her a message?'

Mary thinks, then shakes her head.

'Nah; but tell her I called, yeah?'

Jamie nods. 'Sure thing.'

'Cheers.'

Mary turns to leave.

'Bummer about the holiday cottage,' Jamie says behind her, trying to keep the conversation going.

Mary turns slowly, and looks at him. 'I'm sorry?'

'The cottage? The one that doesn't exist?' He grins. 'Some people will scam anything, right?'

Mary checks to see if he is joking, but his face is open. Or at least as open as it ever is. She shakes her head and takes a step towards him.

'Don't you know which one it was, Jamie? I thought I told you.'

Jamie looks at her blankly. Mary blinks.

'The holiday cottage. Didn't you ask Athene?'

'No.' Jamie shakes his head. 'Didn't want to sound like I thought she was stupid. Showing her up as an outsider, you know?' Jamie raises his eyebrows. 'Why, which one was–'

'It's Blea Fell, Jamie,' Mary cuts across him. Jamie's eyes snap to her face. Mary is bizarrely pleased to see panic there.

'What?'

'Blea Fell,' Mary repeats softly. She can see the confusion and brittle old fear staggering in Jamie's eyes. And behind his eyes. 'Bella's house.'

'Blea Fell? But how... I mean the place has been a wreck for years!'

'Years and years,' Mary agrees.

'Who'd want to go and rent a shell?'

'Here's the thing, Jamie, in the picture Athene had. The one in the brochure scam, or whatever, the house isn't a wreck.'

Mary stares at the man. She can see the creeping fear in his face. Not just the face he is wearing now, but his older face. The face he had when he was younger.

Jamie keeps shaking his head; he's not scoping her breasts anymore.

'That's impossible,' he says, eventually. 'Why would they get a picture, or even *how* would they...?'

Jamie's sentence peters out.

'Exactly. The only pictures of that house that went into the public domain was after the fire.' Mary leans forward, compressing the air between them with the past. 'After the fire and after the crash. And it doesn't look like those. It looks like...' She didn't finish her thought, but the widening of Jamie's eyes, coupled with the fear, tells her she doesn't need to. He looks at her urgently.

'Wait a minute, Mary. You don't think...'

Mary continues to hard-road Jamie with her gaze, and his sentence dies in his mouth.

'I've got to shoot, Jamie. Tell Athene I called when you see her, yeah?'

There is an awkward pause, and then Mary nods and leaves. As she walks out through the little archway she pauses and cocks her head, listening. After a second she continues to the door.

She doesn't explain what she was listening for. She doesn't have to: Jamie already knows.

'You won't hear it,' he whispers, something cold and wet slithering in the back of his mind. Something he thought was locked up and hidden forever. 'You won't hear it because it was never there.'

The front door closes shut with a prison click as Mary leaves.

Mary feels a weight lifting from her as she steps out into the sharp, clear air. The rain from the previous night has swelled the beck that runs down the centre of the village, and its fell waters have given the air a limestone edge; a taste on the wind that is almost salty. Which of course it is, she thinks, walking to her car, limestone being made up of millions of fossils of sea creatures from millennia ago.

All this was underwater, once, Mary muses, opening the door and shaking off the pub – the noises from the past – out of her head. In an odd way, she finds it quite a comforting thought.

13

ATHENE'S PHONE

😈 All going to plan
Blea Fell next to drop off you know what
Did you send email to H?
x

14

BELLA'S LAST DAY: NEW YEAR'S EVE, 1998. 8.45AM

Bella stared into the mirror, trying to read the lines of destruction on the map of her naked body. Her door is bolted, and Mazzy Star is playing softly on the Bang and Olufsen record player – once her father's, given to her as a present. Between the bass of the record, and the snow in her head, she can't hear if her mum is up and playing with her baby sister downstairs. She hoped she was.

She hoped so, but she doubted it.

She reached up slowly, running her fingers through the hacked choppy hair.

In the mirror, she could see all the little cuts and nicks on her body where, like with her hair, she'd tried to take back control. The same with the burn marks on her wrist and lower arm.

Mirror-Bella shrugged.

On the record player the song finished, and the needle arm flicked back, allowing the next single to drop: a song by Joy Division. As the guitars started, Bella felt a little of her armour slotting into place.

She took a deep breath and tried to centre. She felt the

wooden boards beneath her feet. She could feel each knot and whorl. Feel the build-up of all the bits of her she had shed over the years. The resin of her sweat and the dust of her skin. The skin of her tears and the sweat of her fear.

All pointless now. Like they belonged to somebody else.

Bella felt a wetness on her face; a tear slipping out of her eye; a poisoned pearl that slid off her face and dropped to the floor.

She watched its journey in the mirror, wondering if it was real, or in her head, or just in the reflection.

Maybe she'd try really hard, and give her mum a final present.

Maybe, when she went downstairs, she'd try to say hello. Try to be the daughter she used to be.

She smiled softly at herself in the mirror.

'Morning, Mum,' she whispered, practising.

The song finished, the needle pulling back and settling in its retaining hook.

Joy Division. 'Love will tear us apart.'

Bella slowly dressed for the last time.

15

MARY: THE CAFÉ

Mary had just finished with the lunchtime rush – which consisted of two ancient walkers who had bought a cup of tea and asked if they could eat their own sandwiches in the café – when the bell above the door had *pinged*, and Athene had stepped in.

'Hi!' Mary said before Athene was even through the doorway. She immediately felt foolish. Luckily Athene smiled and waved.

'Hello! I've come to take you up on your offer.'

Mary looked at her, momentarily confused.

'On the phone? Cooking me a pie?' Athene said, still smiling.

'Oh, of course. Apple pie! Take a seat; I won't be a minute.'

Athene nodded and sat down at a window table, taking her phone out of her backpack and tapping out a message, probably to her mum. When the walkers had left – without leaving a tip – Mary had dropped two plates of hot pie and cheese on the table and joined Athene.

'Stingy fuckers,' she said, nodding at the backs of the walkers.

'I want to go and look at Blea Fell House,' Athene had said, before even taking a mouthful.

'Why? It's just a shell now. There really isn't much to see.'

Mary takes a spoon of her pie and shovels it in her mouth, trying to disguise her unease. Athene smiles, and shrugs.

'I don't know. I guess it's because that's what brought me here. When my mum showed it to me, I kind of fell in love with it. It looked so gothy!' Athene's eyes gleam. 'Like from a romance novel or something. With the moorland and that strange gnarly bushy stuff–'

'Gorse bushes,' Mary says. Athene shakes her head.

'No, the other stuff. The stuff that looks like petrified trees growing out of the limestone.'

'Juniper,' Mary says quietly.

Athene snaps her fingers. 'That's it! They're amazing! They look like zombie trees! It would be worth going just to see them. Is it far from here?'

'Not far,' Mary says, non-committal. 'Have a bite of your pie. See what you think.' Mary keeps her head down. The image of the juniper trees as zombies sends shivers through her. It is not the first time the trees have been linked to the dead. Bella used to do it all the time. Between mouthfuls, Mary sneaks a look at the girl opposite.

Who are you, she thinks. *Really?* It seems like some sort of portent, the girl wanting to see Bella's house. And last night she had mentioned Heathcliff.

Athene picks up her fork and uses it to break off a corner of the pie. Mary watches as she puts it in her mouth. She feels the little flutter of butterfly wings in her stomach again as Athene's tongue slips out to pull the dessert in.

Stop it. Mary bites the inside of her cheek.

'This is delicious, Mary! Where did you learn to cook?' Athene is licking her lips in appreciation.

Mary smiles. 'My mum and dad weren't very culinary: from about seven I became the main cook of the family.'

'No way. That's like child slavery or something.' Athene's eyes are wide. 'At seven I'd never even learnt how to make a cup of tea.'

'Believe it or not,' Mary says, stabbing a piece of crust onto her own fork, and wiping it in the cream, 'children were meant to do things like cooking meals in my day.'

'Your day,' Athene smirks. 'What are you, thirty? Thirty-five? Hardly middle-aged.'

'You're as old as life has beaten you up to be,' Mary says. 'And you're not equipped to comment.' She points her fork at the folder on the table. 'You're still at school!'

Athene rolls her eyes, smiling. 'Oh please. A masters is hardly still being at school. I hated school. I was really shit at it. I had to do a whole round of interviews to get into uni, my results were so bad. Besides, I was old first. It's only now I'm young.'

'What an odd thing to say.' Mary smiles.

A shadow flickers across Athene's face, and Mary decides to move the conversation somewhere else.

'How come your mum found Blea Fell anyhow?'

Athene shrugs. 'I think it just came in one of those pop-ups. She was looking for quiet places for me to finish my thesis, and...' Athene wiggles her fingers. 'You know, once you start looking, hundreds of other suggestions come at you, offering similar things. Advertisement-targeting or whatever. This was one of those. Anyhow, I took one look at it and fell in love. I thought it would be exactly the sort of place I could curl up and finish my work.'

'On Trauma.'

Athene nods, cocking her thumb and finger like a gun. 'That's right.'

Mary feels a burst of pleasure. Athene is looking at her like she is a real person, and no one has done that for a long time. Working in the café people only ever see the uniform, and in her social life… well, she doesn't have a social life.

She drops her gaze and forks another piece of pie. 'Why Trauma? Is it something you were interested in as an undergraduate?'

'It's something I've been interested in ever since I can remember.' There is a tone in Athene's voice that makes Mary look up. Athene is still staring directly at her, but her eyes are now deep waters, swirling with unknown currents.

'I'm sorry, I didn't mean to intrude,' Mary begins.

'No, it's all right. It's just I had quite an…' Athene pauses. '*Eventful* childhood.' She finishes, clenching the hand that isn't holding the fork. Mary notices that her nails are ragged and torn, like they're the front line of a battle she has with herself on a regular basis.

Mary stays silent, not wanting to put her foot in it.

After a moment, Athene smiles, and the dark depths in her eyes become calm and shallow. 'But survivable.'

Mary nods in sympathy, unsure how to respond. *Fuck it*, she decides. 'I'm glad you came for pie, and I'm happy to show you around what remains of Blea Fell, if that's what you want.'

'Really? Thanks!' Athene throws Mary a lightning smile, before bending her head to scoop up the last of her pie from her fork. As she does, Mary feels her heart stutter, staring at Athene. Time seems to have flipped over. For a moment she saw the smile attached to a different face.

Mary shakes her head, scattering the image. Shaking it out of her brain.

Because of course it can't be; the person who had that smile would be Mary's age if she was alive. And the person who had that smile is dead.

Mary takes her hands off the table and presses them tightly

together out of sight, on her lap. All the colours in the café seem loaded like she'd turned up the contrast. She half expected the radio to burst into life, spewing out static and music from another age.

From the nineties.

It's the Blea Fell coincidence, she mind-whispers. *It's fucking with my head.*

'Mary, are you okay?' Athene is looking at her, face lined with concern.

Mary blinks herself back into the moment.

Nothing ever really goes away, she thinks. *Not really. Not completely.*

'Sure,' she manages, then borrows a smile from the future, and paints it on her face. 'It's just really odd that you got this pop-up, no? About the house? When it's all derelict and everything?'

Athene nods.

'Yes. But like you said, the scammers are everywhere.' She smiles. 'And if I hadn't got it then I would never have gotten to taste your pie, would I?'

'I guess not.' Mary hopes her voice sounds normal, because she certainly doesn't feel normal. 'When do you want to go and look at the house?'

'How about now?' Athene smiles.

It's not only the smile that has triggered her memory, it's the whole package.

Mary stares at the girl in front of her, and feels the cold snow of her past numbing her.

You look a little like Bella, she thinks.

16

BELLA'S SECRET DIARY: AUTUMN, 1992

I made friends with a mouse today!

She was at my new school and spent the whole time hiding in the corner until I gave her some cheese. She isn't really a mouse but that is what she calls herself. Plus the cheese was made-up cheese, really it was a bit of plasticine. The school is built of stone and only has one classroom! Not stone like bricks but stone like a rock. There is a list on the wall that tells what the weather is, and there is a real fire that keeps everything cosy. I think I am going to love it here. For my bedroom, I have a magical tower right at the top of its very own staircase, with its own big wooden door and its own lock.

I can be like a princess or a mad woman or a ghost and I can lock the door and nobody can stop me.

It's like living in a fairy-story house.

Sometimes the fog just appears like it was blown from a dragon's mouth.

There are these strange trees at the front of the house. They are like those Japanese trees that are made to be tiny. I think they are maybe sailors that have died, trying to claw their way out of the ground. My new teacher says that ages and ages ago this entire valley (she calls it a dale) used to be under the sea. She says that all the rocks called limestone aren't rocks at all, but are made up of zillions of fish bones! So maybe these trees are the bones of old sailors who got drowned.

I really really love it here. Everything is upside down.

I'm going to take some real cheese in tomorrow for Mouse. We have a pantry, which is like a fridge but a whole room.

I'm going to sleep now, but I will write more soon.

PS

I love it here, all locked away in my castle with dead sailors as my guards.

17

MARY: BLEA FELL

'My God, it's just so beautiful.'

Mary and Athene are standing on the crest of the moor, looking down onto the ruins of Blea Fell House. The sun is hiding behind fast-moving clouds that hang low over the day and scraps of mist cling to the moor reeds.

'Yes,' Mary whispers. It had been years since she had come up here, and she had forgotten the grating scarring beauty of it. Even with the building in tatters, maybe *because* of the building being in tatters, the place had a foreboding dignity.

'It looks like it grew there, out of the ground,' Athene marvels. 'Like it was part of the rocks or something.'

Mary points to the right of the derelict house; beyond the crumbling drystone walls that once enclosed the field at the back of the property.

'See there, the dip in the moor?'

Athene follows where Mary is pointing, and nods.

'Hidden in the dip is a natural pond. In the summer it's full of frogs and dragonflies. In the winter it freezes over. Kids used to come and skate there during the holidays.'

'You, too?' Athene says. Mary looks sharply at her, but the

young woman is staring at the moor as if she can see through the gorse and the rough grass to the pond.

'Yes, me too. I was actually quite friendly with the girl who lived here.'

Athene turns to her, wide-eyed.

'What, really? That's amazing!' She smiles at Mary, then the smile slips, and she looks confused. 'But when I asked you yesterday, you said at first you didn't know the house. How come–'

'There was an accident, a long time ago,' Mary says quietly.

She's dying, Trent! She's fucking dying in front of us!

Mary hears her own voice on the wind, blown from the past. Smells the fumes and the burning and the copper-wire stench of blood.

Athene tilts her head sideways slightly, peers at her, then at the house. Mary can practically see the cogs turn in her head.

'Oh, I'm sorry. Did your friend...' Athene pauses, as if unsure. 'Did she become ill?'

'Something like that,' Mary says, her voice short. Then, pointing up at the sky: 'Shall we go down? Those clouds look fairly nasty. If you want to take a look around then we'll need to be quick.'

Mary doesn't wait for a reply and strides down the hill, toward the rotting gate and the cattle grid that separated the moor from the track that wound up to the house. After a moment, Athene follows, her backpack banging against her side as she jogs to catch up.

'Look, I'm sorry; I didn't mean to pry.' Athene touches her lightly on the arm. 'I'm just a nosey cow. If I think of a question, it comes out of my mouth. Something must have happened for you to be so wary, I get that.'

'It's okay,' Mary says. She feels Athene's touch slipping from her arm like a burn. 'Over the years I've become wary. Sorry if you think I deceived you.'

The two women cross over the cattle grid, careful not to slide on the cylindrical metal. The grid is slippy, the metal having drawn moisture out of the air, covering the moss that has built up on the grid.

'No problem.'

Athene is first off the grid and holds her hand out for Mary. After a second's hesitation, she takes it, stepping onto the loose stone path. Athene gives her hand a slight squeeze, then lets it go, still keeping a light pressure so that Mary's hand slides out of her grasp, rather than falls.

Mary stays still, watching Athene as she walks ahead, her stride sure, looking over the drystone wall at the juniper trees; at Bella's ghost-forest. Mary swallows the bile that rises in her throat, her insides a confusion of memory and nausea and anger and hopelessness.

She tightens a lid on her emotions and follows her. It's been years since she walked up the path, but it feels the same. The low walls built to last a hundred years. Even the house, in all its dark ruin, is familiar. Although the roof has gone, leaving just the skeleton of blackened rafters, the walls are mostly there. The small windows, with their stone mullions, and the side porch, still stand. And the juniper trees on the moor in front still remain. *Of course they do*, she thinks, looking at them obliquely, *the dead always watch. That's all they've got to fill up their time*. The stunted trees, with their petrified looking trunks, and their strange windswept foliage, would be there forever, she felt. To Mary's eyes they were always frightening, but to her friend, Bella's, they were a grave-wood; something to be walked through at midnight, with a ghost-wind tugging at your nightdress.

Thinking of her friend, Mary suddenly looks at Athene, who

is standing, arms against the stone wall, peering through the broken window.

Is that it? Are you a ghost? Mary wonders, feeling the days of then and now mash together like they'd been braided. She stares at the young woman's back and then shakes her head.

Of course she isn't. Ghosts don't book into hotels, or drive cars, or use mobile phones.

Ghosts are just what lives on in someone's head when the person they love has died, and you never got to say goodbye. Never got to hug them, and thank them for all the times they protected you. Never got to tell them that you loved them.

Mary feels her bones ache inside her tired flesh.

Never got to say sorry.

'There's actual ivy growing up the inside!' Athene shouts delightfully, the noise dragging Mary back out of herself. She takes a hard breath and nods.

'I imagine there is. Not having a roof will do that,' she says dryly.

Athene runs round to the side of the building and looks at the porch door. It is half open – permanently by the look of the vegetation growing out of the bottom of it.

'Do you think it's safe to go in?' Athene is looking dubiously at the ripped porch.

Mary looks at the door. She can see where the paint has been wind-scorched away over the years, leaving the bare wood, which had become saturated with rain, then expanded until it was distorted and warped.

'It's stood here like this for decades; I see no reason why it should collapse now.'

The two women look at each other, then Athene grins and says: 'Let's do it!'

She places her back against the wall, then leans her shoulder against the door. When nothing happens she grunts and applies more pressure. Mary watches as the top of the door bends inwards, but the bottom stays firmly locked in the twines of root that bind it. Scattered around the door are splintered pieces of wood from the broken porch, like clubs. She sees that one has a rusted nail sticking out of it.

'Hang on, you're going to snap it if you keep that up! Come round the back; there's another way in. Maybe that door will be easier.'

'Right,' Athene says, straightening. She is breathing a little heavier from the exertion, her chest pressing against her jumper, and Mary finds herself blushing. Quickly, she moves around the porch, following the overgrown path to the back of the building.

The rear is as entangled as the front, and Mary has to pick her way carefully, mindful of wood and rusty nails.

'The front porch was hardly ever used,' she says. 'It was just for posh, as we used to say. The everyday entrance is around the back.'

'You'd think it would be at the front, so you could see the trees and that,' Athene says behind her.

'Too windy,' Mary explains, trailing her fingers across a wall she hasn't touched in two decades. 'That's why the trees are so stunted. It's only the fact that the roots are coddled by limestone that they stay up at all. The back entrance opens straight into the kitchen, so that food and washing and stuff didn't have to be dragged through the house.'

'Must be a pretty big kitchen,' Athene comments dryly.

Mary stops at the kitchen door, half off its hinges and hanging like a flag, like someone had already tried to smash it in. *Foxes*, Mary thinks, *and twenty years of brutal weather*. There is no porch; but rather a vestibule, allowing for coats and footwear and brollies. Mary looks at the empty racks.

I put my boots there. When I used to come and visit.

'It is. Was. Proper farmhouse kitchen, with a stove and everything. Come on, I'll show you.'

Mary is suddenly feeling reckless. Reckless and released.

All these years, she thinks.

Pulling the door gingerly, it spins on its one hinge and collapses against the wall.

'Careful!' Athene says with alarm. 'Those clasps look rusty; you could get sepsis or something off them!'

But Mary is already past the threshold. She takes a deep breath and steps in the kitchen that once was.

And freezes.

The large refectory table is still there, albeit looking like some kind of driftwood art piece. Bits of it have been gnawed at by animals, and mushrooms are growing from its shiny top.

The old stove, the Esse that Bella used to go on and on about, sits rusting in the hearth.

Even though there is no roof, and a whole army of rodents obviously live in the space, just being in the room is sending Mary spiralling back to when she was younger. For an instant she sees the ghost of herself and Bella sitting by the fire, smoking cigarettes and drinking stolen whisky.

Mary stands motionless and looks toward the door that once led to the staircase. The door is gone, but the stairs are still there. Of course they are; they are made of stone, like the walls. As she looks round, smells and tastes and the sounds from a different life bombard her, like a radio spewing out information from the static of the past.

'Hey, there are scorch marks on the wall!' Athene says, breaking into Mary's thoughts. She takes a raggedy breath.

'Yes. After the…' She pauses, trying to remember what she'd said to Athene. 'Accident with my friend, Bella, there was another tragedy.' Above them, the sky makes an ominous rumble. Mary swallows, and looks at the student. 'Somebody set fire to the building. Due to the inaccessibility of Blea Fell, the emergency services couldn't get here in time to save it.'

'Oh my God, how awful! Was anybody hurt?'

Mary looks around the wreckage where she'd sat with her friend.

'Yes, I'm afraid they were.'

Athene looks at her, as if trying to read her face. She opens her mouth, but before she can ask what she means, Mary's phone suddenly erupts with the opening bars of Julee Cruise's 'Falling', the theme song used for the TV show 'Twin Peaks'.

Mary reaches into her pocket, giving Athene an apologetic grin. 'Sorry.'

Athene smiles and makes a 'carry on' gesture. She walks away and starts an inspection of the room. Mary watches her for a second, then views her screen. There is no name displayed, only a number she doesn't recognise. She swipes the phone and lifts it to her ear, expecting to answer some query concerning the café.

'Hello, Mary Elland speaking. How may I help?'

'Mouse? Is that you?' The voice on the other end of the line is urgent, the tone tight and frantic.

Mary feels the blood drain from her face.

'Mouse, it's me! Are you there?' The voice seems to snake out of the phone straight into her brain.

There is a high-pitched whine deep in Mary's head. The colours of the room become brighter. The air seems to be charging itself. Mary watches as Athene kneels down and looks at something on the floor. Mary turns away, crushing the phone to her ear.

'Trent?' she says, unbelieving. '*Trent?* Is that you?'

'Of *course* it's fucking me!' The words are shouted, distorting slightly in the small phone-speaker.

It was a stupid question; of course it was him. Even though

she hadn't heard from or seen him for such a long time, she recognised his voice. Older, yes, but definitely his voice, reaching out across the years like a lasso.

'How did you get this number,' she whispered. Then: 'In fact, why the hell are you phoning me at all? You know that I–'

'Never mind that. Thank Christ it's you!' There was a pause, then the voice continued. 'Or maybe not. This is so fucked up, Mouse!'

'What is? What the hell are you talking about? Where the hell are you, anyway? Are you out of–'

Trent shuts off her question. 'I'm at work. But I'm going to drive up.'

'What?' Mary feels sick. She imagines it's because all the blood has left her stomach to flood her organs. Flight reflex. 'What do you mean? You can't do that. Trent? You don't–'

'I do; I'm coming. Don't worry...' The man on the other end of the phone laughs quietly; the sound hollow. 'I'll book in somewhere.'

Mary turns and looks at Athene. She is holding something in her hand, turning it as if trying to work out what it is.

'How did you get this number?' Mary repeats.

'That's just it! That's what makes it so weird!'

'What is?' Mary says, her voice rising. Athene looks at her, a question on her face. Mary staples a smile on, shrugging. Athene smiles, turns, and returns to examining whatever it was she had picked up.

'Your number! It was sent to me, along with the other stuff.'

'Sent to you?' Mary leans against the wall. 'What? How?'

'By email. I woke up this morning to find an email in my inbox, with a picture of Blea Fell, and this number. *Your* number, as it turns out.'

'Fucking hell,' Mary whispers.

'Yes. And that wasn't the worst of it.'

'What else?'

There is a pause.

'There was another picture, but this one had been digitally written over.'

'What was the picture?'

Trent's voice has an incredulity about it, like a magic trick had just happened. '*Treachery and violence are spears pointed at both ends*. That's what they'd written. You know what that's from, yeah?'

Of course she does. Bella had quoted it often enough. Mary bites her lip and concentrates. Trent's still talking. 'Then underneath they'd written *I know what happened, and I know why*. How fucked up is that?'

'What was the picture, Trent?' Mary feels like she is in two different places, or in two different times. Now, and that night when it all ended.

'There was a picture of us at the fair, Mouse,' Trent says softly. 'There was a picture of the three of us beside the car at the fucking winter fair.'

If he says any more, Mary doesn't hear. She takes the phone from her ear like it has bitten her and swipes to end the call. Then she turns off the phone and puts it in her pocket. She can feel it like it's radioactive, burning its isotopes into her skin through the fabric.

There was a picture of the three of us beside the car at the fucking winter fair.

She shakes her head.

Treachery and violence...

Impossible. Trent was messing with her for some reason. Playing some sick game, like he used to.

But his voice, she thinks, *he sounded scared.*

The very idea of seeing Trent again makes her feel like

screaming, but the fact he'd been sent her number; that someone is bringing back the past...

'Is everything all right?'

Mary looks up to see Athene standing in front of her. She realises she must have zoned out. She tries to smile, but fails. 'Not really. Do you mind if we go?'

'Shit, no! I'm sorry to have dragged you out here!'

'No it's fine, but I really need to–'

There is a sudden spear of lightning, followed a few seconds later by a growl of thunder. The air feels like it might ignite.

'We'd better get back to the car before it pisses down,' Mary says.

Athene nods, and begins turning, putting something in her pocket as she does so.

'What did you find?'

Athene turns back, smiling. She shows Mary what she has in her hand.

'Look,' she says. 'It's lovely, isn't it? I guess there must have been a baby in the house; there are a few toys half-buried over there. Maybe they had a playpen or something?'

Mary isn't looking at her; she is looking at what she is holding. It is a little wooden animal. A little bird. The paint is faded, and the wood is covered with moss and slime, but Mary recognises it immediately.

Of course she does.

She was the one who gave it to Bella's baby sister.

'It's an owl, you see?' Athene says happily. 'Which is a massive coincidence, because that's my name!'

Mary looks at her, not understanding.

'My name, Athene?' the girl says.

'Like the bird,' Mary says numbly. Athene nods.

'Yes.' She holds up the wooden toy and gives it a little shake. 'But particularly like this bird. Athene is a type of owl.'

'Owl,' Mary repeats, staring at her. 'Your name means owl?'

Athene nods, smiling.

Which is when the lightning and thunder erupts directly above them, and the rain starts dropping like it's the end of the world.

18

BELLA'S LAST DAY: 10AM

Bella walked across the frozen fields to Mouse's house, her boots crunching through the crust of the snow. She started laughing. For some reason it made her feel like she was walking on a cake; like she was like one of those tiny model people you got on wedding cakes, trudging across the surface until, inevitably, she would fall off the edge and land on the table, breaking her little model neck.

Bella laughed harder, higher.

Even to herself, Bella knew the laughing wasn't good.

A lone sixteen-year-old in a field, wearing a coat that looked like a coffin, laughing into the desolate day.

Bella stopped laughing.

She lay down, in the middle of the field, feeling the cracked snow form a Bella-shaped dent. Keeping her legs together, she slowly spread out her arms, dragging them through the crisp, cold snow.

Yes, this looks much more normal, she thought, and giggled a little. She brought her arms back down to her sides.

Carefully, she tightened her stomach muscles, and pulled herself up from her waist, stepping out of the hole she had made in the snow. Once clear she turned and cast a critical eye over her work.

'Not bad,' she said after a minute. On the ground was the ghost-Bella indentation, plus the two semi-circles where she had moved her arms.

Her wings.

When she was very young, her mother had taught her how to make a snow angel, but Bella had always hated the concept. She had never understood why the angels would be laying on the ground. Eventually, she had come to the only conclusion that made any sense to her.

The angels were dead.

Bella looked at her angel a moment longer, then continued across the fields to Mouse's house.

19

MARY'S CAR: BLEA MOOR BACK ROAD

'Her name was Bella, and she died in a terrible accident.'

Mary shivers as she drives her car along the windy road, the heater turned up to the max, filling the vehicle with a low roar, and the smell of burning oil. She rips her eyes from the road for a second to look at the girl beside her.

'Could you keep your eyes on the road, please!'

Athene looks petrified, gripping the car seat, with her feet pushed hard against the front of the passenger well. Mary's gaze stutters across time, seeing a different girl in a different car, also with her legs pressed against the well, a mad smile hanging off her face, unloosed by the night. She stares at Athene for another long second, then drags her eyes back to the road, finally slowing down to a more acceptable speed. The rain is falling out of the sky so hard that it sounds like the car is being hit with concrete bees.

'Fucking shit,' she mutters.

'Thank you,' Athene breathes, unclenching her hand from the seat.

Mary nods, then pulls sharply into a lay-by, skidding to a stop and turning off the engine, killing the wipers. Almost immediately the rain made visibility impossible, sluicing down the windows. The over-revved engine begins ticking as it cools, pinging and clicking.

'Jesus, it's really coming down,' marvels Athene, wiping at the screen.

'How did you get the photo of Blea Fell, Athene?' Mary asks, staring straight ahead at the rain streaming down the windscreen.

'I told you,' Athene says, her voice quiet, soft. 'It was in the brochure my mum got s–'

'Bollocks,' Mary cuts across her. 'The picture in that booklet was from before, when Bella lived there. How did you get it?'

Athene shakes her head. 'Like I said, I–'

'Stop fucking with me, Athene-like-the-bloody-bird! That picture? That's a family picture! Personal! That's not a professional photo! The house has been wrecked for years!'

Mary's voice has risen. Athene stares at her, shaking her head. Mary can see a pulse in her neck, a repeat of the fear ticking in her eyes. Mary doesn't care.

'And that owl,' she spits, jabbing a finger at the old wooden toy upon the student's lap. 'What the fuck is that about?'

'I don't know what you mean.' There is a shake in Athene's voice. 'I found it while you were on the phone.'

'What, after all these years?' Mary scoffs, her own voice buzzing with incredulity. 'It was just sitting there on the floor, was it?'

Athene nods. Mary watches as a large tear forms in the girl's left eye.

'Half buried, along with other stuff. I'm sorry if I've done something wrong,' she whispers. 'I just saw it there and it looked so sad. It was someone's toy and it was laying in the dirt, so I picked it up.'

The tear slips out of Athene's eye and begins a slow roll

down her face, already wet from the rain. Mary watches, the anger and fear replaced by a horror at her shouting at the woman. She puts out her hand, but leaves it hanging in the air, unsure.

'Athene, I'm sorry. It's just that what happened, all that time ago.' She closes her eyes tight for a second, then opens them, withdrawing her hand and placing it on the steering wheel. 'Being in Blea Fell brought it all back. And then seeing you with the owl, well, I guess I lost it.'

Mary lets out a shaky laugh, and hits the wiper bar, causing the rubber blades to scrape across the windscreen. For a second the landscape becomes clear through the glass. The moor and the stone: the green and the grey of the world outside the car. Then the rain obscures it all again.

'And Trent,' Athene says softly.

'I'm sorry?'

'The person on the end of the phone?'

Mary feels the air condense around them.

'What about him?'

'I don't know. You sounded upset.'

Mary nods, tapping the steering wheel with her fingers; beating out a rhythm only she could hear.

'Look, Mary,' Athene's voice is tentative, like she is stroking a tiger. 'I know we haven't known each other very long...'

Haven't we, Bella? Mary's mind is shredded. She knew the girl couldn't possibly be her friend from so long ago. Her friend who she had... Mary shut the thought down, and it was immediately replaced with another. She looked at the student, hard. She couldn't be her friend, but she was the right age to be someone else.

'No we haven't.'

'But I definitely feel we have a connection. I'm not sure what it is, but I feel it...'

Outside the storm has made the day dark, and Mary watches the ghost-like image of Athene tap her chest in the liquid mirror of the windscreen.

'...in here. In fact the whole landscape, and the house and...' Athene shrugs helplessly, and raises up the owl. 'Even this! I don't understand it.'

Mary stays staring straight ahead, watching herself in the windscreen. Watching the reflection of her face being pulled apart by the rain-trails that slipped down the glass. Finally she sighs and turns to face the girl. She sees the tear trails down her face, and bizarrely that makes her feel better.

I never saw Bella cry. Not once.

Mary reaches out and gently touches her cheek. Athene's returning smile is wan.

'The girl who lived there, in Blea Fell, was my best friend.'

Athene nods, her eyes wide.

'She died in a terrible accident.'

'Was it the fire?' Athene asks, her voice barely above a whisper. The rain and the charged thunderstorm air has made the atmosphere in the little car electric.

Mary shakes her head.

What a fucking mess, she thinks.

'No, the fire came later, after she had died.'

20

BELLA'S LAST DAY: MOUSE'S ROOM

'Can you make me a car tape, Mouse? For tonight?'

Bella and Mouse were listening to music, ticking away the day in cigarettes.

'I'm sorry?'

'A mixtape: I've got a list.' Bella reached into her coat, and took out a folded piece of paper. As she did so, her sleeve rode up, exposing the skin on her wrist for a brief moment. Mouse saw the cuts and burns before the sleeve rode back down. Smiling, Bella handed the sheet to Mouse. Mouse looked at it, just for something to look at, because she was too afraid to ask her friend what was so bad that she was hurting herself. Because she was too afraid of the answer. Instead she looked at the list. It had been written on a page ripped from Bella's diary. On it were scrawled five songs.

'Wow,' said Mouse, scanning the list. 'I think we're going to need gin if we're listening to this.'

Bella smiled, picking up her pack of smokes and the Zippo.

'It's for the drive home after the fair.'

Mouse gazed at her for the longest moment, then she took a deep breath and tried to be brave.

'Are you okay, Bella?'

Mouse's eyes flicked to Bella's wrist, safely hidden behind the cloth armour. To her hair, hacked and crumpled. 'I mean you can talk to me if...'

Bella nodded. 'What would you like to talk about, Mouse? Would you like to talk about love? Or friendship? Or trust?'

Mouse stared at her. She wanted to say something, but all the words had run away. Bella looked at her a second longer, then smiled gently. Her face softened.

'I'm *fine*, Mouse, really.' Bella raised her hand and stroked her friend's face. '*We're* fine. I just need to get this year behind me, that's all.'

Bella hugged the flesh and bones of Mouse, and left her bedroom for the last time.

On the way back across the fields she looked at the spot where she had lain down on the iced grass. Her angel had become a black hole, surrounded by the glitter of hardening snow.

'You're such a fucking bitch, Bella,' she said, tears freezing in her eyes.

21

BELLA AND MOUSE'S FIRST DAY AT HIGH SCHOOL

THE SCHOOL BUS, 1996

'Who's *that?*'

'That's Trent. He lives in the next village. And he's *fifteen,* Bella!' Mouse hissed.

If Mouse thought that might put Bella off, she was wrong. Her friend leant closer to the school bus window, her breath misting the glass, her eyes creeping over the boy who stood by the side of the road. He was wearing a smile on half his face like a sideways question mark. Mouse thought he looked like a broken fire alarm in a burning building.

'He looks like Heathcliff,' Bella whispered.

'He's bad news, Bells.' Mouse watched as the bus doors slid open with a hiss, and the boys got on.

'So what?'

Trent paused just past the bus driver, and quickly surveyed the bus, looking for the best seat. The school bus was a war zone, with lines decided on the first day, that would be hard-wired and difficult to break. The back seats were taken by the sixth formers, boys and girls who had earned their spot; had fought their way through the battle of school life. The next few rows were occupied by the wannabes: girls who would put out for the older boys; who thought slutting it up was cool and would make them accepted. The front rows were like the back rows, but in reverse; they were reserved for the freaks and geeks; the refuse-niks who stood outside of the war; who took the front so they could make a quick getaway.

The rest of the bus was a chessboard, with the seats as strategies for developing friendships or protecting from enemies, or sometimes both.

By rights, at fifteen, Trent should have gone near the back, away from Mouse and Bella, who had positioned themselves near the front; but because he was new to the area, like the kids who had come up from middle school, he had to make quick decisions.

He scanned the bus until he saw Mouse and Bella. When he looked at her, Mouse wanted to hide, as if she was eight again. His eyes stayed fixed on her for a nanosecond, passed on to Bella, then continued scanning. He nodded, seeing someone behind them, and sauntered up the aisle. As he passed by their seat he ignored them, even though he must have felt Bella's eyes burning themselves onto him, following him. Mouse grabbed her arm, and dug her nails into the skin until Bella looked at her.

'You've got to stop staring at him!' she whispered urgently.

'Why?'

'Why? Because he's fifteen and if he has any interest in a thirteen-year-old he's sick! Because he's got arrogance coming out of his ears and he's going to be in detention forever! And because... because...'

Mouse ran out of road with her mouth, but kept the accelerator pressed down with her eyes.

Because he'll steal you away from me, she screamed with her gaze.

Bella stayed staring at her, quizzical, then slowly reached up and placed her hand gently over Mouse's.

'It's all right, Mouse,' she said, her eyes locked on her. 'I'm only looking. I'm not going to do anything.'

Mouse stared deep into her eyes, trying to see the woman hiding behind the girl. Her feelings for Bella, so simple and sure in primary school, were becoming... something unknown. She ripped her gaze away from Bella's eyes and down at her friend's hand, gently resting on her arm like a butterfly.

Then she watched as the butterfly pushed, slowly pressing Mouse's hand down, making her dig her nails further into Bella's flesh.

'Bella, stop it...' Mouse whispered. She watched as the hand pushing hers whitened, flattened with the pressure. She tried to push back, but Bella was stronger than her; stronger than anything.

'Bella, it hurts,' whispered Mouse.

Still keeping the terrible pressure on, Bella leant forward and whispered in Mouse's ear.

'Yes, it does,' was all she said, releasing Mouse's hand, and leaning back again. Mouse pulled her hand away feeling, actually *feeling*, her nails slide out of Bella's skin, like she had claws. Bella turned away and looked out of the window. Mouse stared in horror at Bella's arm; the bruised skin and the four crescent cuts. She reached forward with her hand, unsure what she should do; whether to stroke it, or pull the jumper down. In the end she did nothing, just looked at the girl beside her, staring out of the window.

Why did you make me hurt you?

Then she realised that Bella wasn't staring out of the window at all; she was using it as a mirror. Mouse turned around in her seat, and raised her head over the headrest, to see what Bella was looking at. Three rows behind them Trent was sat next to

Jamie, the creepy boy who always seemed to be undressing you with his eyes. The boy with the camera.

And he did not look happy to have Trent sitting next to him.

He looked absolutely petrified.

22

MARY'S CAR: BLEA MOOR

PRESENT DAY

'Wow; the weather in this place doesn't mess about, does it?'

Mary shakes her head. 'Not hardly. It's like a drunk at a party. One minute interesting and funny and giving you the best time ever, then the next throwing up on your cheese plant.'

'Yuck. Nice image; thanks.'

'Welcome.'

The deluge has ended, and Mary and Athene sit in the car, the windscreen covered in diamonds of water. With the breaking of the storm, something has cleared, and the silence they sit in no longer feels dangerous.

She's not part of it, Mary thinks. *She looks a tiny bit like Bella might have if she'd reached that age, and my imagination did the rest.*

The phone call from Trent had freaked her, that was all. That, and the owl, and the fact that she'd been on electric tiles ever since she'd seen the photograph of Blea Fell.

'You were telling me how Bella, your friend, died?'

Athene's voice cuts into Mary's thoughts. She turns and looks at the girl. She really does look a little like Bella, but Mary thinks it's more in the history of the face rather than the face itself. Mary could see pain in it. And survival. There's something in her past that's giving her strength. She hadn't mentioned a father, Mary noted, just a mother. Maybe there was a separation, or a death.

Mary took a deep raggedy breath. 'Do you have any brothers or sisters, Athene?' she says quietly.

'No. Why do you ask?'

Mary shakes her head. 'I don't know, it was just the way you picked up the owl.'

'No, single child, I'm afraid. Just me and my mum.'

'Me, too. Single child, I mean. My parents had me quite late. Very late.' Mary smiles humourlessly. 'So late, in fact, that I was less a happy surprise than a final demand.'

'I'm sorry.' Athene looks at her with such intensity that Mary wonders if she's analysing her; maybe as a case study for one of her trauma essays. She shakes her head.

'Don't be. It wasn't easy, though. They didn't mix with the other children's parents; they had nothing in common. Consequently I never found it easy to make friends. There were no natural invites, and you've seen the way the farms are set out. It's not exactly as if you can just pop over.'

The two women sit in silence, staring out at the total lack of housing in front of them.

'But you said Bella was your friend?' Athene prompts, after a moment.

Mary nods. 'My only friend. Her parents moved up and bought Blea Fell and sent Bella to the village primary school. I can still remember the first day, when she walked in.' Mary smiles. 'I was hiding under a chair.'

Athene giggles.

You probably think that's cute, thinks Mary bitterly, but she doesn't let it show. This girl sitting in her car wasn't to know; wouldn't understand the fear Mary had felt merely living. Of the endless hours in a silent house, her aged parents sat in mute desperation of mortality. The squirming, oily, heavy worm of anxiety that sat in her stomach every time she stepped into school.

'I spent most of my primary school life pretending to be a mouse. I would hide under the chair and scream if anybody tried to make me come out.'

'Okay,' Athene says.

Mary sneaks a sideways glance at her, wondering if she understood. Athene's gaze is open; not amused or surprised or wary.

'In fact that was my name, in the end: Mouse. It stuck right through middle school and into high school. All the way until I got expelled.'

'You got expelled?' Athene looks amazed, her mouth slightly open. Mary tries very hard not to look at the thread of spittle that spanned her upper and lower lip.

'What can I say? It was near the end of the century; the whole world was a little bit crazy.'

'But was it something to do with your friend? Bella?'

'Sort of. After she died everything went a little bit fucked.'

'Jesus, I'll bet. And what about what's his name; Trent? Is he... was he...?'

The sentence stays hanging in the air between them. Mary feels the rattle of the memory-coins inside her.

'He was Bella's boyfriend,' she says after a short pause. 'Or kind of her boyfriend.'

'Oh! Okay. He must have been devastated when she died.'

Mary gives a bitter laugh. 'Oh, he was that, all right. And the rest.' Mary actually thinks she can feel a lock snap inside her, letting out a little of the past.

'If you don't mind me asking, how did she die? Your friend?'

Mary shivers, shaking her head. 'I can't talk about it. Not here.'

'Oh, I'm sorry. I didn't mean to pry.' Athene touches her shoulder lightly.

Mary's body lets off another small shiver, then she smiles at the girl. 'Look, we'll catch our death if we stay here; we're soaked to the skin. How about we go back to mine and have some hot cocoa?'

Athene looks a little wary. Mary blows out an air of exasperation, mainly at herself.

'I'm not trying to chat you up, okay? I'll admit, I am trying to get you out of your clothes, but only so I can dry them, and return them before you get pneumonia.'

Athene grins.

'Okay.'

'Okay.' Mary smiles, starting the car. 'It'll only take five minutes from here. My house is actually only a mile or so from Bella's. Really quick if you cut across the field, but much longer by road.'

Mary checks the mirror, then pulls out.

'So, did you see each other regularly?'

'All the time.' Mary nods, driving carefully on the winding road; the recent deluge has made the tarmac slippy, and the warmth of the road compared to the moor often attracted the sheep that roamed freely on the rough land. 'Every day in the early years. Less as we got older.'

'Why was that?'

Mary takes a small turning off the B road onto a track.

'Oh, you know how it is. Homework. Romance. All that shit that happens to teenagers.'

'Right.'

Mary is acutely aware that she might be oversharing.

But she's asking, she thinks. Then: *Why is she asking?*

Mary negotiates the humps and bumps of the track, driving slowly through the trees.

After a few moments the cottage swings into view, snatches of it revealing itself through the evergreen foliage. Athene whistles.

'That's where you live? It's beautiful!'

'I know, it's a bit scary-single-witch-in-the-woods, but I love it. When my parents died I had the opportunity to sell, but I'd spent so many years alone here when they were alive, continuing after they were dead, it seemed…' Mary shrugs, '…natural.'

She suddenly slams down on the brakes, bringing the car to a juddering halt.

'Jesus!' Athene shouts, rocking against her seat belt. 'What happened?' She looks around wildly. 'Was it an animal? Have we run over something?'

Mary doesn't answer.

'The gate's open,' she says eventually. 'When I left this morning I closed it.'

Athene shakes her head in confusion, clearly unsure of the problem.

'Right. Probably the postman, yes?'

'The postman has a drop-off at the bottom of the track, by the main road. The track is snowbound in the winter. Impossible for the van to get up.'

'Delivery, then? Yodel or whatever,' Athene offers, the bewilderment in her voice increasing.

'Same thing. No delivery ever comes up here. If something has to be signed for, it's delivered to the café.'

'Okay, farmer then, or walker, or tradesperson, dropping in a business card. I'm not sure what the problem is here.'

'Maybe,' Mary says, unsure. She edges the car through the gap between the two walls and past the open gate, on up to the cottage. Athene peers out of the window.

'There's no one here now. I reckon you'll find a business card stuck in your door jamb. We get it all the time back home. Dog walking or window cleaning. Any bloody thing people can think of to make some extra money. I don't know where people get the ideas half–'

'There's something on the door,' interrupts Mary.

'See, I told you!' said Athene brightly. 'It'll be a card from–'

'No.' Mary stops the car in front of the house. She pulls the handle, opening the door, and steps out. As soon as the door opens the smell of the storm hits her. The high notes of charged ion particles, and the end of summer smell of the gorse. The woody earthy smell of the dark between the trees, where she'd seen the birds take flight earlier. Mary looks from her house to the trees.

*Someone was here earlie*r, she thinks, remembering the birds. *Someone was watching me.*

'What are you looking at?' Athene asks, stepping out of the car and following Mary's gaze. 'Is there something in the woods?'

'No; not now, anyway.' Mary, taking a last look into the gloom, turns and walks to her front door. Athene steps in beside her.

'Such a beautiful house, but so isolated,' she says quietly. 'Don't you ever get frightened?'

Mary stops in front of the door.

'Oh my God,' she whispers, taking a step back.

'What?' Athene asks in alarm. 'What's wrong?'

She looks from Mary to the door, then slowly steps forward.

'This?' she asks, eyebrows raised. 'Is it this? It looks like a Christmas decoration.'

Attached to the entrance were two small bells, held together and hanging by a red ribbon. Athene reaches out and pulls the pin that holds them there. As she removes them they make a small chime, sending Mary's hands to her mouth.

'Oh my God,' she whispers again, taking another step back.

'Mary what is it? What's the matter?' the alarm in Athene's voice finally cuts through, and Mary drags her gaze away from the tiny bells in Athene's hand, and up into her eyes.

'My friend who died? All those years ago?'

Athene nods. 'Bella.'

Mary points to the two chimes. 'Her nickname, or the name we had that was our special name. Mine was–'

'Mouse, yes. You've told me. What's going on, Mary? You're beginning to freak me a little.'

Mary reaches forward and gently lifts the chimes out of Athene's hand. As she does they make a small sound, the tone clear and pure.

'Hers was Bells.'

Athene stares at her, the wind tugging at her coloured hair, escaping from under her soaked hat. 'Bells.'

Mary nods.

'You know how kids are. Back in the day there was a thing for putting an "s" on the end of anything. Laters. Tunes. Bella was Bells.'

'I see. Makes sense. But what has this got to do with–'

'It was kind of like my secret name for her. Something we shared between ourselves.' Mary swallows. 'One Christmas I bought her a present; I'd seen it in Woolworths. It wasn't much; my parents didn't really give me any money, and I was too young to have a Saturday job.'

'How old were you?'

'Twelve. It was just before everything changed.'

'What do you mean?'

Mary shakes her head. 'Like I said. Boyfriends and stuff. Going from middle school to the comp.'

'What was it, Mary? What did you buy her?'

Mary holds up the brace of bells. 'This, Athene. I bought her this.'

Mary stares at the bells, then looks back out to the woods.

You waited until I left, didn't you? You waited until I left, then came and stuck these on my door.

The woods stayed dark and secret and quiet.

'There's a card.'

'What?' Mary looks away from the trees and at Athene.

'On the step. It must have been shoved in the door jamb or whatever.'

Mary looks down. On the flat slate outside her door is a plain white envelope.

Athene stoops and picks it up, turning it over in her hand as she stands. 'There's no name or address on it, but I guess it must have come with the bells.'

'Open it,' Mary says, a ball of fear in her chest.

'Sure. At least then you'll know what's going on. It's not sealed.' Athene pulls the envelope open and reaches in. 'It's a photograph,' she says, puzzled, as she slides out a single sheet of photographic paper; the kind that people use to print at home. The image is turned away from her, so Mary can only see the back.

She can see Athene's expression, however. The girl looks confused. Confused and worried.

'I don't understand,' she says, looking at the print. 'Why would someone send you a photo of this?'

'What is it? What's on the print? Is there a message?'

Silently, Athene hands the sheet over. Mary takes it and turns it round. It takes her a second to realise what she is looking at, but when she does the world starts spinning.

'Mary!' Athene grabs her before she can fall, supporting her as she tries to breathe. 'Come on! What is it? Why has someone sent you a picture of that? What does it mean?'

Mary sucks in a deep breath, and looks at the print again. It shows a road covered in snow. The shot was taken at night, obviously with a good camera. The trees at the edge of the road are stark in the blue light of the ambulance framed in the right-hand corner of the shot. Individual flakes of snow are lit by the beam shining from the unit on its roof. The main area of the frame is taken up by the crashed car, laying on its back, shards of glass and blood in the ice and snow around it like a Pollock painting. Mary looks aghast at the body of Bella hanging out of the windscreen; at the twisted metal of the car and broken side windows. At the blood in the ice and snow and the wheels sticking up like the legs of a dead beetle.

'It means that someone is fucking with me,' she says quietly, her voice sounding like it was spoken by a different person. After a second she looks up at Athene. 'This?' She shakes the print, like whoever left it for her might fall out of the image. 'You wanted to know what happened to my friend? This did! That girl is Bella! She died in a car crash on New Year's Eve.'

23

THE CRAVEN HEAD: SUMMER, 1996

'Hi, I'm Trent.'

Jamie looked up from the scuzzy floor at the boy, who he guessed was about his age. Fourteen, maybe even fifteen. He was tall and thin, with a long dirty fringe that had danger written all over it.

'All right,' he muttered, not making eye contact.

They were in the hotel bar. Jamie was clearing up the room; tipping out the ashtrays and collecting the empties; washing the glasses and wiping down the bar. His parents should have done it the previous night, but they had been too mangled. He didn't mind. If it had been a good night then there was always treasure. So far this morning his haul had been a half pack of Benson and Hedges, around a fiver in change, and a wallet. He hadn't looked in the wallet yet: wallets were for saving, once he was alone. Wallets sometimes held secrets.

'I'm staying here,' said the boy, Trent, a smile in his voice. 'At this hotel. My dad is up to look at buying a house. What's it like round here?'

Jamie didn't answer. He wondered if the boy could smell the stale ash on his clothes.

'I bet it's a shithole. I bet there's sod all to do except push over cows and race ferrets, am I right?'

Jamie let out a little giggle. He couldn't help himself. The boy chuckled along with him, and stuck out his fist.

'What's that for?' Jamie looked at it, wondering if the boy was threatening him.

'You bump your fist against it. Like the boxers, or Mick Taylor. It's like a handshake, only much cooler.'

'Mick Taylor?' Jamie continued to eye the fist.

'The cricketer? For Australia?'

'Right.'

'I love the Aussies, me. The cricket. Crocodile Dundee. I'm going to emigrate there, first chance I get.' Trent raked his other hand through his hair, pushing back his fringe.

Jamie nodded, smiling shyly at the boy.

'Better than this shithole,' he said, echoing the boy's comments. He stuck out his fist. 'Jamie. That's my name.'

Trent grinned and gently hit the offered fist with his own. Jamie felt a little thrill run through him.

'Good to meet you, Jamms. I reckon you and me could be mates, if my old man moves up here.'

The elation Jamie had felt when Trent had touched him disappeared like it had never been. He turned away and picked up butts off the carpet and put them in a metal waste bin.

'If you move up here you wouldn't want to be mates with me. I'm way too uncool.'

'Oh, I don't know; I'm not really into cool.'

Trent sat on a table and took a little box out of his shirt pocket. He looked at it, then began tapping.

'Is that a pager?' said Jamie, slightly awed.

Trent nodded. 'Yeah. My dad insists I have it. He says it's so that he knows I'm safe, but that's bollocks. It's so he can keep tabs on me.'

Jamie stared at Trent, open-mouthed. He'd never heard someone speak about their parent like that. Like they were enemies.

'Why does he need to keep tabs on you, Trent?'

Trent finished typing and put the pager back in his pocket.

'So he knows I'm not going to burn the hotel down,' he said, grinning. He pulled a Zippo out of his jeans pocket, flicked the lid and raised an eyebrow at Jamie. 'Now, mate, I bet you find all sorts when you clean up around here, yeah? How about any fags?'

Jamie stared at Trent for a moment, then grinned.

24

ATHENE'S PHONE

😈 H phoned: M freaked
Bell and photo found, about
to have a heart to heart
Maybe something will slip
x

25

MARY'S HOUSE

'I'm not actually a lesbian, by the way,' Mary remarks, walking back into the living room from the kitchen carrying a tray with the hot chocolates. She hands the steaming mug to Athene and sits down on the floor opposite her, by the fire. 'In case I gave you that impression.'

'Sorry; answering a message from my professor, letting him know that my work might be delayed.' Athene swipes her phone and places it on the little table by the settee. Then she shrugs. 'None of my business; straight or gay is all the same to me. Love is love, right?'

Mary nods thoughtfully, staring at the flames. 'Love is love,' she repeats. 'I never really understood what that meant. Love is... unasked for.' She watches as the flames grow and change colour, always in motion, never still.

She sighs and licks her lips, not looking at Athene. She'd semi-composed what she was going to say while she'd been making the drinks.

'When Bella came into my life I was ten, in my last year of primary school. She was so different to all the local kids. She had this tenderness about her, like she'd seen things, done things.' Mary shrugs, staring into the fire. 'The way she was curious and kind, but somehow separate...' She quickly takes a sip of her drink. The hot liquid scalds the roof of her mouth. 'I don't know. She was just nice to me, really. Actually saw *me* instead of around or through me... I guess I fell in love with her almost straight away. She became my best friend and my sister and I suppose even my parent. She seemed so certain of who she was and where she was that I just... let her run me.'

'Run you?' Athene's voice is soft. 'What an odd phrase.'

Mary smiles at the flames.

'Yes; it sounds funny, doesn't it? But my parents were so distant, and the rest of the kids acted like I didn't exist, that it felt nice to let go of control. Let somebody else make the decisions.'

In her peripheral vision she watches Athene. The girl nods once, like she was agreeing, or maybe just confirming that she has heard.

'Being a child is like being an island with treasure on it; you have to guard it from pirates,' Athene says.

Mary turns and fully looks at her, open-mouthed.

'That's exactly it! Everybody wants to occupy you. Have I heard that before: is it a saying or something?'

Athene smiles shyly.

'Probably. It's something my mum said.'

'She sounds very wise.'

Mary sees a shadow cross Athene's face.

Definitely some trouble in the past, she thinks. She doesn't push it, not wishing to intrude. Instead, she turns back to the fire. Outside, the day has started weeping again, leaving its rain-tears on the cottage windows.

'I like to think that we were very happy, me and Bella. In our childhood. We would walk over to each other's houses and go exploring on the moor. In the summer we'd spend hours watching the dragonflies up on the pond. They were so big some years it was like having insect birds buzzing over the water; or mechanical rainbows.' Mary takes another sip of her cocoa and smiles at Athene. 'Like your hair.'

Athene self-consciously tucks the wet strands behind her ear. 'So, did you spend a lot of time in each other's houses? I bet it was fun having sleepovers at Blea Fell! In the middle of the moor.'

'No, hardly ever. My parents would get nervous if I stayed away. I guess it was because they were so old. They'd lost their ability to be reassured if I wasn't near them. And Bella never really liked me sleeping over. I think she struggled with anyone in her private space.'

Mary smiles at a memory.

'And then as we got older, sleep became less important. We'd stay up by the fire and talk and smoke and just... be.' Mary shrugs. 'You know how it is when you enter your teens.'

'Oh, yes,' Athene says. 'Difficult to ever forget.'

Mary nods and smiles, but then feels the smile slip. 'Anyhow, for three years I had Bella all to myself and she was all that I needed, everything that I wanted.' Mary takes a shaky breath.

'And then?' Athene leans forward slightly.

Mary shrugs. 'And then Trent came along, and everything was ruined.'

'He broke up the friendship?'

Oh, you have no idea, Mary whispers inside her head.

'The first time she saw him was on the school bus. It was like she had been waiting for him all along, and everything that *we* were, was just passing time,' Mary mused, the distance between then and now nothing more than a bitter blink of the eye.

I'm sorry.

'We were thirteen, and he was fifteen.'

'That's... wrong,' Athene says, after a pause.

'I know, but it didn't seem so, somehow. Trent was a wild

card. New to the area, with a shady history he never told anyone about directly. He was like a movie character. He used to smoke those white-tipped American cigarettes you couldn't even buy round here then. He looked like a rebel.'

'Like James Dean?' Athene asks.

Mary pauses and blinks cat-slow at the fire, remembering how Bella would always go on about the actor. 'Yes, exactly like that,' Mary says slowly, turning to look at Athene. 'What made you think of him?'

Athene shrugs. 'A girl I roomed with at uni; she had a picture of him. The one where he's standing in a busy street, lighting a cigarette? He's wearing this big overcoat, in Manhattan or somewhere, and the whole world is moving around him, but he acts like it doesn't even exist.'

Mary cocks her finger at her, like she's holding a gun, the gesture almost an exact copy of the one Athene had done to her earlier, in the café. 'Bingo. That was Trent. That was exactly what he was like, even at fifteen. Like the world was somebody else's joke.'

'So he was a bad boy, then?'

'Not bad,' Mary says slowly. 'At least not *bad* bad. He was...' Mary shrugged again. 'It was like his heart was painted black. The first time Bella saw him she said he looked like Heathcliff.'

Athene looks confused for a second. 'What, from *Wuthering Heights*?'

'The very one you mentioned in the café last night,' Mary says, the memory momentarily creasing her features. She shakes her head. 'Anyhow, Trent came onto the scene just as our friendship might have...' Mary paused, unsure how to continue.

'Become physical?' Athene suggests.

Mary barks laughter, startling the young woman. 'It was *already* physical, love. Or at least from my perspective. Once puberty set in it was nothing *but* physical. Not sex; just... aching.

Deep, right inside the body, aching. Like she was a loose tooth. She was pain itself for me to be around, but I couldn't help it.'

'Jesus, I remember what that was like,' Athene agrees. 'The lying awake at night smelling them, feeling them like ghosts that have stitched themselves to your skin.'

Mary eyeballs Athene, impressed.

Defo she's been hurt before.

'Yes,' she says gently, 'to your skin, and through your skin, right down into your DNA. You think you can't live without them.'

'What did you do?' Athene asks, her eyes wide and clear.

Mary looks at her, not smiling. She feels a tear diamonding behind her eye.

'I lived without them.'

Athene's gaze clouds, confused, then a shock of understanding flashes across her face.

'Oh Christ, Mary, I'm sorry, I forgot! I didn't mean to–'

'It's all right. It was a long time ago. After the crash, well... the world just lost its colour.' Mary juts out her chin, pointing at the small bells lying at her feet. 'Those brought it all back. Whoever stuck these to my door knows about the nickname.'

'And you say they were a present you bought? For Bella?'

'A decoration for her tree, yes. But now the shock has worn off...' Mary picks up the bells and shakes them between her fingers. 'It wasn't these. Someone has tried to make a replica, but the originals made a different sound. These are made of plastic; the ones I got from Woolies were metal. Brass or copper, I think. They cost me all the money I'd saved.'

'Did she like them? Bella?'

Mary nods, staring at the bells. 'She did. She loved them. She hung them up on our tree in the ghost wood.' Seeing the question on Athene's face she waves a hand toward the door.

'The juniper wood outside her house. She said that the bells would guide her home if ever she got lost.'

Mary lowers her head, and sees a perfect tear drop down onto her floor.

'Oh dear,' she murmurs. 'I am sorry, I don't know–'

Another falls to join it, Mary's vision blurring. She feels Athene's arm around her, stroking her hair.

'Shh,' whispers the girl softly. 'It's all right. Don't be sad.'

'Except it didn't fucking work, did it? She never came home again.'

Athene doesn't say anything.

After a moment, Mary rests her head on the younger girl's shoulder and closes her eyes.

Then opens them again, feeling a burning in her palm, where Bella scarred her; feeling a clenching in her throat.

As Athene strokes her hair, and tells her it will be all right, Mary can smell her skin, smell the scent coming off her. She smells like Christmas oranges.

Smells like Bella.

26

BELLA'S HOUSE: 1998

AUTUMN BEFORE THE WINTER FAIR

Bella stared at the thin blue line. As she sat on the toilet in her empty house, she wondered if she was going to cry. After a minute, she stood up and carefully placed every piece of the pregnancy kit back into her bag.

Thin. Blue. Line.

She repeated the words over and over in her head, like loading bullets into a gun.

27

THE GHOST FOREST: BLEA FELL HOUSE

WINTER, 1997

'Shh!'

'How can I be "Shh", when every step sounds like I'm walking through polystyrene! I feel like I'm in an episode of some shitty old sci-fi!'

Bella giggled, then slammed her hand to her mouth, smothering the sound.

'Okay, well, be as *shh* as you can! And wrap yourself up, It's about to snow!'

Mouse looked up. Bella was right; flakes of white crystal were floating down through the blue-black sky. Mouse pulled the overcoat tighter around her pyjamas, and followed her friend over the wall.

Bella and Mouse were visiting the ghost forest in the field at the front of Blea Fell. Mouse was staying for a rare sleepover, and once everyone was in bed they had snuck out to be in the woods. Mouse watched Bella as she stroked the trees, pressing her face against the bark and caressing them. Mouse pulled a pack of cigarettes out of her pocket and tapped one out. She held it up to the moonlight. The smoke was crumpled and slightly bent. She smiled to herself as she watched the snow fall around it.

Crumpled and slightly bent. Like her. She looked up at the snow, squinting her eyes against the cold flakes. The bell she had given Bella the previous Christmas tinkled in the night, making the trees appear even more eldritch.

'I think we should do it on this one,' said Bella.

Mouse stayed staring into the sky. The snow was falling like kisses in the moonlight. She creased her brow.

'How does it work that it's snowing, but I can see the stars and the moon?' she whispered. 'I mean I should just be able to see clouds, no?' She stuck out her tongue, and stayed still until a fleck landed on it, melting and leaving a taste of the sea.

'It's because we're in a snow globe,' Bella whispered back. Her voice was like her body; full of static, disrupted and scattered by the falling snow. Mouse turned away from the sky and looked at her. Bella was kneeling by one of the trees. She had a Swiss army knife in her hand, and was hacking at its bark.

'What are you doing?'

'Tattooing my name onto the sailor's arm.'

Mouse watched her for a few moments, then walked over and lay down next to her, staring up at the sky. The moon was full, and as the snowflakes spiralled down they seemed to be lit from within. *They are what angels would look like, if they were weather*, thought Mouse, stroking the snow beneath the tree. In the branch above her the bell chimed a gentle note.

'What do you mean, we're in a snow globe?' Mouse said.

The sound of Bella's knife was like an insect gnawing at the tree as she cut.

'I mean you and me, Mouse. I know you think it's all changed because of Trent, but it really hasn't. Deep down the only ones who count are you and me.'

Mouse's breath was smoke as it came out of her, the hot air from inside crystallising as it hit the cold; the smoke from the cigarette only making it thicker. She closed her eyes. She so much wanted what Bella said to be true. As she lay there she felt the snow caress her. Like the last bed before dying, she thought. She imagined being found in the morning. Her and Bella next to each other, just indistinct shapes under the snow, holding hands. She took a final drag on her smoke, then flicked it into the night.

'There!' said Bella, triumphantly, stepping back and admiring her work. 'Now it's your turn!'

Mouse sat up and looked. Bella had carved her name into the trunk of the tree. In the moonlight, the white of the flesh beneath the bark looked like bone.

'You and me, I get,' Mouse said, taking the knife. 'Will always get. But I don't understand about the snow globe.'

The girls exchanged places; Bella laying down in the snow whilst Mouse began to carve her name. She took off her fingerless gloves to grip the handle of the knife better; the blade was sharp and she didn't want to cut herself. The soft smell of tobacco filled the air as Bella fired up a cigarette.

'What I mean is everything in the world is for you and me, Mouse. Maybe not all the time; but when we're together. Trent and school and all the shit that happens around us, that's just the skin of life. It doesn't matter. It happens to the sky and the birds and to everything that lives. It's what our imagination does that really matters.'

'And you're imagining a snow globe, are you?' Mouse whispered, smiling.

'Of course; one in which only you and me live, forever. Even after we're dead.'

Bella sat up, took a drag from the cigarette, and held it out to

Mouse, the end reversed so she could put it between her lips. Mouse stared into her eyes, willing her to notice how much she loved her, then leant forward and took the cigarette, her lips gently pressing against the filter. For the briefest of moments she felt Bella's cold fingers on her lips, and then they were gone.

'I'd like that,' Mouse whispered.

'Just me and you, in this prehistoric forest, surrounded by snow that happens every time our world is turned upside down.'

'And what's turned our world upside down, Bella?'

Mouse was looking as deep into Bella's eyes as she dared. Bella's eyes were grey, and Mouse was fairly sure that they had no end to them; that if she were to fall into them she would just spin down forever and ever and never come out.

'I'll tell you after we've finished,' Bella said, smiling.

'Finished what, carving our names? It's done, look.'

Mouse pointed at the tree with the knife; at the names glowing on the bark, like stories trying to be born.

'That's only part of it,' Bella whispered, the snow sticking to her long hair, making her look pixelated. 'Now we've got to seal it. Give me the knife.'

A question in her eyes, Mouse handed Bella the knife. Before Mouse could do anything, Bella grabbed her wrist and squeezed, causing her hand to open, exposing the palm. Bella slid the blade of the knife quickly across her skin. Mouse watched in disbelief as a line of red appeared. There was no pain. Part of Mouse's brain supposed that her hand was too cold, or the knife was too sharp.

'What...' she began.

'Shh,' Bella said, tugging at her own glove, and handing the knife to Mouse. 'It's not deep, and it's important. Now you do me.'

Bella held her hand up, like she was making a stop sign. 'Then once you've done it, we need to hold our hands together, and let the blood mingle. That way we can always come back here. It will be like a magical portal or something.'

Bella's eyes were on fire, the full moon replacing each of the pupils. Mouse felt dizzy and floating at the same time. She looked from Bella's eyes to her upturned palm. The cut on her own hand felt full, like the blood.

Slowly, as if her actions were somebody else's, she brought the knife up to Bella's palm. Bella nodded sharply, and closed her eyes. Mouse watched as the tip of the blade pressed into Bella's skin. The silver of the blade shone in the moonlight, but Mouse couldn't tell how hard to press; Bella's hand was white with cold, the blood retreated deep inside.

'Bella, I can't...' Mouse began, but then stopped as Bella pushed her hand forward, causing the tip of the knife to disappear into her. Bella opened her eyes and stared at Mouse.

Thank you, she mouthed, then pulled her hand down. Mouse watched, mute and immobile, as the knife appeared to slide upward, creating a slit in Bella's palm. Blood, slow and unbelievably red, seeped out. Bella let out a sigh.

'Right, put the knife down and hold my hand.' Bella lowered her hand and held it out, like she wanted Mouse to shake it.

Mouse shook her head. 'This is so surreal! Why are you even doing this?'

The snow stopped falling and Mouse looked around in confusion. The snow hadn't petered out, or thinned in its descent, but just... stopped.

'See,' Bella whispered, her face a bear pit of emotions. 'That's what happens in a snow globe; all the flakes settle on the ground and the snowing stops, until the next time it's shaken.'

Mouse stared at her. Bella grinned, wiggled her eyebrows, then edged her bleeding hand nearer. Mouse didn't know what else to do; she laughed softly.

'You're bloody nuts, you know that, Bells?'

Bella solemnly nodded in agreement. 'Just exactly the amount I need to be. Now are you going to do the blood-sisters thing with me or what?'

Mouse nodded, and clasped Bella's hand. Her hand was so cold that she couldn't feel her friend's skin against hers, but she felt her heartbeat, pulsing their blood together.

'That's great, Mouse,' Bella whispered, as if they'd done something monumental. 'Now all we need to do is to seal it with a kiss.'

'What?' Mouse said, unsure if she'd heard correctly, but before she could say anything else Bella leant forward and kissed her. It was a cool kiss, with their lips barely touching, and over before it had ever really begun, but Mouse could feel the heat behind it; deep down in Bella's throat. Like a snake wrapped around her heart, she thought, leaning forward, closing her eyes. She could smell the fire, from where they had sat in front of the stove, eating oranges and putting the skins on the hot plate, filling the room with a burnt citrus odour.

'There,' said Bella, leaning back and smiling. 'That's all done and can never be undone. Like Heathcliff and Cathy.' She clapped her hands together and jumped up, wrapping her massive coat around her small frame. 'Let's go back in and tell ghost stories 'til it's light.'

Mouse stood up slowly, not taking her eyes off Bella.

'What just happened?'

'I told you! Our world got turned upside down.'

'By what?'

'By my mother,' Bella said, a coldness creeping into her voice.

'Your mother? What's your mother got to do with anything?'

Bella looked at her friend, all laughter and playfulness gone like they were never there.

'She's pregnant, Mouse. I'm going to have a baby brother or sister.'

Mouse stared open-mouthed as Bella turned and began walking back to Blea Fell, her footsteps sounding like slowed-down stabbing as she crumped through the snow.

28

MARY'S HOUSE

It's not attraction, it's something else, Mary thinks, trying to shuffle through the emotions playing in her head.

Athene is still stroking Mary's hair, holding her gently in her arms.

As if she is my mother, or someone trying to protect me, she realises, keeping her eyes closed. The smell of Bella is strong; oranges and cinnamon and the salt of the wild western winds that came in from the North Sea. Mary rationalises it must be because of Blea Fell, and the photograph and the bells: that all the memories were being unlocked inside her.

Bella was dead, and Blea Fell burnt down, and nothing of that past could possibly be happening now.

Mary opens her eyes and looks at the photograph that had been left. The twisted metal of Trent's car looks as bare and brutal as it did the night of the accident, when she had been thrown out of it. As she stares, the sounds of that night sweep through her. The wet rasp of Trent's breathing; his lung punctured by the broken ribs when his body slammed into the steering wheel. The hissing of the snow as it evaporated on the underside of the car. The glass spider-splintering-in-ice-song as the weight of the car crushed the windows. The empty piece of air that had been filled with the sirens of the ambulance, suddenly switched off as it slipped and slid to a halt.

And the silence from the still form of Bella, half in and half out of the car; a doll with her stuffing coming out.

Mary closes her eyes again, takes a deep breath, then gently pushes Athene away.

'Come on,' she says, standing. 'The clothes will be dry by now. Let's get you back to the pub.'

Athene looks at her with concern. 'But what about all this?' She indicates the photo and the tiny bells. 'Shouldn't you take it to the police or something?'

Mary smiles. 'What would I tell the police? That somebody is fucking with me? Me and Bella and Trent.'

'Trent?' Athene asks.

Mary nods. 'Somebody sent him a picture from the past, like they did you. Maybe the same person who put this stuff on my door.'

'But why?'

'Good question. And why you? Raking up the past with me and Trent makes sense, but why you? It's just so random!'

'Why does it make sense? I mean with you and Trent? If your friend died in a terrible accident what is there to rake up? I mean what's the point?'

Mary looks at Athene a moment, then looks away. 'It's... complicated. After the accident, there was the fire at Blea Fell.'

Athene nods slowly, a confused look on her face. 'But what's that got to do with–'

'It was arson,' Mary says. 'And somebody died.'

Athene stares at her, her mouth slightly open, clearly unsure what to say.

Mary sighs. 'Come on; I need to go with you to the Craven Head. I want to see Jamie.'

'Jamie? What's he got to do with it?'

Mary shakes her head again and gathers up the photograph and bell.

Five minutes later they are back in her car heading for the village.

It's only as they're driving into the village that Mary realises Athene deflected her question; that she never answered why she had been targeted too. Why she was even here.

29

BELLA'S LAST SUMMER: THE BEDROOM

'You could be locked up, for going with a fifteen-year-old, you know that?'

Trent looked down at her, as he pulled on his 501s. He tried to do it like the man in the advert did; cool and fluid, as if he was pulling on a second skin.

How things looked were important to Trent; they were all he had.

Like now, with the girl spread naked on the bed in the gloom. He could see the shape of her body. She was lying on her stomach, with the detritus of sex around her. The discarded clothes and twisted sheets. The pillow on the floor and the duvet scrunched up into one corner. The stale smell of lust, cooled down and coagulating, like used cooking oil in an old pan.

'Could, but won't,' he said, smirking. He was good at smirking. He spent hours in front of the mirror practicing. 'Someone would have to care, for that to happen.'

Smirking when anything close to emotion might be wanted or expected.

Smirking when seriousness was required.

Trent had practiced and practiced and now it was armour-perfect.

'And who's going to care about you, Mouse?'

'Wanker,' Mouse muttered, dragging on her cigarette.

Trent silently agreed. In fact, he'd go so far as to say 'prize wanker'. If the armour wasn't so firmly in place he'd probably hate himself.

Mouse got up off the bed and walked across the room to the window. Trent felt a sudden pang of panic, then remembered where he was. He began to walk over to her.

'Don't,' she said, without turning around.

Something about her tone made him pause. Normally *he* controlled the situation; held the power. But somehow the balance in their relationship seemed to have shifted. He was beginning to lose himself; become undone.

'Don't what? I'm not doing anything.'

She didn't turn around, just stayed staring out at the darkening sky.

'It'll be winter soon,' she said, finally. She said it so quietly, and with such a blanket of sadness, that he found himself wanting to hold her. Protect her. Instead he reached down and stole a cigarette from the soft pack of Marlboros on the floor.

'And then it'll be a new year, and the whole sorry dance will start over again,' he said, lighting his smoke.

She finally turned around and faced him, completely uncaring of her nakedness, like it was pointless.

'What if I'm pregnant? What if what we've done has made me pregnant?'

Trent stared at her for a long beat, then laughed. It was the sort of laugh that could get away from him. It was mad Blackpool-rock laughter, the lunatic locked-away-in-an-asylum razor-blade laugh he kept bottled up, but which ran all the way through him, right down to his very centre.

'Don't worry, I'm not father material: there's no way you would get pregnant.'

She stared at him some more, then turned back and looked out of the window. 'I'd like you to leave, now.'

Trent gave a mocking bow to her back, and dragged on the rest of his clothes. While he did it he placed his stolen cigarette on the wooden dresser, like he would on the rail of a pool table. In the washed-out reflection of the window, Mouse watched it burn down, blackening the edge of the scarred top.

'That's a bad habit,' she said.

'What is?' Trent said, making his voice flat, like he was bored. With his clothes on he felt more himself. More in control. 'You?'

'No; I'm not a habit, Trent. I'm just something in your past.' She nodded. 'The cigarette.'

Trent looked at the butt. The smoke had burnt the wooden top, causing the wood to char.

'Whoops,' he said, smiling, hoping to get a smile out of the ghost-girl in the glass. He didn't.

'One day it'll be more than "whoops". One day you'll burn the whole fucking house down.'

Trent looked at her back, taut and soft at the same time, and felt like screaming; felt like screaming backwards.

'When did you stop being a mouse, Mouse?'

Mouse's back became more taut, closing herself further from him. He felt himself wanting to take it all back: to reach out and stroke the girl in front of him.

Tell her he was sorry.

Tell her about the real him, hidden away since beyond early.

But he didn't. He just blinked, turned, and left.

By the time he'd made his way out of her house through the kitchen, walked round the side, and looked up at her bedroom window the day was full dark.

There was nobody looking out at him. The glass pane was just a black space.

Trent pulled the coat around himself and trudged down the track to the road, feeling heavier with each step.

30

THE CRAVEN HEAD

Jamie looks up as Mary walks through the bar-saloon door.

'Mary!' He jumps to his feet. 'Thank Christ you're here, I've been ringing the café! *Trent* phoned me! Can you believe it? I didn't even know he was released! Right out of the blue, he said–'

As Athene comes into view, walking in behind Mary, Jamie stops talking like someone had unplugged him. He rearranges his features into a poor semblance of the manager of a quaint tourist hotel.

'Oh, Athene, hi! Did you have a good look around the village?'

'Don't worry, Jamie, she knows about Trent.' Mary's voice is clipped and matter of fact as she slips out of her coat and flings it in the direction of a bar stool. It lands on the circular leather seat, stays for a moment, then slides off onto the carpet like the skin off a drunk.

'Fuck,' Mary comments, looking at it. 'I used to be a much better aim than that.'

'Hi, Jamie!' Athene gives him a little wave.

'What do you mean, *she knows*?' Jamie says, ignoring the

wave and the collapsed coat, looking from Athene to Mary, his eyes wild. 'Knows *what*? Knows about what happened? You didn't say–'

'Knows about Trent,' Mary interrupts. 'She was there when he phoned me.'

'Trent phoned *you*?' Jamie looks with confusion at his mobile on the bar, as if somehow Mary had borrowed it.

'Yes; while we were at Blea Fell.'

Jamie's eyes swivel back to Mary and lock on. 'Bella's place? Why the fuck were you at Blea Fell!' All semblance of quaint-manager has vanished, revealing a double barrel of fear and confusion.

'Swearing in front of the guests, Jamie?' Mary tuts.

'Sorry, Athene,' Jamie mutters, eyes still fixed on Mary. 'But there's a bit of a crisis from the past happening here.'

'So I'm gathering,' Athene says.

'Jamie, listen to me carefully.' Mary walks forward and stands in front of him.

'What?' Jamie's breathing is hard and fast. 'What, *Mouse*?'

If the use of her old nickname was meant to transfer power in some way, it doesn't work: Mary merely nods and smiles, like he's just done something she expected. 'Trent is coming here–'

Jamie cuts across her, eyes bugging. 'I know! He left a message! He said he was arriving this weekend! Maybe sooner!'

'Trent is coming *here*, Jamie,' Mary continues as if he hadn't spoken. 'Because somebody sent him something.'

Jamie looks at her. 'Sent him what?' he says quietly, suspicion filling his tone.

Mary shakes her head. 'I don't know everything, but what he told me was enough. Somebody sent him a picture of back then, of Blea Fell, along with my mobile number.'

There is a pause while Jamie's face tries to both express, and hide, his thoughts; confusion and fear and incomprehension scuttling themselves across his features.

'Plus a picture of me, Trent and Bella at the fair,' Mary finishes softly.

'The fair?' Jamie's voice is quiet. 'The winter fair?'

'And not just any winter fair, Jamie.' Mary takes a step forward. 'But *that* winter fair. The *final* winter fair. *That* photograph, Jamie. The one you took.'

'What's the winter fair?' Athene asks.

Nobody looks at her. Jamie's eyes stay locked on Mary's. He shakes his head slightly.

'That's not possible,' he manages, after a few seconds.

'Oh it's possible, all right,' Mary comments breezily, taking another step forward. 'If somebody had decided to fuck about.'

'What's the winter fair?' Athene repeats.

'Mouse, this is so fucked-up. I wouldn't–' Jamie retreats a step.

'It's possible if somebody manages to get hold of the photo somehow, out of wherever the police put photographs after *twenty years*.' Mary's eyes are blazing.

'Not me. Maybe Trent–'

'The police?' Athene says, slightly louder, but nobody is paying attention to her.

'Somebody *sent* it to Trent, Jamie. Somebody not only got hold of the photo, but knew who to send it to.'

Mary's voice has gone from breezy to danger-quiet. As she advances, Jamie takes another step backward.

'Where he lived? How the fuck would I know where he lived, Mouse? I didn't even know he was out of jail!'

'Maybe it was the same person who sent me a photo too. Pinned it on my door like a fucking scene from *Deliverance!*'

Mary reaches into her back pocket and brings out the photograph of the car crash. Jamie looks at it, shaking his head, eyes wide.

'Wait, Trent was in jail?' Athene says, alarm in her voice. 'What was he in jail for?'

'Not been out to my house, today, have you, Jamie?' Mary says, still ignoring Athene. Her voice, although soft, seems to cut through the silence of the room.

'Where did you get that?' Jamie stares at the print, his voice is hoarse with tension.

'Look, can somebody tell me what's going on?' Athene looks from one to the other. 'Why did Trent go to jail? Was it something to do with the crash?'

Mary's eyes stay locked on Jamie, who is staring at the photo like it's car-crash pornography. He licks his lips, and his fingers twitch, reaching out for the print. Before he can take it, Mary puts the photo back in her pocket.

'Any idea how this wound up on my door, Jamie?' Mary asks.

Jamie's skin has become pale and blotchy, like it had been made up out of the wrong ingredients. He licks his lips again. 'How would I know?'

'When they questioned me, Jamie, back in the day; just after the crash; they showed me this picture. When I say just after, I mean when I could talk. Once the leg had healed. Or healed enough for me to be off the sleepy-meds. They showed me and asked me how the crash happened. I couldn't believe it when I saw it.'

Jamie looks around the room, then back to where the photo was hidden.

'I–' he begins, but Mary steps forward suddenly, her face inches from Jamie's.

'I remember not understanding, because it didn't make sense. If someone was close enough to take a picture they were close enough to help.'

'I don't...'

'They wouldn't tell me where the photo came from. They said that the ambulance was there already, and it was taken by a passer-by, but I knew it was you. The picture was too good.'

Jamie looks at her. For a moment there's defiance, then he seems to deflate.

'It was such a fucked-up night,' he says softly.

Mary nods. 'Especially for Bella.'

'When the ambulance shot through the square it was just after the fireworks. It seemed...' He shrugged his thin shoulders, searching for the right phrase. 'Fun.'

'Fun?'

He nods. 'Like it was something off the telly. *Casualty* or whatever. I grabbed my satchel – the one I kept my camera in – got on my scooter and followed it. It couldn't go too fast because of the weather, so it wasn't hard. When it reached the...' He struggles for words again. 'When we came across the accident I didn't know what to do! They wouldn't let me help; told me to keep back! In the end all I could do was... record it. Photograph it.'

'Jesus!' Athene mutters.

'Then the police came, and they took my camera. I swear! They took my camera so there was no way I could make copies! They said they needed it for evidence!'

Mary stares at him, long seconds knifing out between them.

'So how come it ended up on my sodding door then?'

'I don't know! I didn't have anything to do with it, Mouse, I swear!' Jamie looks like he's about to cry. 'The police took the film before it was even developed!'

'And what about the other one, Jamie?' Mary asks. 'The one that was emailed to Trent? I suppose that has nothing to do with you, either? That's...'

'If someone doesn't tell me what the hell is going on I'm going to bloody well...'

Mary and Jamie turn and look at Athene, her angry outburst finally getting through.

'I don't know what I'd do, but it wouldn't be pretty,' Athene finishes, wilting somewhat under Mary's clear gaze.

'And not just the photo of the fair,' Mary says, her eyes thoughtful, appraising the student. 'There's the photo that was sent to you and your mum, Athene.'

'You mean the one in the brochure?'

Mary turns to Jamie.

'It's a photo of Blea Fell, but not Blea Fell now.'

'But I didn't know that,' adds Athene.

Mary shrugs.

'How could you? You've never been here before.'

'What does it matter?' Jamie says.

'Not just from before, but Blea Fell *then*,' Mary continues. 'I never clocked it when I first saw it; I was too muddled just by seeing it not in ruins. But I'm certain. It was Blea Fell in that summer.'

Jamie sits down on a stool. He looks like someone has beaten him up from the inside.

'Which summer?' he whispers, but it was clear from his face he already knew the answer.

'From *that* summer, Jamie. The summer before Bella died. The summer after you and Trent were expelled and he went on remand. The summer that fucked everything forever.'

31

LAST DAY OF SCHOOL: SUMMER, 1998

'For fuck's sake, Trent, stop it! Stop it, or you're going to kill him!'

It was difficult to know what shocked the crowd most: the fight in the corridor, or Mouse swearing at the top of her voice, her eyes wild and scared, her voice high and ripped through with terror.

She slammed herself against the metal lockers, her hand stuffed into her mouth to stop herself screaming. Her entire body was in conflict, the fight and flight impulses locked together. The noise the locker doors made as she smashed into them echoed around the corridor. The fight was almost silent; only the sound of scuffing as Trent held the boy in place with his body, sitting astride him as he threw his fists down again and again. The crowd of students that made up the loose fight ring stared, seemingly struck dumb by the viciousness. Normally there would be jeering and crowd noise; something to encourage the animal display in front of them.

But not this time.

There was something about the ferocity of the pummelling; something in the way hate was radiating off Trent.

If Trent had heard Mouse, he gave no sign. He kept punching the boy's face, over and over. The noise was like meat being slapped down on a butcher's counter. Little sprays of blood made patterns around the two boys, a grotesque modern art painting of pain and betrayal.

The boy was not even protecting himself. Just letting his face slowly turn to a mush of red and white, with his eyes dim cushions of pain.

'Please, stop,' Mouse whispered, sliding down the locker until she was sitting on the hard linoleum floor. Nobody heard her, or if they did, they didn't acknowledge her. They stood silently, watching the fight. Mouse could see Trent through the body of the crowd, and let out a gasp.

He was no longer looking at his opponent. Trent was still hitting him, like he was on automatic, but he was no longer looking at him.

He was looking at her.

And his eyes were flowing with a battleground of emotion. They were leaking thick, viscous tears. The crowd of students looked from the fight to Mouse, trying to understand what was going on. How the invisible girl could be involved in the pain and destruction happening in front of them. Trent continued to gaze straight at her, his clockwork fists slowly running down until, finally, they were still on either side of the broken boy beneath him.

Once the hitting had stopped, the silence became harder; more solid, a stretched rope between Trent and Mouse.

Trent nodded, the oil tears slipping from his face and landing on the ruin of the boy beneath him.

'This is for you,' he said into the silence. Mouse shook her head, but couldn't speak.

'This is for you. Because of what he did.'

Mouse stared in horror at first Trent, then the beaten boy beneath him.

A small, bloody, bubble of spit formed in the gap between the boy's broken mouth. It expanded as he breathed out, then broke with a wet snap. Trent looked down and smiled. Slowly, he brought his hand up to his face, forming a circle around his eye with his thumb and forefinger.

'Say cheese for the camera, Jamie,' he said.

'TRENT BARROW, GET OFF HIM! WHAT THE HELL IS GOING ON?'

The crowd, a moment before in a drunk of body violence, snapped and ran at the thunder of the teacher's shout. There was the squeak of a dozen trainers on the linoleum floor as they scattered, then only Jamie and Trent, the teacher, and Mouse remained, as if they had never been.

'What's happening here, Trent?' the teacher asked, staring in disbelief at the schoolboys. For some reason, Trent's face seemed to be covered in ash.

The teacher turned and looked at Mouse. 'What's been going on? This is...' He petered off, as if unsure how to finish. Mouse shook her head. He looked back to Trent and Jamie. 'Christ,' he muttered. He stepped forward to pull Trent off, but then stopped, the sheer violence of the scene overwhelming him. He looked around wildly then, spotting the rag of students peering around the corner at the end of the corridor, shouted, 'Go and find a teacher! Tell them to call an ambulance and get me the first aid box from Mrs Croft!'

The children just stared wide-eyed past him at the two boys on the floor.

'Now!' the teacher shouted, before turning back to look at Trent.

'Jesus, you've practically killed him! Stand up and step away.'

The teacher stepped forward, then stopped again as Trent shook his head.

'Nah, he's all right, sir. I was just explaining the finer details of composition to him, when we got a bit carried away.'

'Carried away?' he stared at the boy incredulously. 'He's going to need to go to hospital, Trent! I'm going to have to call the police! This is way beyond...' The teacher ran out of words again.

Trent looked up at him, wide-eyed. 'The police, sir?'

The teacher nodded. 'Get off him, Trent. I need to check his airway. Go and stand by the lockers.'

Trent blinked and looked down at Jamie. His face was swollen, a Halloween pumpkin, with his eyes almost completely shut. Trent stroked his face gently.

'I said get off–'

Trent slapped Jamie backhanded, ripping the flesh off his temple with his ring. Mouse screamed as the pumpkin skin split open. The ring must have been sharp, as blood and fat oozed out of the long gash.

'You know, Jamie? I think that might leave a little scar,' Trent said pleasantly, as the teacher lunged forward and dragged him off the boy's body.

The last thing Mouse saw, before the scene went blank and she shut down, was Jamie, with his ripped face and his strange limp body.

The last thing she saw as it all went blank was Jamie, with the teacher and Trent in the background behind him.

The last thing she saw as the world tilted and everything disappeared was Jamie, smiling at her with his almost-closed eyes and broken-teeth mouth.

32

THE CRAVEN HEAD

Jamie turns away and walks behind the bar, pulling a glass from the shelf and slotting it under the gin optic. He is amazed to see his hand is steady.

'I'm not getting this.' Athene looks between Jamie and Mary. 'Why was Trent expelled, and sent to...'

'Remand,' Mary says.

'Remand. Did it have something to do with what happened with Bella?'

'It was a misunderstanding that got blown out of all proportion.' Jamie shrugs one shoulder. 'Trent beat up a student at school, and they expelled him. It was no big deal; it was his last year and he was going to fail his A-levels anyhow. The whole remand thing was way over the top.'

'No big deal? Are you fucking joking with me or what?' Mary's voice is tight, as if she was trying to choke it. 'He nearly blinded you, Jamie! If he'd caught you any lower, your eye would have been bouncing along the school floor like a bloody ping-pong ball!'

'What? The student was you?' Athene looks at him, confused. 'Why did he beat you up?'

Jamie shrugs. 'Like I said, it was a misunderstanding. Anyhow it's twenty years ago! It doesn't matter anymore.'

'Except it clearly does, Jamie.' Mary walks forward a couple of steps and hooks a finger at Athene. 'Because somebody sent mystery-girl here a picture of Blea Fell in the summer before Bella died, and got her to come up here and start digging up the past.'

'Hang on a minute, Mary, what do you mean *mystery-girl*? I–'

Mary raises her hand without looking at Athene, keeping all her attention on Jamie.

Athene looks at the hand, held in front of her like a warning sign.

Mary continues. 'And Trent, *your* Trent, Jamie, not long out of prison, is also sent a picture, not just of Blea Fell, but of me and him and Bella, leaning against the car. A picture you took. The car that a few hours later will be involved in a fatal accident. The accident that, incidentally, sends Trent to jail.'

'What do you mean, *his* Trent?' Athene asks. 'I thought you said he was Bella's boyfriend?'

Jamie and Mary ignore her. Mary still has her hand up, looking like a demented lollipop lady, and Jamie is bleeding daggers from his eyes.

'Not my Trent, Mouse. He was Bella's Trent. Her Heathcliff.' Jamie's voice is soft, but his words seem to slice into the room. 'Bella's, and yours,' he finishes.

Nobody speaks.

Athene finally breaks the silence, moving a couple of steps abruptly towards them.

'Right. You two clearly have some issues to discuss; I'm going to the shop to get some supplies, then I think I'm going to pack. It's all getting a bit intense for me, I'm afraid. I don't think there's any way I can work in this environment.'

She nods sharply at them, then turns and walks quickly to

the door. With her movement the tension seems to break in the room.

'Athene, I'm sorry...' Mary begins, but the student doesn't slow down; just continues, disappearing through the doorway and into the hotel lobby. Mary and Jamie listen to the front door open and close.

In the silence that follows, Jamie smiles at Mary, his face twisting. 'That went well, don't you think?'

'Fuck off, Jamie,' mutters Mary, staring at the doorway. She glares at it a moment more, then swallows, the fizzing fear and anger that had been buoying her up dissipating. 'I haven't got the energy for it.'

Jamie slings back his glass, pouring the gin down his throat. Wiping his mouth, he puts down the empty tumbler.

'Do you know how they make gin,' he says, turning the glass on the scarred bar with his fingers. Watching as it slowly revolved.

'What?' Mary turns away from the doorway and looks at him. 'What are you even talking about?'

'Gin. Did you know that they have to throw most of it away? That in the process of making it, the first bit of it is poisonous?' He raises his eyebrows at her, making his scar crinkle.

'Fascinating, Jamie.'

'No, really! You make up the batch, add your botanicals – herbs and spices and whatever – then you have to throw a third of it away because it's pure ethanol. If you drank it, it would kill you.'

Mary looks at him, then looks back to the door, where Athene had left a moment before.

'You've fucking lost it, Jamie, you know that?'

Jamie nods. 'That was Bella, at the end. She was the poison.'

Mary stares at him, disgust colouring her voice. 'What are

you saying? What do you mean, *she was the poison*? She died, Jamie. She died screaming.'

'Before then.' Jamie's voice is flat. 'Before that night. Before the fight at school. Before even–'

'I held her in my arms, Jamie, and she wasn't poison, she was broken. She was a rag doll with bits of stuffing poking out. She wasn't *poison*, Jamie, she was a fucked-up girl who got killed!'

Jamie shrugs. 'Whatever. You were always in her pocket, ever since you were little. You never saw her without your Bella-glasses on. You never knew what she was really like.'

'What do you mean? Of course I knew her! I was her best friend, Jamie!'

Jamie sniggers. 'Sure. That's why you fucked Trent.'

Mary's mouth drops open. Jamie raises his hands, palms out, his face a picture of mock amazement.

'What, you think I didn't know?'

Mary shakes her head. She feels hot with shame and anger.

'You think *Bella* didn't know?' Jamie whispers, his voice snaking through the air.

It was as if Jamie had slapped her. She actually feels herself reel from his words.

'She didn't.' It sounded like somebody else was saying the words. Mary's head is full of snowstorms and stunted trees. Of moonshine and a kiss from the past that meant more to her than anything. 'Trent would never…'

'You know he would, Mouse. Trent had his own agenda.' Jamie's lizard eyes flick over her body. 'Anyhow, you'll be able to ask him soon.' He looks at his watch and swallows. Even in her shocked state, Mary can see that he was frightened. She suddenly has a memory of Jamie on the school bus, when they were all just starting high school. It was the same look; like he was terrified a secret was going to be found out.

Mary takes a ragged breath, and straightens up, binding her

emotions until later. 'Fuck you, Jamie, and fuck Trent too.' She leans down and picks her coat off from the floor; begins walking out of the bar.

'You know who she is, don't you?' calls Jamie.

Mary stops and turns slowly. 'Who?'

'The mystery girl, Athene. You know who she is, who she must be, yes? I mean, otherwise nothing makes sense. Photos for you and Trent. And a photo of Blea Fell for her. That can only mean one thing. That she's connected somehow. That means she must be her.'

'It can't be,' says Mary quietly, not even believing herself. 'She was given a new identity. A new name and everything. She wouldn't remember anything. There would be nothing to connect her to here.'

Jamie shrugs again. 'But she looks like Bella a bit, doesn't she? And she's the right age. And she's trying to find out about Blea Fell, and the fire.'

Mary feels the past shiver through her; sees in her mind's eye Athene picking up the owl in the carcass of the house.

It's funny, because my name means owl.

Mary takes a step back into the room. 'You think she's Bella's sister, Jamie?'

Thing.

Mary hears Bella's voice in her head, calling her sister by The Addams Family nickname she had for her, but isn't sure if it's conformation or derision.

Shut up, thinks Mary. *You're no use: you're dead.*

'You think she's Martha? You think someone tracked her down for some reason, sent her a cryptic clue to come here?' Mary smiles at him, arranging her face into bemused amazement. 'Sent Trent one too?'

Jamie looks uneasy; unsure.

'Why?' said Mary simply. 'What could the possible point be?

Her sister's dead. Her parents are dead. Who would gain from it?'

Jamie doesn't say anything. Mary continues to gaze at him, and eventually, he looks down at his empty drink.

'What aren't you telling me, Jamie?'

Jamie stays staring at the glass on the bar, until Mary eventually shrugs, and turns away.

'I'll see you, Jamie. Say hello to Trent, for me. Wish him a good journey home.'

'For what it's worth, I'm sorry,' Jamie says before she can turn fully away again.

Mary stands motionless. 'Sorry for what, Jamie?'

Jamie shakes his head, then points at the wall to the left of her. 'I saw you looking. Looking and listening. When you came in before.'

'What the fuck are you talking about?' she asks harshly. But she knows what he's talking about. What they've never talked about, and she doesn't want to hear it. Not now; maybe not ever.

'The pinball machine,' Jamie continues. 'In the back room. Dad got rid of it that winter.' Jamie smiles, but the gash in his face looks painted on. Black and cold and badly formed. 'It kept on breaking, so he just got shot.'

'Great, Jamie. Thanks for sharing.'

'It didn't though.' Jamie's words tumble out of his mouth like a cork has been popped. 'Break, I mean. I mean it did but I did it. I kept on breaking it. I couldn't stand the sound.'

Mary stares at him, incredulous.

'You couldn't stand the sound?' she says, wonder in her voice. 'You couldn't stand the *sound*? Well, poor you.'

'Like I said; I'm sorry.' Jamie doesn't look at her; just stays looking at his empty glass.

'Too late for sorry, Jamie.'

Mary is quite impressed that she doesn't fall over as she

leaves the barroom and walks out of the hotel. When she gets outside she leans against the door and breathes in the crisp autumn air, replacing the stench of the past that had filled her lungs. What had happened that night with the pinball was something she had locked away; and she wasn't going to unlock it now.

Across the road, sat on the bench by the beck, is Athene. The girl was jabbing at her mobile phone, no doubt letting her mum know what a bunch of nut-bags she's gotten mixed up in.

She really does look like Bella, thinks Mary. Or at least, maybe I want her to. Maybe I want to finish everything and stop being turned over by the past.

Mary checks the small road for non-existent traffic, then crosses over toward her.

If it is *the past*, a small voice says inside her.

33

BELLA'S SECRET DIARY: 1992

I have found a secret about my room!

Yesterday it rained and rained and I spent the whole day in my room.

Mum came and lit the fire, which is a real fire, and I locked the door and was going to spend the whole day reading.

Anyhow, after a while the fire started spitting, so instead of reading I just watched it, because it was alive and talking to me in crackles and light and heat. Every now and then a bit of coal would spit out and land on the floor, and that's when I noticed that it must have happened loads of times before because the wooden boards were covered in burn marks! All over the floor around the fire. It is like the fire was trying to escape but could only get a little way. The further away from the fire the less burn marks there were. It was like a fire-tide. Anyhow I forgot about my book (*Wuthering*

Heights, again! When I grow up I want to be Cathy, not Isabella!) and decided to spend the afternoon with my fire. Outside the day was so dark it was almost night, and the fire was so sparkly and pretty, with its spitting coal like a volcano, that I couldn't concentrate.

Anyhow, one bit spat so far that it got the record! I watched it skitter across the floor, then fall down a massive knothole in the wooden board. I was worried it might set the house on fire, even though the house is made up of under-the-sea stone, so I went and tried to look down into it, to make sure it wasn't burning the rafter or whatever, but I couldn't see anything.

But I could smell something! The smell of burning paper, like when you leave it by the stove at night so it's all crackly dry in the morning, so it will set fire easily.

I was very excited! If the house burnt down it would be like *Jane Eyre*! Or like London, with me as Mr Pepys!

Anyway, I ran to the drawer and got my big torch. I keep it there in case of power cuts (they happen a lot!) or burglars (none yet, but still hoping) or to light up my ghost forest at night.

I switched it on and pointed it down the knothole.

And guess what I saw?!

There, under the floorboards, was a pile of books! I couldn't see what they were called, but they looked old. There was bits of dust and fire on top of them.

I can't tell you how thrilled I was! Maybe there was a treasure map down there! Or a dead girl's secret diary!

First I stuck my finger in the knothole to see if I could pull the floorboard up, but it wouldn't budge. That's when I noticed the screws. The bit of the board with the treasure map (hopefully!) under it was held down with four brass screws. I got my Swiss army knife and used the screwdriver bit to undo them.

I was given the knife by Mum for my twelfth birthday. I am going to use it to cut my hand and form a blood bond with someone one day. And then we'll run away and be happy together!

Anyhow. Once I'd done it I removed the plank so I could see what was underneath. Sadly, it wasn't a treasure map, or a suicide note from a broken-hearted girl. It was a book of Greek myths and a little leather bracelet. The bracelet had a name carved in it in odd symbols that I imagine is Greek, so I couldn't understand it.

But that's not the exciting thing! The exciting thing is I have a secret place where I can hide my diaries! I can write whatever I want, and no one will find them except after I'm dead, way, way in the future when everyone will probably live in space, and they'll be able to read all about me.

I think there is enough room for a dozen diaries.

I'm going to ask for a rug for Christmas, so that the secret hidey-hole will be extra safe.

That's it.

I'm going to my ghost forest now, to dance in the rain and shout for Heathcliff to come and take me away.

I wonder if he'll ever hear me?

34

ATHENE'S PHONE

😈 H on his way up; maybe arrive soon

👻 good. Arranging everything now

😈 something happened between M & J. Also between J and H. Data?

👻 no. J bullied by H. Nothing else. J recognise photo?

😈 yes. Freaked

👻 recognise source?

😈 no

👻 check. Carry on as planned

😈 check

x

35

SUMMER BEFORE HIGH SCHOOL, 1996

'I saw you and Bella the other day.'

Mouse jumped, startled by the voice, her ice cream slipping out of her hand. The cone cracked on the granite bank of the beck, spilling the contents over her boots. She had been staring into the slow-moving water, watching the midges hatching. Swarms of them, with only hours to live, breaking free of their watery cradle to go on a mating frenzy. She often came down to the village to watch them. They were like the weather: upside-down clouds of life that skimmed along the water as if it was the sky. Never getting too high. Always staying near to where they started. She liked to look at them, knowing that she was different; that she would never stay here. Never.

She had it all worked out. She would run away with Bella, and they would live happily ever after in some loft flat in the middle of a ruined city, and smoke and smoke until they were dead, stick-thin and cold in each other's arms, like Cathy and Heathcliff should have been.

'Bollocks, Jamie, you made me drop my 99!'

'Sorry,' Jamie said, his head angled to his feet, face downcast, like even to look at her was too much for him. 'I wanted to give you something.'

Mouse sighed. Even though she'd spent her life making herself invisible, Jamie had always managed to see her. She supposed it was because she hadn't laughed at him, or run him down. Ever since primary school, Jamie had been picked on. She had never really understood why. She supposed it was like that; some kids were just picked on, because a pack needed someone outside the pack to help define itself. That's what schools did. Everything in them was designed for it. From the narrow corridors that led nowhere, to the hidden places all around the building where students could get cornered and trapped. As if the building itself encouraged it.

Jamie glanced up through his greasy fringe and snuck a look at her embryonic breasts. Mouse felt a spasm of revulsion.

She had never picked on Jamie, but he was hard to like.

'You gave me a bloody fright, Jamie, so well done.'

Mouse wiped her Docs against the dry grass by the path, trying to scrape off the ice cream.

Jamie didn't say anything. He stayed still, head bowed at the ground, like he'd been switched off.

Mouse sighed. 'What is it you wanted to give me anyway?'

Jamie's gaze strayed toward the bridge, by the post office. His tongue was slightly out of his mouth. Mouse turned to see what he was looking at. On the bridge there was a slim boy, looking at them.

'Who's he?' she asked, frowning. She'd never seen him before, which was fairly interesting in itself. The village was not big, and everyone knew everyone else. 'Who's your friend?'

'Just someone staying at the pub. He's up with his dad. They might be moving here.'

Mouse looked at the boy. Even from a distance she could see that he had a presence about him, like he was wearing a magnetic coat. He was lounging against the bridge not really looking at anything, with a smile on him that looked like a question mark, as if the world was an answer to something he hadn't bothered to ask. As she stared he turned his face slightly, taking in her gaze. She blinked and looked away, feeling herself flush.

'In fact, forget what you wanted to give me. What do you mean, you saw us? Where?'

Jamie paused, as if unsure what to say. 'By the pond,' he muttered.

Mouse looked at Jamie. He had an old army messenger bag slung over his shoulder, and was fingering the strap.

'The pond? What pond?'

'The one on the moor.'

'The one near Bella's house?'

Jamie nodded.

'What were you doing there?' Mouse asked, confused. 'That's miles from the village!'

'I wasn't spying on you!' Jamie said quickly, seeing the suspicion in Mouse's face. 'I'm a bird watcher! You know, curlews and that.'

Jamie patted the leather satchel. 'I've got a book on them. Birds. I like to walk the moors; see how many different ones I can spot.'

Mouse looked from his bag to his face. Jamie stared earnestly into her eyes.

After a second Mouse sighed. 'Yes. I bet you do.'

'It's because I haven't got any friends.'

Mouse stared at him. He said it so matter-of-factly that any anger Mouse felt at being observed evaporated. *What must it be like to be you?* she thought.

She almost reached out and touched him, but then he licked his lips, making them a little too moist, and looked his hungry look at her body from behind his fringe.

Mouse crossed her arms over her chest.

'You should have come and said hello, if you saw us there,' she said, her voice colder than she meant. Jamie practically flinched.

'I would've, but you might have thought I was spying or something.'

Mouse studied him, her mind ticking. 'This bird watching,' she began.

'Curlews. Sometimes lapwings and skylarks,' Jamie said.

'Whatever. I guess you have binoculars, yes?' Mouse looked at his bag.

Jamie nodded. 'The skylarks go really high. You wouldn't be able to see them otherwise.'

He gave another sideways glance at the boy on the bridge. Mouse watched a number of expressions squall across Jamie's face. Lust and longing, but also fear.

'And what do you do after you've looked at them,' Mouse asked. 'In your binoculars?'

'I've got a book,' Jamie repeated, tapping his bag again. 'I tick them off when I've seen them. Like trainspotting.'

Mouse nodded, her mind beginning to drift with her eyes. 'What's your friend called?'

'Trent. His name is Trent.' There was a longing in Jamie's voice, like water kissing the hull of a ship. 'I don't think he's really my friend. He says he is but…' Jamie shrugged a shoulder.

The pathetic self-pity of the statement made Mouse's teeth hurt. 'Trent? That's an odd name. What's he like?'

'Says someone called Mouse.' Jamie smiled shyly.

Mouse nodded, smiling back.

'It was him who told me to give them to you.' Jamie looked suddenly miserable. 'I didn't mean anything by it. It was for the birds.'

'What was?' Mouse saw the boy, Trent, languidly push

himself off the wall of the bridge and stroll over in their direction.

'The photographs.' Jamie fumbled at the straps of his messenger bag. 'The ones I took of you and Bella.'

Mouse watched the beck water slink by. She blinked slowly, taking in what Jamie had just said. Finally, she lifted her head and looked at him. 'You took pictures of Bella and me? Why?'

Jamie nodded, pulling an A4 envelope out of his bag. 'It was a heron. It flew down to the pond, looking for fish, I guess, and I was following it with my camera. And then I saw you there.'

Jamie looked pleadingly at her, offering up the envelope. Slowly, Mouse took it.

'You weren't doing anything! You were just watching the dragonflies!'

'Weren't doing anything? Of course we weren't doing anything! What are you talking about?'

Mouse felt herself flush, and ripped open the envelope. She pulled out a glossy photograph. In it, she and Bella were doing exactly what Jamie had said; they were watching the dragonflies. In the stillness of the picture the insects looked incredible; a rainbow of colours that seemed to shimmer around them, bleeding into the buzz of the air. Bella was smiling, and pointing at the scene, her thin arm covered, as ever, by a long-sleeve top.

And Mouse was looking at Bella.

Can anybody else tell? she wondered, looking at herself looking at her friend. Can anybody else tell what I'm thinking?

She slipped the print into her other hand, exposing the next shot. It was the same, only closer. Mouse guessed that Jamie's camera must have a telephoto lens. The whole frame was filled with her and Bella, with hardly any pond visible.

'Can't see any herons in these, Jamie.'

'It must have flown off,' Jamie muttered, looking down and

left, following the rapid approach of the boy on the bridge. Mouse shrugged and shuffled on to the final print.

'What the hell?' she whispered.

'You looked so happy,' pleaded Jamie. 'The shot sort of took itself.'

The final picture didn't contain a heron, or the pond, or even Bella for that matter. It just contained Mouse. It was so clear and so close that she could see the individual lashes surrounding her eyes. Could see her chipped tooth where her mouth was slightly open. Could see the curve of her neck. Mouse stared intently at the picture, feeling the day tighten around her. She was fairly certain she could see the frozen pulse of blood in her vein that she had felt when she had looked at Bella that day by the pond.

The picture clearly showed the love shining in her eyes.

'You shouldn't have taken this, Jamie. This is... private.'

'Which is why I told him to hand it over to you,' said a carefree voice.

Mouse looked up into the laughing eyes of the boy from the bridge.

'Hi, I'm Trent,' he said, smiling and sticking out his hand.

36

THE CRAVEN HEAD, ATHENE'S ROOM

Jamie stands perfectly still in the centre of the room, listening.

He is not listening for Athene returning; he imagines she is with Mouse, who would be trying to explain away the scene Athene had witnessed; trying to make it normal and all right, somehow.

Good fucking luck with that.

He is listening to the room.

It was a trick he learnt when he was young, when he used to clean rooms for his parents. How to listen to the room and let it tell him all the secrets.

Where the valuables were hidden. The jewels or the money.

And then later... the other valuables.

The pornography, or the photographs of an affair: things he could convert into cash or relief with his hand. Things he could use to soak up the terrifying static that made a constant background itch right in the centre of his brain.

Jamie turns a full slow circle, breathing deeply through his nose. Slowly, he walks over to the bed.

He's not worried if Athene comes back; he's brought the little trolley of cleaning products with him, so can spin some tale about how he's valeting the room. He even places a spray can of polish on the side table as a prop.

Jamie is feeling wired; he needs to do something to get back in control. The years are spiralling away and he is becoming undone inside himself.

He pulls back the sheet and checks for any treasures; any little stains or hairs that he may be able to make use of. He slides his hand under the pillow, and strokes the sheet where he imagines she might have lain. He leans down and sniffs the fabric, letting his mouth open slightly, and releasing a thin string of saliva. He stays like that for a soft beat, just putting himself in the same space as Athene's naked imprint, then straightens and smooths the duvet back up. He opens the drawers next to the bed, but all that is there is the new world bible, a blister pack of paracetamol, and a novel. Jamie closes the drawer and looks at the socket next to it. The bedside lamp and Teasmade have been unplugged, and there are two chargers in the double unit; he guesses one for a mobile phone and one for a laptop. Jamie glances around, but the devices aren't visible. He looks for her backpack, then remembers that she was wearing it when she left the bar. He scratches his scar absently and looks around the room again. After a moment, he walks into the en suite bathroom. He opens the cabinet above the sink and surveys the contents, tutting slightly at the banality he finds. There is only a toothbrush, floss dispenser, and a pack of tampons. Jamie takes a tampon out of the box and slips it into his pocket, shutting the cabinet. As the door closes he sees his reflection. He quickly looks away; unsettled by the expression on his face. The fear in his eyes, laced with a look that he has only seen on the inside.

Hate.

He stares at himself for an extra beat, until he has slackened his face into a resemblance of banality, then turns away and leaves the bathroom.

Silently, he walks back into the bedroom and stands still, clicking his teeth together. After a moment, he strides over to the tatty wooden wardrobe and pulls open the door. There is nothing hung up; just a bunch of clothes haphazardly thrown on its floor. Next to the raggle-taggle of clothes there is a hessian laundry sack. Jamie can see the corner of a pair of briefs sticking out of it. He feels his groin give a lazy throb at the sight of it, but does not reach down. Losing control could put him in a daze of sensation, and he might not hear Athene return. Being caught holding a duster was one thing; walking in on him caressing old underwear was quite another. Sighing, Jamie casts his eye over the rest of the wardrobe, opening and closing the drawers. The only paperwork he uncovers is some student ID and a library card in a belt bag. Back in the day he used to find all sorts of things: membership to strange clubs, or business cards of escort agencies. Now, everyone stores all the juicy stuff on their phones.

Sighing in frustration, Jamie carefully puts everything back where he found it and looks around the room again.

His gaze strays back to the bed. He breathes in slowly, through his nose, taking in the scent of it. He notices the bottom corner and creases his eyes, crinkling his scar.

'That would be stupidly clichéd,' he says quietly, staring at the untucked sheet. 'But then again...'

Jamie walks to the bed and kneels down beside it. Gently, he reaches forward and slips his hand between the base and the mattress, pushing against the pressure along the flat surface. He finds the feeling intensely sexual, and spreads his fingers as he searches, pushing his arm further in, moving it left and right as he reaches for anything that might be hidden there. He gives an almost coital sigh as his fingers brush against a flat card-like structure. The surface is laminate-slippy, and has the shape and feel of a bank card. Grasping it softly between his thumb and index finger, he slides the object out, turning as he does so, so he is leaning with his back against the bed. Jamie holds the object in front of him.

It is not a bank card; it is an ID card.

Jamie scans the picture and name.

'Oh dear,' he mutters, feeling ice fill his balls and lava bubble in his stomach.

The name on the card is not the same as she booked in with. The picture is of the girl, but the name is different. Jamie supposes it could be fake, but imagines that that would be quite hard.

'Well, well,' he whispers. 'Everything's just got a lot more fucked-up, then, hasn't it?'

The card is a warrant card: a police ID card stating that the bearer is a Student Police Officer with the Bristol Constabulary. In the picture she is in full uniform, and is smart and unsmiling, with her hair tucked under her cap. Jamie guesses the hair is all one colour.

C. Merrin. Student Police Officer.

Carefully, as if it might go off, Jamie returns the card to its hiding place under the mattress and stands up. He feels numb and on fire at the same time. He holds on to the cleaning trolley for support. That Athene is a police officer, albeit one still newly qualified, was bad enough. But the fact that she hadn't told them; had deliberately hidden her identity, given them a false name, was absolutely terrifying.

Because that meant that it wasn't a coincidence. Because that meant that what she had said about being scammed to rent Blea Fell was a lie.

She was here because of what happened.

Jamie feels the acid in his stomach rise, filling him with nausea and a deep throb of fear.

Still clinging to the trolley, he quietly wheels it forward, and opens the door leading to the corridor. He sticks his head out, making sure no one was around.

But the burning question in Jamie's mind was whether she was here in a professional capacity, or whether it was personal?

'Who are you?' he whispers.

Jamie wheels the trolley out of the room and pulls the door closed, locking it behind him.

37

BELLA'S LAST DAY: SPARROW ROCK, 4PM

'Trent, I'm pregnant.'

Bella looked down on the market town, a bustle of activity as it prepared for the new year. The words left her mouth, then were whipped away by the wind. The outcrop of rock hung over the town like a judging post. Up here the wind was bitter, blown in from Norway with no impediment.

'TRENT, I'M PREGNANT!'

Bella shouted the words. It didn't matter. No one was there to hear them. Bella just needed to scream them out loud, releasing the pain. She dragged her arm across her face, spreading tears and snot and loss and loneliness.

She sniffed, and blinked until she could see again.

She took the battered diary out of her army satchel and opened it. Looked at the page.

`Time to run away, Heathcliff, I'm pregnant.`

She looked at the words, trying to make them fit the thought in her brain, but they didn't seem to have the same power. The same finality. They were like the wind. She could rip the page out and burn the paper, like they had never been there. It wouldn't stop what was growing inside her.

She turned the page; grabbed her pen with her frozen hands.

Then quietly, she said the other thing. The thing that she'd never said aloud, even of herself when alone.

'Mouse, he raped me.'

`Mouse, he raped me.`

More words. More wind. More poison leaving her body.

She looked at the spider marks on the page.

Seven days earlier, Bella had not known what she was going to do. She had left the surgery crying tears that had burned their way out of her body, straight from the white-hot ball of hate at the centre of her mind. She had walked to the woods that sat above the little market town where she sat now, and lit up a cigarette with her Zippo. As she sat there smoking, she had reviewed her life. Her choices, and her manoeuvres within the choices she had been given. As the bitter wind dried her tears into shiny snail tracks down her face, she had smoked herself out of fear and self-loathing into hate and resolution. On the hills in the distance, white caps of snow covered the grey scars of rock that normally smeared the green of the moor.

She had pulled out her Sony Walkman from her army bag and put her headphones on. As the cold synth soundtrack of her life flooded her brain, she had immediately felt in control. Distanced and safe. That time, when she smiled, she let it reach her eyes without touching her mouth.

Sixteen weeks was how long the baby had been growing inside her. That's what the doctor had said. She had spoken seriously, because it was a serious thing. Something sixteen weeks old growing inside someone fifteen years old. The doctor had asked if she'd told her parents, and Bella had just laughed. She couldn't help it.

Then she had gone home and hacked all her hair off.

Bella had thought about it all over Christmas.

Sixteen weeks. That would put the conception at the end of the summer holidays. The rape. When the heather was burning on the moor and the dragonflies were buzzing above the pond.

When Trent had returned and wanted to find a new way to be.

Sixteen weeks.

Sixteen weeks of growing and changing and colonising.

Bella stared down at the town below her, willing her heart to become stone.

It had to stop.

It had to end.

38

THE BECK

Mary sits down next to Athene. The younger girl was texting a message on her phone, but closes it down and puts the device in her holster belt as Mary settles onto the bench.

'Just messaging my mum,' she says curtly. 'I'm letting her know that I'll be back later tonight, or maybe tomorrow, depending on how quickly I can finish off here.'

'I'm sure she'll be pleased to see you.' Mary says quietly, looking at the slow water in the beck, taking the fallen leaves to the next valley like sad, desiccated ships from a fallen season.

'I doubt it. To be honest we'd had a bit of a confrontation before I left. That, as well as the masters, was one of the reasons I needed to get away.'

Mary turns from the water, studies the girl's face. Athene doesn't look at her, only watches the river pass by. Now that Jamie had said out loud what she had been secretly thinking, about Bella's sister, and concretised the thought, Mary could allow herself to see it. The bone structure was similar to Bella's, with the blunt nose and high cheeks. All she needed was a ton of eyeliner and fuck-you hair and she could be Bella's older sister. On the girl's lap is the packet of cigarettes.

Mary suddenly remembers something from their first meeting, in the storm at the café.

'Who was the cigarette for?'

Athene looks at her, confused. 'I'm sorr–'

'Yesterday. When I told you you couldn't smoke in the café. You told me that it was okay, because you didn't smoke.' Mary raises her eyebrows and smiles. 'Then you said it was because you'd given up.' Mary leans forward, pointing down at the soft box. 'Bella used to rip the corner of her packet like you did. I think you were lying to me, so who was the cigarette for?'

Athene looks at the pack of smokes on her lap, then searches Mary's face, skimming her with her eyes. It's an odd feeling. Intimate, yet judgemental at the same time. Like the younger girl is trying to assess her in some way.

'You're right, I'm afraid I might not have been completely honest with you,' she says eventually.

Mary takes a breath. 'Why should you? We don't know each other, and just about everything you've seen must be a little bit...' Mary tries to think of a word that would describe how Jamie and she had just behaved in front of her in the bar of the Craven Head.

'Fucking weird?' Athene suggests, smiling tentatively.

'And the rest.' Mary nods. 'I'm sorry you witnessed that; it must've looked really messy. It's just that all of this is bringing back such... difficult memories. When Bella died it was a real explosion in our lives.'

'I'll bet,' Athene says. Her body relaxes a little.

'Not just mine and Jamie's and Trent's, but others, too.'

Athene nods her head in understanding. 'A small community like this: it must have been devastating on so many levels.'

'It was,' Mary says carefully. She turns back to watch the

creeping beck, keeping Athene in her peripheral vision. 'Especially for her sister, Martha.'

Mary holds her breath, concentrating all her senses on the girl beside her.

'I'm sure,' Athene agrees, still nodding. 'What happened to her? Is she still around?'

Before Mary can answer, Athene suddenly swings towards her.

'Oh my God!' She reaches out and grabs the older woman's arm. 'Did she die in the fire?'

'What? No! I thought you... never mind.' Mary, flustered, runs her hand through her hair. 'She was fine, thank God. What do you mean, you weren't completely honest with me?'

Athene shrugs. 'I'm not really up here to write a masters.'

Mary keeps very still.

Here it comes, she thinks.

'Then why are you here?'

Athene stares at the beck for a moment, as if collecting her thoughts. When she begins to speak, her voice is much quieter, and Mary has to lean forward to catch what she says.

'I finished uni, like I said, but I was burnt out. The fact is I had a bit of a breakdown. I'd had quite a... tricky upbringing. There was some trauma in my life.'

'You don't need to explain yourself to me, Athene.'

'But I do, that's the thing!' Mary is taken aback by the pain in Athene's voice. 'Because I think it's all connected, somehow. My childhood was a war zone, Mary. I didn't know why, but I just couldn't seem to fit. I got into trouble at school. Was always fighting with my mum.'

'Your mum?'

'Yes.'

'What's she like?' prompts Mary.

Athene smiles. 'She's lovely. I haven't made it easy for her, but she's always supported me. Ever since I arrived.'

'What an odd phrase.' Mary smiles.

Athene doesn't smile back. 'But correct. When I turned eighteen my mum told me I was adopted. My biological mother... well she wasn't very well. Not well enough to look after me, anyway, apparently. My mum... the woman who'd looked after me all of the life I could remember... turned out not to be my mum, after all. My... birth mother – that's what they call them – let's just say that she was somewhat incapacitated.'

Mary feels frozen inside, and each time Athene speaks it is like little bits of her are being snapped off.

'I'm sorry.'

She doesn't know! thinks Mary. She remembers the trauma of Martha being taken into care. How the police said that she'd be given a new identity. That Mary mustn't try to contact her. Mary who was half crazy with grief and guilt at Bella's death. Who wanted to find Martha and hold her and hold her until the snow came, like Bella had promised.

As if the girl had read her thoughts, Athene says, 'My mum, the woman who brought me up, offered to help me get in touch, but I was so messed up.'

And then everything begins to slip into place for Mary. Why she felt so emotionally drawn to Athene. Why the girl had flashes of Bella running over her features like liquid lightning. Maybe even why Athene seemed to be drawn to Mary. When Martha was a baby they'd shared, or at least they had in Mary's eyes, a special bond. That's why she'd bought her the owl.

Why she'd shut that part of her heart away, after the fire.

Mary shakes her head, pulling out of her thoughts and concentrating on the present; Athene's still talking.

'And when I finally got well enough to pursue it, it was no good.'

'What do you mean?' Mary's voice is soft, like she doesn't want to scare Athene off, but inside she is reeling.

Athene shrugs. 'There was no record of me, or no follow-through or whatever. Some bollocks anyway.'

'What?' Mary says slowly. 'They couldn't find you in the system?'

'Oh, no; I was on the system all right,' Athene says bitterly. 'But apparently it needs to be both ways.'

'What do you mean?'

'Apparently I don't have a right to track my mother down. Not an automatic right, anyhow. She has to want me, it seems.'

'Right. Okay.'

A memory knives into Mary's brain, of Mrs Moss, Martha and Bella's mother, screaming at her parents' front door.

'She's dead!' Mrs Moss' face was dead-daughter white, and streaked with murder-lines that said she would never sleep again. Mary had watched from her upstairs window, hiding behind her curtains, covered in bruises and broken futures. Trent was in jail.

'She won't ever see me again!' the mother had screamed, spittle flying from her mouth. 'How am I expected to live with that?'

Mary grinds her fist into her leg, diffusing the pain, pulling herself back to the present. 'What about your father?'

'Fuck knows. There was no record of him.'

'Right.'

Mary pictures the fire, burning hot and fast, sending ashes into the sky, like anti-snow. She watches, from inside her head, the figure stumbling away toward the pond on the moor.

Trent.

For whom one death wasn't enough. A dead Bella had broken her, but not Trent. Trent had gone for more.

'Anyhow that's what I meant about the cigarette,' Athene finishes. 'I went off the rails, then got myself cleaned up. I stopped drinking and smoking,' she grimaced. 'Other stuff too, but I still carry a pack with me, to remind myself. Whenever I feel under pressure, I get one out and kind of look at it.' She shrugs one thin shoulder. 'Like a Zen thing. It sort of calms me inside.'

'And you needed calming last night? And now?'

'Yes,' Athene says simply.

'Why?' Mary smiles. 'Because of the storm?'

'No.' The young woman's face is serious. With no make-up on, Mary can see the family resemblance even clearer. 'Because I'm afraid I was about to lie to you.'

'What do you mean? You mean the cigarette?'

'No. Maybe "lie" isn't the right word. You see the brochure wasn't the only thing that was sent to me.'

'What do you mean?' Mary's brow furrows with confusion.

Mary watches as Athene reaches into her pocket and pulls out her wallet; a stylish piece of leather with a brass pop-rivet. She opens it and takes out a photograph. Puzzled, Mary leans forward. The photograph is passport sized, like it was from a booth. Silently, Athene hands it over. When Mary sees what it is she lets out a gasp.

'When the holiday stuff arrived this was attached to it, along with an address for your café. I didn't have a scooby what it meant.'

Mary can barely breathe. The photograph is of her, back when she was young. It is in black and white and she is staring directly into the camera. Cigarette smoke trails up in front of the frame, obscuring the image, but it is definitely her. Before the years and the deaths and the pain like a clock inside her, ticking away her hope. Before the car crash and the fire.

'Where did you get this?' she whispers.

'As I said, it was sent to me, like the holiday cottage.' Athene shrugs. 'Turn it over.'

Mary can't feel her fingers as she does so. Written on the back, in Bella's handwriting, are three words.

'You see why I might want to play it careful?' Athene says. Mary nods dumbly. She can't stop staring at the words. 'Obviously when I received this I didn't know what the hell it was, or who you were, or anything; still don't, really. But when I saw you in the café I recognised you immediately. You still look like the girl in the photograph, underneath. You're still beautiful, you know? And when you started telling me about Blea Fell, and how you were connected...' Athene shrugs again.

Mary drags her eyes away from the words and stares at the girl. 'Who are you? Are you Martha?'

Athene raises her eyebrows. 'The sister? Is that what you think? You think someone has found me and done all this...'

Athene holds her hand out for the photograph, and Mary can see old burns on her wrist.

I went off the rails, then got myself cleaned up. I stopped drinking and smoking, but I still carry a pack with me, to remind myself.

Of what? Mary thinks. She watches her hands as they return the photograph. It is like watching the hands of a stranger.

'Good question: maybe I am; let me know when you have an answer. Maybe this Trent knows something? Right now I'm going to get some stuff from the shop, supplies and that, then I'm going to the police station to see if they have any update of this scam done to me and my mum. Maybe there'll be a clue as to who or why. I'll catch you later, yeah? When you've had a chance to think.'

Mary nods again. She doesn't say anything; doesn't trust herself. The past and the present kaleidoscope around and through her. She just watches as the young woman stands up and leaves.

Don't trust her.

That's what was written on the back of the picture, in Bella's scrawling handwriting.

Don't trust her.

Which meant Jamie was right. Bella must have known about her and Trent. Must have known and said nothing. Must have known and said nothing but felt everything. Mary feels sick all the way through herself. Blackpool-rock sick.

Don't trust her.

'Fuck,' Mary says, watching Athene walking away. 'Fucking hell, Martha.'

39

BELLA'S LAST DAY: 6PM

Bella lay on her bed, looking at the blue lights metronoming off her ceiling.

Blue. Black. Blue. Black.

She could look at them all night, if she didn't have things to do. She loved the way they made everything darker. Made separation easier.

Without her really knowing, Bella caressed the slight swelling of her stomach. The embryo that one day would become a girl or boy.

Or at least it would, if Bella let it.

Although she had woken up certain of what she was going to do; now, in the dark, she wasn't so sure.

It wasn't the baby's fault that its father had raped her.

But then again it wasn't her fault either.

That was a realisation Bella had come to slowly. For the longest time she had thought that it must have been something she had done. Some signal she had given out, but she had realised that that wasn't true.

It wasn't her fault.

It wasn't her fault.

'What am I going to do?' she whispered into the darkness.

40

THE CRAVEN HEAD

Mary storms back through the pub, her heart pounding. She enters the bar and spies Jamie, helping himself to another drink. She strides over to him, excited.

'You're right, Jamie! She's Martha, has to be, but she doesn't realise it! She's adopted! Her history must have been wiped or whatever, because of what happened. I think someone's fucking with her, like they're fucking with us.'

Mary plonks herself on a stool at the bar, her mind buzzing. She doesn't see the look of fear on Jamie's face.

'I don't know who it could be, but someone's dragging up the past.' She puts her hand flat on the table, her eyes shining.

'She's the Feds, Mouse,' says Jamie, flatly.

Mary stops talking and looks at him. He's clearly had a few more gins since she'd left.

'What?'

'She's a policewoman, Mouse! She's up here investigating us! Undercover. Athene isn't even her real name.'

'What?' Mary repeats again. 'Investigating us? Why would she be investigating us?'

'Fuck knows. Maybe something to do with Trent?'

Mary sighs, suddenly feeling like she wants to lie down on the floor and close her eyes.

'What's going on, Jamie? What do you mean she's a policewoman?'

'I found her warrant card upstairs, hidden in her room.'

Mary shakes her head. 'What were you doing in her room?'

'Like we said, she seemed to be involved, so I had a quick butchers.'

Mary looks at him. There were so many things wrong with what he was saying she barely knew where to start. 'You can't just let yourself into her room and search through her private stuff, Jamie! That's not right.'

Mary jumps as he first bangs his fist down onto the table, then raises it to hit the side of his head.

'Missing the point, Mouse! It's not going in! She's the fucking police! Even if she's Martha with a new name, she's the police! She kept it hidden! That means...'

Realisation suddenly breaks across his face.

'It's her! That's how she got them!'

'What are you talking about?'

Jamie looks at the door, then at the ceiling, as if he has X-ray eyes and can see into the room above. 'The photos. If she's the police then she has access to them.'

He drops his gaze and looks at her.

'It's all Athene or whatever her name is! She's the one who sent the photos. She's the one who tracked down Trent. She's been lying to us all. She's playing some fucking warped game with our heads.'

Mary looks at him, feeling the truth of what he is saying. If Martha really was with the police then it all made a kind of horrible sense. She'd have the ability to find out about the car crash; have access to the evidence, maybe. But it didn't explain the subterfuge. Didn't shed any light on why she'd need or want to manipulate them like this. Trent had gone to jail for what had happened. The whole thing was history.

Mary swallowed.

Except, of course, it wasn't.

There were still secrets.

Still things that were buried.

41

BELLA'S LAST DAY: TRAVEL DIARY

AFTER THE CIGARETTE

I've just done the worst thing ever, but I couldn't help it.

There wasn't a choice. She cried and cried no matter what I said.

I had to write it down because she deserves it, but I'm going to rip the page out later, because I don't want it to contaminate the rest of it. I've written it because I'm so ashamed. I tried to tell her but she didn't understand.

How could she?

I hate myself for doing it.

Even though I know it's the right thing.

It had to be done, otherwise they may not believe me.

I'm so sorry, Athene. If you ever read this you'd probably hate me.

But I'm doing it for you.

42

THE CRAVEN HEAD: ATHENE'S ROOM

Athene steps into her room. If Mary could see her now, she wouldn't recognise her. The wide-eyed look has disappeared. She looks older. Harder. More like the rocks that scatter the landscape than the girl she has been playing for the last day.

She closes the door quietly and is about to walk to the bathroom when she stops.

On top of the bedside table is a can of polish.

Athene looks at it, working out the meaning, then walks swiftly to the wardrobe and opens the door. She looks down at the laundry bag, feeling relief spread through her, then back at the table.

'Okedoke,' she says softly, and reaches into her pocket, pulling out her phone.

43

BLEA MOOR, 1998: THE END OF SUMMER

Blea Fell through the lens of the camera looked like it was a secret in stone. The windows were mirror-blinded by the sun shining on them, preventing any chance of observing what was going on within. There was no car parked on the track; both parents being out, doing something with the baby, probably. Maybe taking it to the doctor. Apparently it would never go to sleep at night; would stay up screaming until morning.

A real night-owl, Bella had said.

Jamie smiled when he thought about Bella, and panned the front of the house, eyeing the building through the camera lens, trying to see through the windows.

Bella, Bella, Bella. Jamie muttered her name under his breath like a mantra.

Jamie settled himself into the coarse grass, rocking his hips against the ground. He was lying down on his stomach, his camera on a stubby tripod. Beside him was a book of moorland birds, on the off-chance he was spotted, and a bottle of diet Coke. In his Nike backpack he had a selection of chocolate bars, a half loaf of white sliced bread, and a packet of cheese and onion crisps.

Jamie looked through the lens at the house for a moment longer, snapped off a couple of shots, then sat up.

On top of the hill overlooking the house, Jamie had positioned himself between two gorse bushes; not enough to impede his view, but hopefully enough so he couldn't be spotted from the house, should anybody happen to look his way. And if anybody got curious, he had his ornithological book, where he had marked out local birds with a highlighter pen. He was dressed in a pair of army combat trousers and a fleece. Although the sun was out, there was a brisk wind, bringing the smell of the sea in from the west.

Jamie began building himself a chocolate and crisp sandwich.

So far he had managed to photograph Bella in the kitchen, making herself a coffee, then sitting down on the tatty sofa writing in her diary. Or diaries, he corrected himself, biting into the sandwich. The chocolate was just the right side of soft, and as he chewed, it mixed with the crisps and white bread, until the whole thing became the consistency of slurry in his mouth. He'd stolen the crisps and chocolate bars from behind the bar when he'd left that morning; his parents still asleep. Jamie wouldn't be surprised if they were still there, lying in their bed, reeking of alcohol and old-people sex.

Sometimes Jamie would watch them, sleeping. Sometimes he would watch them, and wonder what it would be like to stab them with the kitchen knife. Over and over.

Jamie felt a slight shiver as the sun went behind a cloud. Stuffing the rest of his sandwich into his mouth, he lay back down and positioned himself behind the camera. As he looked through the lens, the house suddenly sprang forward, the beaten stone of its walls in sharp focus. Jamie moved the camera slightly so he could look through the kitchen window. The room was almost half of the ground floor, stretching from front to back, with a whole dining room and living space included. From his angle, Jamie could see the stove, and the sofa in front of it where Bella had been writing in her diaries. The telephoto lens hadn't been powerful enough that he could see what she had been writing, but it had definitely been passionate. As he had watched her, she had practically been etching the words. He could see her grip on the pen, white and hard. And the expression on her face had actually frightened him a little. Bella, whose features were normally so guarded, had looked so angry. Like there was a rip in her. He had watched as she'd flung one book aside, and picked up another. Jamie wasn't sure he knew how, but he knew they were diaries; something Bella was putting her secret-self into. There was something about the intimacy of her gaze on the page. There was no thought process going on there, like if you were writing a story. What was in her head was spewing straight into the book.

And it wasn't pretty, whatever it was.

Jamie smiled, and wondered if it was about Trent. Or Mouse.

Bella wasn't in the kitchen anymore; or at least not anywhere the camera could see. The diaries had been cleared away, and the sofa was empty. Jamie kept the camera looking through the window a minute more, in case she returned into shot, and then moved it across to the window that looked into the other part of the ground floor; a sort of study where the father worked.

Jamie didn't like the father. The father had hungry eyes. Jamie had seen him at various school functions, and very occasionally in his parents' bar, sipping whisky. The father's eyes were always watching; eating. Eating up whatever they were looking at, like they couldn't get enough of whatever it was. Not just eating; consuming. Gobbling. And never satisfied. Always hungry.

Jamie looked through the camera at the empty room. Bella wasn't in there, and neither was the hungry father. Jamie gave a cursory look around the room. There was a nondescript picture on the wall, an old-fashioned metal safe, much like the one his parents had in the cellar, and a home computer on the desk. Other than that the room was strangely empty. The space seemed to be barren, like a film set. Not real.

Jamie felt the shiver again, and moved the camera to the upstairs window. The hill he was hidden on rose above the house, putting him slightly higher than the upstairs windows. Having never been in the house, he picked the top left at random, and caught his breath as the camera picked up Bella's back. It was just a flash as she walked in front of the window, but it was enough to cause his heart to leap into his throat. He quickly pulled his face away from the camera and looked around him. He knew it was irrational; that even if he was being observed, no one without a camera with a telescopic lens of their own would know what he was looking at, but nevertheless he felt the sick slug of fear in his stomach.

Jamie looked around the moor, empty other than the lapwings and the skylarks. He glanced at the sky, and saw there was a large bank of clouds, meaning he'd have a viewing window of at least a few minutes. He lay back down and pressed his eye against the lens.

The room was the bathroom, which explained the lack of clothes. Despite him viewing from the hill, the angle wasn't acute enough to see if Bella was completely naked; the window sill obscured anything lower than a hint of curve at the base of her spine. Not taking his eye off Bella, Jamie fed chocolate into his mouth, pushing it in slowly between his teeth, and resting his tongue on it, feeling it melt under his heat. Bella was standing in front of the sink, with the bathroom mirror in front of her. She wasn't doing anything; just staring at her reflection.

Jamie wondered if she was about to have a bath; she hadn't been gone from the kitchen long enough to have had one already. After a moment, Jamie decided she wasn't. There was no steam in the bathroom; he could see her face clearly in the mirror. It was not a large mirror, so he couldn't see her breasts; just her face and neck.

What are you doing, Bella? he wondered, the chocolate slowly becoming liquid in his mouth, filling it. He pushed in a little more. *What are you looking at, with those eyes?* Bella appeared motionless, just... still. Jamie noticed her right shoulder was moving slightly, meaning she was moving her arm.

Are you touching yourself? His head hummed inside his skull. Chocolate dribbled out of the corner of his mouth.

After what seemed an age she looked sideways and down.

Something in the sink, he thought, or by the side of the sink.

Then her hand appeared, holding something small. Light from the mirror slid off it, and Jamie realised it was a razor blade; not one of those disposable ones his dad used, but a metal rectangle, the type you put in those razors with the wind-up middle.

Safety razors, Jamie remembered. Which was a stupid name for them, because it looked anything but safe. He watched as Bella got hold of her hair with one hand, and held it up and out from her head. Bella stared at her reflection a moment longer, then brought up her other hand; the one with the razor blade, and sawed at her hair. She must have been pulling tight, because after a few moments the hand holding her hair jerked away, the tress still held in it.

'Jesus!' whispered Jamie. Bits of molten chocolate came out, splattering the camera, but he didn't notice. Bella placed the hair somewhere out of sight, and grabbed the next lock. Slowly she brought the blade to it, and repeated the process. And the next. And the next. Jamie watched, hardly breathing, as he witnessed Bella massacre her own hair. And all the time she did it, Jamie noticed, her expression never changed.

Subconsciously, Jamie nodded.

What happened, Bella? What did Trent do?

The buzzing in Jamie's head increased, no longer connected to any sexual desire. He stayed stone-still, and then let out a shaky breath when Bella finally finished and placed the blade in the sink.

Bella looked at her work in the mirror, then turned around.

And everything got worse.

Jamie let out a gasp as he saw Bella's bare front.

She had not been touching herself, just before she hacked off her hair, or at least not in the way Jamie had imagined.

There were cuts all over her chest; slashes of red where she had sliced herself with the razor. There was no gushing; the cuts weren't deep, but they must have hurt. He saw with a kind of blunt horror that bits of the hair hacked from her head were stuck in the blood.

Despite himself, he looked closer, his eyes pressed hard against the lenses. Bella reached out of shot, her hand returning holding a towel. She turned and wet the towel, then turned back and began wiping the blood off herself.

Now that the blood was cleared off, Jamie could see that there was so much. As well as the new cuts and slashes, there were older ones; ones that had scabbed over. Ones that had faded. Ones that had scarred.

Jesus, she must have been doing this for months; maybe even years, he thought, pressing the shutter mechanism that would take the picture.

And then something else occurred to him.

Why hasn't Trent said anything? He must know about this! He must have seen them? Bloody hell, he must have felt them!

And then the thought doubled down on itself, raising the stakes.

Maybe he caused them.

Jamie photographed Bella's face. She was staring out of the window, looking out at the weird collection of trees in the field opposite her house. Watching her, Jamie felt a shiver of dread wash through him.

Bella was smiling broadly, but only with her mouth. No mirth or joy or even hate reached her eyes. Her eyes were grey buttons. Her eyes were slate pennies.

Jamie clicked one more photo, then shut down the camera and crept away.

As awful as what he had witnessed was, Jamie felt happy.

Maybe he had something he could barter with.

44

ATHENE'S PHONE

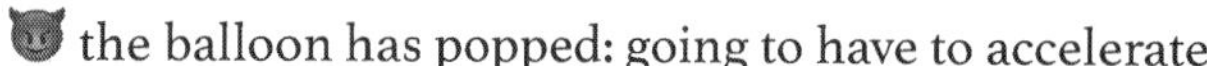
the balloon has popped: going to have to accelerate

what's up?

J searched room, found ID.

shit. Did he find d's?

no

right. Things all on track this end. Time to wipe phone and boogie.

agreed.

xx

x

45

BELLA'S LAST DAY: BLEA FELL HOUSE

BEFORE THE CIGARETTE

'Do you like your name, *Thing*?'

The baby fell over and giggled, her fat legs sticking out in front of her like oars from a body-boat.

'Martha.' Bella tried it in her mouth, then shook her head. 'I'm not sure. It sounds like you should be wearing an apron and sweeping a yard.'

She picked up her sister and swung her out of the playpen, putting her down on the rug. In her hand was the owl that Mouse had given her. Bella looked at it. Just even looking at it sent arrows of hurt shooting into her heart.

'What about Owl?' she whispered. 'Do you think Owl is a good name? Like Wren or Robin or Jay?' Bella reached down and stroked Martha's face, causing her to crinkle her features with happiness. 'I think I like Owl. I think Owl is a good name. There's owls in Auntie Mouse's favourite TV programme.'

Martha belched, releasing a tiny stream of saliva. Bella smiled, and gently placed a book in Martha's playpen. It was the book she had found hidden under her floorboards.

'There's a girl in this book I found who has the name of an

owl, or at least very nearly. In fact she's not a girl at all: she's a goddess!' Bella opens her eyes wide. 'Her name was Athena and she was a warrior! She wasn't born, or anything boring like that, she split open her own father's head with a spear and jumped out of his brain! What do you think of that?'

What Martha seemed to think of it consisted of sucking on the head of the toy owl.

'And then later her name got changed to Athene, which became the name of a type of owl, which became a toy for you to eat. From Greek Goddess to Martha's rusk; how cool is that!'

Martha stuck out her chubby little arms and Bella picked her up.

'Yes, *Thing*, I think Athene is probably a much better name, all in all.'

She held Martha tight, breathing in her special baby smell.

'I don't think I'm going to see you again, little sister, so I want you to know that I love you, okay? I want you to know that I'm sorry.'

The tears Mouse had never seen Bella cry leaked out, acid through the white foundation. She gently lifted Martha's shirt, exposing the skin on her chest and stomach.

'No romper suit? What a fucking surprise.'

If Martha was shocked by the swearing she didn't show it; she just blew happy bubbles of saliva in her sister's face. Bella could see little scratches on her skin, but nothing bad. Martha could have done them herself. She winked at Martha and turned her round. There were more marks on her back, plus what looked like a couple of old burns. Some bruising.

'You didn't do these yourself, did you, Mar-ma?' she said, studying her skin. 'But I don't think it's quite enough.'

She took a long pull of her cigarette, making the tip glow orange. She pulled her sister tight.

'I'm sorry but I can't seem to find another way,' she whispered, watching from a distance inside her head as she turned the cigarette round in her hand.

The scream Martha made seemed to rip the stone house in two.

46

THE CRAVEN HEAD

'I'm not sure about this,' Mary says.

'I don't care. She lied to us, Mouse; we need to find out what she wants.'

Jamie pulls the set of master keys from his pocket, unlocks the door, and walks into Athene's room. He strides in, not knocking; Mouse had told Jamie about Athene going to the police station in Skipton, to see about any news on the house scam.

Jamie smiles grimly. He bet she had. All the way to her cosy little mates at CID or whatever, planning to fuck him up all over again.

'But this is breaking and entering; or invasion of privacy.'

Mary wished she hadn't followed him up here. It made her feel dirty; as if she was doing something with Jamie that no one else knew about, and she really, really didn't want to feel like she was in some sort of secret with Jamie.

'Bollocks. She started it. That girl is a snake in the grass, Mouse. She's not been fucking scammed; she's been scamming you; messing with us.'

Jamie pauses in the middle of the room and turns to stare at her. Mary thinks he looks unhinged. He has alcohol stains down the front of his shirt, which is hanging untucked from his trousers, and his hair is fear-greased to his scalp.

'Why are you so worried?' she asks. 'It's not as if you have anything to hide.'

Jamie gives a half shrug. 'Business hasn't been fantastic lately. I may have been...' he pauses, as if trying to work out where he is, '...diversifying.'

Mary stares at him, her mind ticking. She thinks back to their youth, back to school and the drinking she and Trent and Bella used to do in the pub. Then she remembers the shifty teenagers she'd seen this morning, when she was waiting outside, looking for Athene. She shakes her head.

'You've not been dealing again, Jamie? Don't tell me you've been–'

'Oh fuck off from your high horse! It's not like you didn't get the odd thing from me.'

She looks at him astonished.

'Yes, when I was *fifteen*, for God's sake! When we were kids! I–' Mary stops, hearing the ghost-bells of a pinball machine; becomes acutely aware she is alone in a bedroom with him.

She takes a step back.

Jamie's eyes are wild, not noticing her discomfort. 'Whatever,' he mutters, walking over to the bed.

'What are you doing, Jamie?' Mary takes another step back.

'It's under the mattress,' he says, still unaware of the change in Mary's voice.

'What is?'

'The proof,' he snaps, getting down on his knees, and shoving his hand between the mattress and the baseboard.

Mary looks at him, incredulous. 'That's where you found it? Before?'

Jamie nods, his arm disappearing into the bed like he's using it as a giant puppet. 'Yeah; it's a shit hiding place. Almost everybody does it. Idiots. Probably in a film or something.'

Mary realises that the man didn't just come in and look round Athene's room, but did a systematic search, including under the mattress. And saying everybody does it meant that it wasn't the first time.

How many drugs are you dealing? she wonders, looking at him, crushed to the floor.

Mary watches as his expression turns from dark triumph, to confusion, to fear as he pushes further into the bed.

'Where the fuck is it?' he shouts.

What else do you do in their bedrooms? The skin on the back of Mary's neck crawls as she watches him.

Suddenly Jamie stands up, bringing the mattress up with him. He tips it on its side, then sends it, along with the duvet and the sheet, spinning off the other side of the baseboard. He stares at the bare-wooden bed support, bewilderment and disbelief marching across his features.

'It's gone,' he says dully.

'I think you've really lost it, Jamie,' Mary says, the muscles in her legs tense, her voice full of quiet wonder.

'Her ID. It's gone.'

'What?'

'Her police ID.' Jamie looks at her, all anger gone, replaced with a kind of hunted fear. 'That means she must know. She must know that I'd been in her room.'

Before Mary can say anything, the silence is broken by a burble of synthetic sound coming from the head of the bed. She turns and sees Athene's mobile phone, on the table next to a can of polish.

'Fuck.' Jamie points to the polish. 'I must have left it in here when I snuck in before.'

But Mary isn't listening to him; she is collapsing to the bare-threaded carpet, all thoughts of creepy-Jamie forgotten. The burble has resolved itself into the opening notes of a song. Like Mary's *Falling*, or a million other people, Athene must have a music track as her ring tune.

'What the hell's going on?' whispers Mary, tears springing from her eyes. She doesn't feel the rough carpet under her knees. Doesn't see the look of shock on Jamie's face. All she sees is the phone on the table, grinding out its song.

'How can she have this?' Mary looks at Jamie, and it's like she's looking through him, to the younger Jamie. 'How can she have this on her phone?'

'Coincidence,' says Jamie, but she can see he doesn't believe it. Of course it isn't coincidence. How could it be, given who they were and the fact that Athene is a police officer, with access to the original case? Mary stays staring at Jamie a beat longer, then turns her head slowly back to the phone, playing the song she watched Bella die to. The last track on her playlist, making up the soundtrack of the car journey that ended in Bella lying cold and unmoving, crushed half out of the shattered windscreen.

Yazoo's 'Only You'.

Only you.

'I'm so sorry, Bella,' Mouse whispers.

And then the tune stops, and the phone goes dead.

47

BELLA'S LAST DAY: ONLY YOU

Bella isn't moving. The snow is falling gently and all the sound has been turned down to zero except Bella's music still coming from the upturned car. Mouse looks at the still body of Bella for a heartbeat, then crawls towards her.

Only you, only you.

Mouse keeps her eyes on Bella, and doesn't understand why she is veering to the right as she crawls. She keeps putting herself on track, but then slides off-beam. And all the time the snow falls and the sound stays hidden. It is only when she looks away from Bella and down at herself that she realises her leg is broken. More than broken. Mouse stares at the glistening piece of bone protruding from her jeans, unsure at first what it is. When her brain finally works it out, it is as if a switch has been flicked. Pain floods into her like a dam has burst, sending great gobs of searing agony. It is so staggering that it takes her sight away for a moment, replacing it with a black blanket of crushing hurt. Her arms collapse from under her, sending her face-first into the ice and snow. As she hits, her mouth fills with icy shards, clearing away the blackness.

'Trent!' She tries to scream the word, but all that comes out is a croak, a pain deep in her chest where something is broken. She swallows and tries again.

'TRENT!' She raises her head slightly, twisting it round so she is facing the wreck of the car. She thinks she can see a silhouette, crouching over Bella's body. She blinks, clearing away the tears, and sees Trent. His army jacket is ripped, probably when he had been thrown out of the car, and the T-shirt underneath sodden with blood. Trent doesn't register that he's heard her; keeps leaning down and hugging Bella, then straightening and running his hands through his hair, shiny with melted snow and hot blood.

'I'm sorry I'm sorry I'm sorry.'

His voice sounds like the wind, reaching Mouse across the ice-packed ground in a whisper.

'Trent! Is she...?'

'BELLA! BELLS!' Trent screams, and grabs Bella's exposed shoulders and shakes her.

Even through the pain in her leg and spear of hurt in her chest, Mouse can see there is no resistance; that it looks like Trent is shaking a doll. Mouse makes a tight, wet, moan deep inside her and tries to crawl towards them. As soon as she moves she screams. Now that she was becoming aware of herself, she can actually *feel* the bone sticking out; snagging on her jeans as she moves, causing it to rip something deep in her leg. A muscle, maybe.

Her scream startles Trent, and he turns and looks at her. For a moment his eyes are blank, like he had forgotten about her. As he stares he puts his hands back up to his hair. Then something clicks behind his eyes, and he looks imploringly at her.

'Mouse! What do I do, Mouse?' he pleads. 'I don't think she's breathing, and half the fucking car is on her! What do I do?'

'Mouth to mouth,' Mouse whispers. She isn't sure if the

words are loud enough to reach Trent, but then he suddenly leans down and places his mouth over Bella's.

'I can't tell!' he says after a few moments of breathing into her. 'My lips are so cold, I can't tell if it's working!'

Trent is crying. He keeps leaning forward as if to shake the still girl, then leaning back, afraid to touch her. As if he doesn't want to know. As if not touching her might make it not real. But Mouse can tell. In the moonlight, amplified by the snow and the ice and the skewed headlights of the car that bizarrely are still working, Mouse can tell.

'There's no mist,' she whispers. The pain in her leg is like a bell. Every time she moves it sends peals of hurt through her. But she can't help moving; she is crying so hard, although all the tears seem to be frozen inside her. All she can do is shake.

'What?'

'Out of her mouth. There's no breath. You'd see it. She's not breathing, Trent.'

'Ohmygod. Ohmygod.' Trent springs up and takes a step back, as if maybe he thinks giving her space might help. Mouse can hear a high pitched wailing at the back of her head, like part of her brain is ripping away, but then realises it must be an ambulance. She can see blood dripping off Trent's fingers, slow and thick and steaming in the freezing air.

Not Bella's blood, she thinks, looking at his sodden T-shirt. She tries to crawl again, but the pain takes her breath away.

'Imsosorry imsosorry.'

Trent is squatting next to Bella, his hands back in his hair.

'Not your fault,' whispers Mouse. 'She pulled the wheel. I saw her.'

Trent turns slowly to look at her. Through the pain Mouse can't see any colour in his eyes.

'She crashed the car, I saw her. She tried to kill us, Trent.'

'Not true,' he says, shaking his head. Little drops of blood and sweat and ice fall from him, glittering in the light. 'Don't say that.' The words cut across the distance between them.

Trent stands up and strides towards her. As he gets nearer, his features come into focus, and for a second the pain in Mouse's leg switches off.

Trent looks demonic. 'Don't say that. It's not true! She–'

'But I saw her, Trent. She told us we were going straight to hell, and then she spun the wheel.'

The sound of the ambulance is nearer, Mouse thinks, but it was hard to tell. Sound in the valley had a way of bouncing off the hills and folding in on itself. Blood is dripping off Trent and spattering around her. He is standing above her, his fists clenched and his whole body shaking.

Shock, thinks Mouse. *We're both in shock.*

'DON'T SAY THAT! NOT TO ANYONE! IT WAS ME! MY FAULT!'

Mouse stares up at him. Her vision is fading in and out and she knows she was going to lose consciousness soon.

'I crashed us. I blanked out when she told me... when she said about...' Trent is weeping, looking back toward Bella, who is covered in snow.

'I think you're really hurt, Trent.' Mouse can't believe how much blood is on his shirt. Trent ignores her.

'She said she wanted to die! But then... Bella was trying to save us. I was pissed and jacked and it was my fault! That's what you saw, okay? She was trying to get us back onto the road.'

Trent collapses down onto his knees.

'I was so fucked, Mouse! I think I zoned out. The car just started sliding and Bella tried to get us back straight and now she's dead. Now she's dead and she'll never know!'

'Know what? Know what, Trent? Why did she want to die? Is it because of us?'

Is it because of me? Because I betrayed her?

Mouse is fading fast. Trent was just a dim planet spinning round the sun of her pain, everything shutting down.

'Know what, Trent?' she whispers to the shadow of him. 'What doesn't she know?'

'How much I love her,' he says helplessly.

Mouse nods. She can hear the ambulance skidding to a halt, sirens winding down to silence.

How much we both do, she thinks, as she fades to black.

48

BELLA'S LAST SUMMER: ONLY YOU

'How come you only listen to songs from like a million years ago?'

Bella laughed and slammed her hips against the pinball machine, the force nudging the ball away from a hole and onto her flipper. Punching the button, she sent the silver sphere up through the playfield, causing the lights and the sounds of the machine to go into overdrive.

'Modern music's rubbish!' she said happily, then swore as the ball ricocheted off a rail and sped down the middle of the field, disappearing from sight with a sad succession of bleeps and pings.

'Bollocks!'

Bella and Mouse were in the games room at the back of the Craven Head, drinking blackcurrant snakebite and playing the machines. They had taken half an E each – scored from Jamie a couple of hours earlier. The MDMA was making Mouse feel both shivery and hot, and she had a repeating note in her head like she was on hold to heaven. She couldn't believe how happy the lights on the game were making her.

'My go!' she said, using her body to move Bella aside, and

pulling back on the spring lever that would send the ball shooting into play. Bella shifted over, but kept her body brushed up to Mouse's. Mouse suspected it was because of the drugs, and the fact that they were supremely wasted on cider, but she didn't mind; she'd take what she could get.

Trent was due back tomorrow, and Bella seemed to be on a mission to keep tomorrow as far away from today as possible. Hence the drinking and the pill.

'Not going to sleep tonight,' she'd said, glassy-eyed, and with a chemical smile plastered on her face. 'Then I won't wake up and it will still be today!'

'Why don't you finish with him,' Mouse said, sucking down her snakebite through a straw.

'Why, do you want a go?' Bella replied, raising an eyebrow. Her face was beautifully framed by her shaggy long hair. In Mouse's state her skin seemed to be glowing.

Mouse flushed and looked away.

'Of course not. It's just that you never seem happy when you're with him, that's all. And then after what he did to...'

Both the girls glanced through the door into the saloon bar to see if Jamie was in earshot, but all Mouse could see were tourists and the Local Dead. That's what her and Bella called them; the old farmers and retirees who came to the pub every night.

'Did he ever tell you what it was about?' Mouse flipped both flippers, causing the ball to judder between them, then slide onto the extended arm. She paused for a moment, then flipped it up the ramp, locking it away for a multi-ball.

'I can't believe you're asking me now, just before he comes back!' Bella sounded amazed, but Mouse knew better. It wasn't only that they had barely talked about the incident that got Jamie expelled, and Trent sent to reform school, it was that they had *never* spoken about it. Not once. There had been talk around the school. It was well reported what Trent had said; about doing it for Mouse. There was talk also about Trent and Jamie's lockers being searched. Everyone assumed that drugs must have been found. Hence the expelling. In fact there were burned ashes in Trent's locker, and everybody wondered if he'd been smoking crack.

But it hadn't felt like drugs to Mouse, as she'd watched Jamie being ripped apart. It had felt more personal.

Mouse blinked and slammed her flat hand against the button, ramping a second ball.

'Wow, you should take drugs every time you play pinball,' Bella said admiringly. 'I can't wait to see what you're going to do to the Space Invaders!'

'Space Invaders haven't existed since the eighties,' Mouse exclaimed, finally losing the ball and moving aside. 'Like the music you love.'

Bella staggered back in front of the table. It took her a couple of giggling seconds to pull back the ball-fire lever.

'Yes, but like a fine wine my tunes have matured!'

'Dad says can you keep the noise down, or he's going to have to throw you out.'

The two girls turned to find Jamie leaning against the games room door, staring at them. There was a waxy sheen of perspiration covering his face, and his eyes were slightly out of focus. Mouse wondered if he has been sampling a little of his own product.

'And why would that be, Jim-jam?' Bella said sweetly. 'Because we're underage, because we're drunk, or because we're mashed out on the drugs you gave us?'

Jamie smiled queasily and looked over his shoulder. 'Look, the pub will be closing in an hour, and we can have a lock-in, then you can make as much noise as you like, but until then just chill, all right?'

Jamie turned and left, his shoulders hunched against the girls' spluttering laughter.

'Just chill? What the actual fuck was that?'

'Maybe he's gone all hard with his new scar and OG connections.' Mouse said it as a joke, but inside she felt shame crawling through her.

This is for you.

'Maybe,' Bella said, nudging the pinball machine so hard that the tilt sign snapped on, cutting all the power to the game. She watched as her ball rolled down the field and into the gaping hole at the base. 'I'm bored of this,' she said, turning away in disgust. 'Let's sit down and talk.'

'Sure.' Mouse didn't mind. She was having difficulty keeping her thoughts going in one direction; sitting down sounded like a fantastic plan. Sitting down, or possibly lying down under the pool table. Possibly with Bella. The song on the jukebox finished, and there was a sonic pause before Cher's 'Turn back Time' ramped up.

'See!' Bella said triumphantly as she collapsed into her chair. 'Absolute fucking guff!'

Mouse sat down opposite, carefully placing her snakebite on the little round table between them. She pointed at the jukebox. 'Cher...' she said, then pointed at what she was sitting on. 'Chair!'

Bella looked at her a moment, then burst out laughing.

I know it's just the drugs, Mouse thought, *but I'm so happy in this moment*. 'It's like old times,' she said, before she could help herself.

'What do you mean?' Bella asked.

'You and me, Bells,' Mouse said quietly. 'You and me, with no one else and just having fun.'

'Yeah, well maybe we should make the old times the new times,' said Bella, raising her glass of purple alcohol in salute.

'Except you were always mean to me,' Mouse said without thinking.

'What?' Bella looked at her incredulously. Realising what she had said, Mouse put her hand to her mouth, as if she could stuff the words back in.

'You think I've been mean to you? When? When have I been mean to you?'

Bella looked genuinely amazed.

'I'm sorry. It's just the drugs talking. Let's–'

'Let's not,' Bella interrupted. 'Let's stay on topic. All I've ever done is try to look out for you, Mouse! How can you think I've been mean?'

'I didn't mean it.' Mouse felt her world slipping away; sand on a turning tide. 'I love that we're friends; that you've looked out for me all these years.' Her face contorts for a second, a spasm of true confusion. 'Although I've never understood why. You could be friends with whoever you wanted. And you picked me.'

'So what do you mean with the mean?' Bella said half smiling. Mouse stared at her helplessly.

'You must know,' she whispered. The song finished on the juke and the bubble of silence seemed to coalesce around them. 'You must! Like on the bus!'

'The bus? What fucking bus?' Bella stared at her with Ecstasy eyes; all pupil and unblinking, like she'd stolen them from a seal.

'When you made me hurt you.' Mouse's voice was soft. She could barely get the words out. It was as if all the air had been stolen from her lungs.

The jukebox started with the next tune, 'Falling', and Julee Cruise began singing, her strange voice seeping out of the speakers like mist. Bella stayed staring at her friend a moment longer, then blinked and smiled.

Mouse felt a flush of relief, a warm wave washing over her feet on an evening beach.

'This song,' Bella said. 'You talk about me and my choices. Why do you love it so much?'

Jamie kept a selection of discs on the juke especially for them, scattered amongst what Bella called the *tits and fists* that passed for chart fodder.

'Because it reminds me of you,' Mouse said simply. The whole show, for which it was the theme, did. From the rural setting to the fucked-up tragedy of it. From the beginning, with the dead girl wrapped in plastic, to the owls and the love and plain weirdness of it. 'Because it reminds me of us.'

Bella looked at Mouse with her seal-eyes, staring at her and in her and through her. Mouse felt like she was melting under her gaze. Then Bella reached across and gently stroked the back of her hand with her finger, so softly it was like being stroked by a shadow.

'Poor Mouse,' she said. 'I'm so sorry.'

And then Mouse got really scared, because it looked like Bella was going to cry. Bella who was always in control, always the captain of her own narrative.

'Bella...' Mouse began, unsure where the rest of the sentence was going, but wanting, needing, to start it. 'Bella, I just want–'

'I'll leave him for you,' cut in Bella.

Mouse stopped speaking and stared at her. She opened her mouth, but could think of nothing to say. The room seemed to be breathing, like they were on the inside of giant lungs. Like they had flown through the lyrics of the song pouring out of the jukebox like honey.

'What do you mean?'

'We're nearly sixteen. Soon we can do what we want.' Even through the drugs, Mouse could tell that Bella was serious. Even through the heave and swell of the snakebite she had drunk she could see the determination in her friend's eyes. 'No one can stop us.'

'Why, is Trent trying to stop you doing what you want?'

Mouse thought of Trent's face as he looked at her, straddled over the pulp of Jamie's face. Thought of the violence he wore like an overcoat.

'Bella, is Trent ever violent to you?'

Mouse thought of Bella's arms. Of the cuts like ticks and tocks, marking out a timetable. Then she thought of Bella forcing her hand down on the bus. Making her cut her friend. Pressing her hand down against her will.

'The rules of attraction,' Bella said. 'Broken things need breaking.'

The words were hard but Bella's expression was soft.

Mouse held her breath. 'Your eyes. They're like the snow globe,' she whispered.

'What?'

'The snow globe. Like when we carved our names on the tree.'

'Of course they are.' Bella smiled. 'I told you, Mouse. The world is just for you and me.'

And then the song changed, and the opening synth notes of Yazoo's 'Only You' began.

'See!' Bella grinned. 'They're playing our song.'

Bella staggered to her feet and put out her hand. After a moment, Mouse grabbed it and was hauled to her feet.

'Careful! We'll both go flying.'

'Better hold on to me then.' Bella wrapped her arms around Mouse and began to dance to the song. Mouse resisted for a moment, then let herself relax into the girl.

If I didn't, she'd fall over, Mouse thought, but she closed her eyes and rested her head against Bella's. She could hear Jamie calling time in the saloon bar; the grumble of the Local Dead as they shuffled to their feet.

'Let's run away and get married, and then do a *Thelma and Louise* to this song off a tower block.'

Bella's voice was like tiny stones being dropped in a pond; possibilities rippling out from the weight of her words.

'They die at the end; Thelma and Louise.' Mouse kept her eyes closed, gently pressing her hands against Bella's back. The music throbbed through her body like an electric current.

'We all die in the end,' Bella whispered back.

An image of Trent flashed across the wall of Mouse's closed eyes.

Some of us die every day, she thought in a dark part of her brain.

'Hey, Bella, your dad's here to drive you home!'

Mouse opened her eyes and looked at the door. Jamie was back, standing there, staring at them with his napkin eyes.

'What?' Bella slurred.

Jamie shrugged, his eyes spinning. 'My father phoned him and said to come and pick you up. I told you to keep the noise down.'

Bella glared at him, then turned back to Mouse. With difficulty she focused on her, then shrugged and smiled.

'Only you, Mouse: remember that. Only. You. Nobody else matters. Just me and you in the snow globe.'

'What about Trent?'

'Heathcliff?' Bella smiled without any humour. 'He's lost on the moor. I'll come back and get him when I'm a ghost.'

Mouse looked at her, her gaze flicking from eye to eye, trying to understand.

'He's waiting outside,' Jamie said. For a moment, Mouse thought he meant Trent, then realised he was talking about Bella's dad.

'All fucking right, I'm coming!'

Bella stretched out a finger and stroked Mouse's face, then turned around and walked past Jamie.

Hardly weaving at all, Mouse thought, touching her cheek where Bella had touched her. The E was pedal to the metal now, making the music and the lights the best story ever told.

I should go with her, she thought suddenly. *I'm completely mangled.*

'Give me five minutes then we can have a pinball tournament if you like?' Jamie said.

Mouse turned to look at him. He was smiling hopefully at her. Then she thought of sitting in the car with Mr Moss, trying to have a conversation with him while drugged out of her mind. She nodded. 'Sure. Why not? But you'll need to order me a taxi home for later, cos I'm not staying here, no matter how high I am.'

Jamie nodded and grinned.

49

THE CRAVEN HEAD

'Fuck! Fuck, fuck, fucking fuck!'

Jamie kicks at the wooden base of the bed, breathing hard.

'How can she have that as her ringtone? How can she even have it?'

Everything Athene did seemed to resonate with the past, punching it into the present.

'Because I told you!' Jamie shouts. 'She's the police and she's here to fuck us!'

'But even if she is the police – which I only have your word for – there's no way she'd know about the mixtape: what it meant.' Mary pauses, then looks at Jamie. 'In fact, neither would you.'

Jamie looks down, his face reddening.

'Except it wasn't only on the mixtape,' Mary says slowly, unpeeling memories like clothes off a corpse. 'It was also the song playing on the jukebox, wasn't it? The night you–'

'I don't fucking know! But she's clearly off her trolley! Maybe the care home fucked her up and she obsessed about her original past. Made up some wicked-witch fairy tale. Maybe she's come back to seek revenge for her shit life. Or her dead sister.'

'Have you any idea how mad you sound, Jamie?' Mary looks at him pityingly. 'Jesus, and you were dissing me! Martha was taken into care right after...' Mary swallows, feeling a stone of pain constrict her throat. 'The fire. Right after everything came out. She was given a new identity or whatever. Even if she found out who she was there'd be no reason to come back here! Everything that was here was gone! All that was left is us! Trent was in prison, her Dad was burnt to death in the fire, and her mother...'

Mary pauses again, hearing Bella's mother screaming on the step, screaming that she'd never be able to hold her daughter again. 'Her mother was gone, too.'

'Which is why she's after us! We're the only contact!'

Before Mary can reply, the ring tune starts again, the sad electronic opening notes of the song filling up the room. Jamie stares at it like it's going to explode.

'I can't cope with this anymore.' Mary hauls herself to her feet. In three short strides she crosses over to the bedside table and grabs the phone. Swiping the screen she crams it to the side of her head, ramming it against her ear.

'Hello?' says a familiar voice. 'Hello, who am I speaking to?'

'What?' Jamie asks, seeing the colour drain from Mary's face. 'Who is it?'

'Hello? I was texted this number, saying to ring urgently. Is there a problem? Who am I speaking to, please?'

Mary takes the phone away from her ear and looks at it. On the screen is a picture of the band: Yazoo. Below, rather than the name of the song, is: Bella's final tape mix: track 5.

Mary stares at it, not comprehending, then slowly puts the phone back up to her ear, a sense of déjà vu smothering her. She takes a deep breath.

'Hello, Trent.'

50

BELLA'S LAST DAY: BLEA FELL HOUSE

'What time will you be back? Will you be back in time for the bells?'

Sheila looked at her daughter and saw a stranger looking back. Bella had plastered her face with white foundation and thick grey kohl eye make-up. On the back of her head sat a leather beret, with her DIY hair poking out. There was one of her French cigarettes burning in the ashtray, and a glass of gin held in her black nail-varnished hand.

'I'm not coming back tonight; I'm going to stay over at Mouse's.'

'Right.' Sheila couldn't keep the disappointment from her voice, but she didn't blame her daughter; the atmosphere in the house these last months had been toxic.

Ever since the end of the summer when that boy had come back, she thought bitterly.

'We're going to go to the winter fair, then on to a disco at Jamie's.'

'So it'll just be your father, me and Martha then.'

At the mention of her name, the baby looked up from her pen by the stove. It was clear she was unsettled; she was mithering and looking around uncertainly. Sheila supposed she might be about to teethe.

'Where's Dad, anyway?' asked Bella.

'Where else? In his study.'

There was a swing of lights on the wall as Trent's car drove up the track and passed the house, ready to turn around by the derelict barn.

Bella nodded, taking a final drag of her smoke before stubbing it out. She stood up, pulling on her duster coat.

'Wish him a happy new year from me, won't you?'

'Don't you want to do that yourself? Before you go?'

Bella looked at the thick heavy door that led to her father's study and shook her head. She drained her gin and placed the empty glass carefully on the table. 'No. I don't think I do. But tell him I'm sorry I've been so distant recently. Tell him I'm going to try and make next year really special.'

Sheila looked up at the odd tone in Bella's voice, but before she could say anything there was a loud knock at the porch door.

'There's my crew, I'm out of here.'

Bella walked to her mother and gave her an awkward hug. 'I'm sorry.'

Her mother smiled. 'That's all right, love. Go and have a nice time with your friends. I'll see you in the morning.'

Bella shook her head, and glanced at her father's door again, then down at Martha. 'No, I'm not sorry for that: I'm just... sorry.'

Then she shrugged and walked away, toward the door. Sheila watched as she opened it and slipped out into the night, the sound of her boyfriend's greeting slipping in. As the door closed behind her it made a click, like someone had turned something off.

Inexplicably, Sheila started to cry.

51

THE CRAVEN HEAD

'Mouse? Mouse, is that you?'

Mary can hear the sound of motion through the earpiece; ambient sounds that suggested Trent was driving. 'Yes, it's me.'

Mary is amazed that she isn't shocked that Trent was speaking to her; that he had been given Athene's number. She isn't even surprised that Athene had left the phone, with Bella's death-song, the car-crash song, as its ringtone. She supposed she must be in shock, but there seemed an inevitability about it, like falling off a cliff.

'What is it?' laughs Trent down the line. 'Are you a whizzy businesswoman or something, now? You need two phones?'

Mary realises that he must think it was her who texted him; that he assumes that the phone belongs to her. Jamie is blundering around the room, pulling out drawers and opening cupboards searching for the police ID he said belonged to Athene.

'Where are you, Trent? Are you on the road? You said you were going to come up?'

So many questions, but not the ones she wants to ask.

'Yes! I'm just coming off the motorway, actually. I should be with you in an hour or so.'

'What?' Mary snaps out of the daze the song had wrapped her in. 'You're nearly here?'

'An hour, tops.'

Mary grips the phone tighter. 'Fine. I'm at the Craven Head with Jamie. I'll see you when you arrive.'

'With Jamie?' Trent sounds surprised. 'Wow; just like old times! Getting the gang back together and all that, eh? Tell him he should get his camera out; take a picture for the family album.'

Trent hangs up. Mary looks at the dead slab of metal and glass in her hand, her brow furrowing.

'How the fuck did Trent get Athene's number?' Jamie says. Mary looks up at him. Jamie is standing by the wardrobe, his hands clenched. In one of his fists is what looks like a pillowcase.

'What happened to the photographs?' she asks him.

Jamie looks momentarily confused, then, Mary notices, suddenly secretive; like he's been caught out. 'What photographs?'

'The ones you took of me and Bella. By the pond.'

'What? From when we were young? What the hell are you asking about that for? We need to find the girl! Find out what the fuck her game is.'

Jamie looks about as angry as Mary has ever seen him. As if he is not in control.

'She must have come back here and grabbed her stuff, then left the phone on purpose. She's messing with our minds, Mouse!'

Mary ignores him. 'I remember; you gave me the photos, but not the negatives. That camera of yours; it was pretty snazzy I think. It wasn't like a camera with a cartridge. It was the sort of set up where you can develop it yourself. I never really thought about it before.'

Jamie says nothing; just stares at her like she is going mad.

'You know, Jamie, there was something about that time when Trent attacked you that I never really understood.'

Mary's mind is in auto-shuffle. The disruption Athene, or Martha, or whoever she is, is raking up the past like autumn leaves ready for a fire, scattering her memories and then settling them down in new patterns, making her think about things she hasn't thought about in years.

'He did more than attack me, Mouse, he nearly killed me!'

Mary nods. 'I know; I was there.' *This is for you.* That was what Trent had said. 'I always thought you might have had a thing going.'

Jamie looks like he's trying to say something. His mouth is moving but there is no sound, like someone has forgotten to draw the speech bubble.

'I never understood what he did before he really hurt you. He made a camera action with his hands. Do you remember, Jamie?'

Jamie says nothing; just looks down at the pillowcase in his hands. Mary sees that it actually is an empty laundry bag.

'Did you take any other pictures, Jamie? Pictures of Trent, maybe? Is that why he hit you?'

The silence between them is a solid presence.

This is for you. What Trent had said before he ripped open Jamie's face.

Mary hears the sound of a long-gone pinball machine in her head. 'Or maybe pictures of me?' she says, cocking her head. 'Different pictures of me, Jamie?'

The silence between them is a weight, as if they had reached the limit of something. As if a dam that had built up for years and years is about to break.

'This was full,' says Jamie finally, holding up the empty laundry bag.

Mary creases her brow, trying to slot what he was saying into the conversation they were having. She can't. 'What?'

'When I came in before it was full; there were knickers and stuff on the top, and I just thought it was full of old laundry. You see it all the time.'

Mary blinks, and in the microsecond her eye is shut she has an image of Jamie pawing through a thousand laundry bags full of underwear. She shudders. 'There are so many things wrong with that sentence, Jamie.'

Jamie shrugs. 'Whatever. The thing is it was full and now it's empty.'

'So what? She cleared out and took her laundry with her.'

'Except she's only been here one night.'

Mary stares at him, realising what he's saying. 'Okay. So what was it full of, then?'

Jamie looks down at the laundry bag, then slowly around the room. 'I don't know; I never checked.'

'You surprise me.'

'But the edges were all hard and angular now I think about it. Odd shapes sticking out, like a Christmas sack.'

'What? You're telling me it was full of presents?'

'No. Old cassette tapes, maybe. Or videos.'

Mary blinks slowly, thinking of all the knowledge that Athene/Martha seems to have. Mentioning Heathcliff, and the bells left on her door. Even the owl.

Everything linking back to Bella.

And suddenly it all makes sense.

'Not videos,' Mary says, nodding again. 'Books.'

'Books?'

'Diaries.'

On the bedside table Mary sees the brochure Athene had

shown her. The fake holiday let with the picture of Blea Fell on it. She remembers the final section.

The section that listed her café.

And the police.

And the hospital.

'Jesus fucking Christ. It was all there. She was showing it to me right at the beginning. Like the plot of a novel on the very first page!'

52

THE CRAVEN HEAD: 2010

'I'm leaving, Jamie; I don't even know what I was thinking when I married you!'

Louise's voice was harsh with emotion.

'It's not the affairs or the drinking, it's the pictures, Jamie. It's the photographs.'

Jamie stared straight ahead, not looking at his wife. He sat in the cold bedroom with no lights on and counted under his breath, as if the act of numeracy would have some magical effect and make everything all right.

'Nothing to say?'

Louise glared at him from the door, just beyond the threshold, as if even being in the same room could contaminate her. Make her in some way infected. Her face was dry and papery, all the moisture either cried or sweated out. 'Not going to try and explain, like you normally do?'

Jamie didn't look at her, just stayed staring at the wall, counting the cracks in the paint.

One, two, three...

'Good,' said Louise after a pause. 'Because it wouldn't do any good.'

She looked at him, fear and disgust and the destruction of a thousand little histories crossing her features. Her lips were chapped and flaky from all the worry-biting.

'You know, Jamie, when I first met you I knew there'd be affairs.' She laughed bitterly, half at him and half at herself.

One, two, three...

'I wasn't stupid. New guests in and out. Everybody pissed at the end of a night. I had my eyes open. Fuck knows, my expectations weren't high.'

Jamie stayed staring at the wall. He could feel little pockets of himself expanding and contracting; tiny islands of emotion in a sea of dead.

He shut himself down a little more.

Four, five, six...

'But it was the photos, Jamie. It was the pictures.'

Louise bit her lip, seeing in her mind the images she had found on Jamie's laptop.

She wished she couldn't, but every time she closed her eyes they returned, staggering out of the back of her mind with all the pain and hurt and nausea they had created the first time she'd seen them.

Seven, eight, nine...

'And the sites you go on, Jamie,' said Louise softly, as if even talking about it out loud could make them invade the space. 'All the dark stuff you've been viewing; it's sick.'

Ten, eleven.

'Some of those people, Jamie. Some of those girls.'

Jamie licked his lips, but stayed looking at the wall.

'It looked real, Jamie.'

Jamie shook his head. 'Actors,' he whispered. 'Not real. Just...' he searched the wall for a word that would work. A word that would mean that everything could be all right. Or if not all right, something that was not jailable.

He couldn't find one.

'Entertainment,' he finished.

Louise blinked, trying to fit the word with the images she had seen.

'Goodbye, Jamie,' she said finally, and turned away.

Jamie didn't look at her; didn't stand up and run after her and beg her to stay. He just listened to the sound of her leaving, watching the wall for messages from the past.

One, two, three, four.

53

BELLA'S LAST DAY: TRENT'S CAR

Five minutes after she got in the car with Trent and Mouse, Bella thought she was going to throw up. What she had done to Martha was gnawing like ants at her stomach. She wondered if her sister would ever understand; could ever forgive her. Bella wished she could stay to explain, but there was no way that could happen. This night was going to be her last night, one way or another, then everything would be different. Everything would be changed.

Bella took a swig of her gin from the half bottle nestling between her legs. Next to her on the front bench seat of the Viva, Trent was gang-boying; driving with one hand loosely at the top of the plastic steering wheel, the other wrapped around a bottle of Red Stripe. Bella concentrated on breathing through her nose, and looking at the world blur outside the window.

'Careful, Trent! The roads are still icy.' Mouse: shouting from the back seat.

She was right; the roads were suicide-slick with black frozen water covered with booby-trap fresh snow. Trent just laughed and yardied his beer, chugging it down and tossing the empty bottle into the back footwell. Bella watched as he reached into his jacket and pulled out a doobie. Within seconds the sweet, chemical, smell of factory-skunk filled the car. Bella cracked the window down a notch, the half-grin on Trent's face increasing her nausea. She supposed it might be a bit of a thrill for him, knowing that he had slept with both the girls in the car. Then she hated herself for thinking that way. Trent was her Heathcliff, wild and dangerous, but also emotionally vulnerable and loyal.

Like Mouse.

Bella knew she had driven him away; driven them both away. It was very probable she had driven them both to each other. Fuck knows that she didn't control them anymore. The picture she had seen, pinned to their tree like a wanted poster, of Mouse, had ripped up her childhood Mouse and replaced her with something else, more complicated and separate. A Mouse who was unknown and an unseen and untrusted.

Like Trent again: they were two of a kind.

In fact, that's what she had written on the back of the photo when she had taken it up to her room.

Don't trust her.

Then she had written it on the back of *all* the photos she had of Mouse, right back to the first.

Don't trust her.

Like going back in time, changing her own past, painting it in darker shades.

All unfair, of course, just action and reaction to what was happening to her. Really it should have read:

Don't trust me.

I'm not who you think I am.

I'm not in control.

It didn't even matter who had put it there; not anymore.

Tonight she was going to take back control.

Tonight she was going to kill what they had all become.

Bella took another swig of gin and stared out of the window.

She barely flinched as Trent draped his free arm over her, heavy across her shoulders. The weight didn't feel like intimacy to her; it felt like the weight of earth on top of a coffin.

She was so tired, sitting in this metal tear with Trent and Mouse, so lonely, that she could stop right now. It would be easy. Reach over and pull the wheel, spinning the car off the road. She can even feel the tingle in her hands, as if wire was in them, pulling them like a puppet.

She took another slug of gin and glanced at Trent.

But that wasn't enough. Just killing them all wouldn't solve anything.

It wouldn't take back her rape.

It wouldn't rewind her pregnancy.

It wouldn't bring back trust.

All she would be was the paper the map was drawn on, not real in herself.

And she couldn't live with that.

Couldn't die with it, either.

Bella turned round and looked at Mouse, stretched out on the rear seat, her back against one door and her booted feet propped up against the window of the other. Like Bella, she was drinking from a half bottle of gin.

'Hey, Mouse, did you do the tape for me?'

Mouse was staring at the roof of the car, at the stained plastic lining where they had all written their names in black Sharpie one night when pissed.

Bella and Mouse and Trent 4ever

Like they would never grow old and never die. Like they would be friends until the end of time and drive off into the sunset together.

Bella smiled coldly. At least one of those was right.

Mouse nodded and reached into her coat, removing a cassette. 'Sure. Are you going to put it on now?'

She tossed it, and Bella caught it one-handed, the sound like a slap.

'No, it's for on the way home, after the disco.'

Mouse made a face, and Bella could see that underneath the make-up she was pale and ill looking. Like she had cancer, or was throw-up worried.

Which Bella imagined she was.

Not for much longer, she mouthed, smiling. Mouse frowned.

For a mad moment, Bella wondered if she should tell Mouse about the baby? Or maybe even Trent? She actually turned and looked at him; studied his face. She could see the man struggling to escape the boy in his features, but like a boat in a storm she thought it would fail. That the damage to the boy was too much to escape from.

Shame.

And anyway she knew the baby wasn't the reason she was going to do what she was going to do, it was just the punctuation. It was just the full stop.

As they drove down out of the hills the bright glitter of the frosted moor slowly turned into the sad neon of the street lights of the small town. First a lonely house, then the quarry, and finally the bridge across the coal-black river.

Trent pulled down a side street parallel to the square and found somewhere to park. Even from inside the car, Bella could hear the screaming of the fair. The kids and the rides, and the music pumping from the speakers. Lights and shadows kaleidoscoping the brick wall of the library opposite. Now they had arrived, Bella felt calm. Somewhere in her ship, a window had opened for the last time, letting her see the beauty. She grinned to herself and pulled on the metal handle, opening the car door.

The cold and the fizz of the fair slid down the alley to her from the square, slipping down her throat and up her nostrils and punching at her pores. They could all feel it, she could tell.

Mouse and Trent and all the other kids in the street, necking snakebite and smoking joints; popping pills and sniffing powders. Laughing and slip-sliding their way to the lights. Everybody wrapped up in coats and hats and scarves and snoods.

Feeling the bite of the night, Bella reached back in and grabbed her Parka.

'This is going to be some night.'

Trent swaggered around the car, not bothering to lock it. Bella thought he was loving the moment, playing it like a movie. Arriving at the fair with two girls, arms around both like they're supporting him, but really he was just showing off their leads and their collars.

Unkind, unkind.

They began to walk towards the fair, then Mouse suddenly stopped. Bella looked at her.

'What?' asked Trent, eyebrows raised. 'What is it?'

And then he saw Jamie, ahead, in a scrappy duffle coat with his camera slung around his neck. Trent grinned.

'Well, if it isn't Jimmy! How's it going at the *Daily Planet*, Jimmy?' Trent's voice is light. Jamie, already in the shadow of the library wall, seemed to shrink back further, as if trying to press himself into the Victorian brickwork. Trent and Jamie hadn't met since Trent got back. Not since Trent nearly ripped his face off. Not since they both got expelled.

But it wasn't Trent that Bella noticed; it was Mouse. She moved in an almost exact reflection of Jamie; stepping back and pressing herself against Bella. Like she was petrified.

Jamie flicked one of his porn-glances at the girls then focused on Trent. He smiled sickly and subconsciously rubbed the scar above his eye.

'Just the local rag,' he said lamely, stroking the strap of the camera. 'I'm hoping to sell them some shots of the fair.' He shrugged, his gaze sliding away and slipping between the three of them. 'You know, ringing in the new year and all that.'

Trent nodded. 'Yeah, I get it. Taking pictures of people having fun. I understand. You've always had an eye for it, haven't you, mate?'

'I don't know what you mean,' Jamie muttered, his eyes snaking to Mouse.

Trent smiled and looked at the scar on Jamie's face, bone white against the raw meat of the surrounding skin. Jamie licked his lips.

'Sure you do. In fact maybe you can take one of the three of us, yeah?' Trent's grin widened and he took his arms off Bella and Mouse, spreading them above the girls' shoulders. Jamie looked like he was going to be sick. 'Maybe you can click one off now. Get ahead of the curve.'

Trent winked at Jamie.

'For fuck's sake, Trent,' Mouse said.

Bella felt the bile back in her throat; the tightening in her womb. She knew Trent was only posturing; trying to get a rise out of Jamie, but it felt too violent. Too full of poison. She staggered a little, falling back against the car.

'Hey, Bells! Are you okay?' Mouse said, holding her up, a look of concern on her face.

Bella nodded, the moment of dizziness passing. There was a sudden flash as Jamie took a picture. 'That's right!' said Trent, oblivious. 'Make sure you send me a copy, yeah. Maybe pin it to my locker.'

He paused. 'Oh, hang on, I don't have a locker, do I? Cos I got fucking expelled.'

Jamie's features spasmed. Bella looked at him quizzically. Pathetic, lonely, lost Jamie. Looked at him and realised it must have been him who had taken the picture; taken the picture and then pinned it to the tree in her ghost forest for her to find. The picture of Mouse and Trent.

Before she could say anything, Trent laughed dismissively and dropped his arms back over Bella and Mouse's shoulders, dragging them away and towards the fair.

'See you at the disco, Jimmy! Remember to save some drugs for me!'

Bella looked over her shoulder at the boy as they slipped and staggered away, and was surprised to see the level of hurt in Jamie's eyes. The hurt and something else. Something like a worm coming to the surface before a thunderstorm.

The hate.

Jamie's stare disappeared with the rest of him as they turned the corner, and the full visceral force of the fair hit them. Bella stared at it, wide-eyed.

The square was snow-packed and dazzling. The lights from the Waltzer reflecting off the ice like they were swimming just under its surface. Around the ride were all the stalls. Bella saw people throwing hoops and tossing balls. Firing at tin cans with bent rifles and aiming blunt darts at hardened dartboards, all for the chance of participation in the dance of the fair. The noise was deafening, with no buildings in the way to soften it. The sirens and the music and the mechanical suicide of the Waltzer booths, as they were spun by the roustabouts that ambled along the spinning boards, as if they were indestructible; the gypsy boys that were like a truer version of Trent.

Bella breathed it all in. The air was thick with the smell of popping corn and candyfloss, hot dogs, and the final explosion of adolescence. Bella looked at it all for a long second, then dipped her shoulder, slipping from beneath the weight of Trent's arm, and dived into the throng of the fair. She heard someone shout; maybe Trent, maybe Mouse, but she didn't stop. She smiled wide with her mouth and her eyes and her body as she pelted toward the noise and clatter, the pain and fear of a moment earlier forgotten.

She took a deep breath, breathing in the beauty, then threw herself into the madness for one last rodeo of innocent fun and joy and magic.

54

HIGH SCHOOL: JUST BEFORE

Trent stared at the picture pinned to the door of his locker, feeling a worm of guilt and shame turn lazily over in his stomach, like it was just waking up from a nap.

'No fucking way,' he breathed, unbelieving. 'No. Fucking. Way.'

The photograph was slightly blurred, but Trent guessed it would have to be, because whoever had taken it hadn't used a flash. If they'd used a flash, Trent would have noticed it. So the only light that would have been available would have been the ambient light; the moon and the porch lamp. Trent couldn't remember. Trent looked at himself in the picture. Slightly blurred not because he was badly shot, out of focus or whatever, but because the lens or aperture or whatever the hell it was called would have had to have been kept open; soaking in all the light it could. Slightly blurred because he was moving. It looked like he was leaving a ghost of himself behind as he left the house.

Trent found it hard to breathe. The school went on around him but it was like he was an island. All he could do was stare at the photograph.

How did it get here? he wondered. He always locked his locker. Always. Which meant not only had they taken the photo, but they had also broken into his locker. He reached out and touched the print that was taped to the door; felt its glossiness. He used his forefinger to cover his picture-face. Now it could be anybody. Any young man pulling on his coat and leaving his house in the middle of the night. Going to work, maybe. Or the pub.

Except it wasn't his house, was it?

He held his breath and moved his finger off his face, tracing it up the wall of the house until it reached the first floor, then slowly moving it along until it reached the window. Mouse's bedroom. He remembered turning and looking up at the window, seeing it empty.

Except here in this photo it wasn't empty. Mouse was there, naked and sad and looking down at him. She was indistinct, because there was no light on in her bedroom, but she could be seen. He supposed she must have watched him go, then retreated back into her room before he turned round. He didn't blame her. The only person he blamed was himself.

And the person who took the photograph. The person who must have followed them there, then stood outside while they... Trent felt his mouth spasm... then photographed him when he left.

And then sent the picture to him.

Why? Trent wondered. As a message? But what message? Was it blackmail?

Trent gently removed the print, peeling off the sticky yellow electrical tape that held the corners to his locker, then folded up the photo. Taking out his Zippo, he flicked the lid and fired it up, creating flame. He touched the heat to the corner of the print, then watched as the chemicals ignited, erasing the image as if it had never existed. The picture seemed to shrink from the flame, as if running away before it could be burnt.

Trent smiled humourlessly and dropped the photo onto the locker's metal shelf. Once the flame was out he rubbed the ash into his hands and onto his face.

Then he shut the locker and went in search of Jamie.

55

THE VILLAGE STORE

'I'm sorry, she left here about ten minutes ago.' The old woman who volunteered at the village store beams at them.

Why is she smiling? Mary thinks. *There's nothing funny going on here.* And then she realises that she wasn't smiling; her false teeth were too big for her mouth, causing a permanent grin. And then Mary decides she is wrong; it wasn't that her dentures were too big, it was that the rest of her face had shrunk with age.

'Right,' says Jamie. 'I don't suppose she said where she was going, did she? Only she's left her phone at the hotel, you see, and we thought she might need it?'

Jamie waves Athene's phone in the air, as if the very fact of its existence explained the urgency.

The old woman shakes her head and continues to smile at them, her tombstone teeth gleaming. 'Sorry, I'm afraid not. She just came in and bought her cigarettes, then left. She seemed a bit distracted, to be honest.'

'I bet she bloody did,' Jamie mutters.

'I'm sorry?' the shopkeeper says.

Mary can't seem to stop staring at her teeth. With a

conscious effort, she drags her eyes away and smiles at the woman.

'Nothing. It's just that she's a policewoman so we really wanted to get her phone to her in case there was an important message or something.'

'A policewoman?' The lady laughs. 'Oh I don't think so, dear! Not with hair like that! And she's too young, surely?'

'I think she's a trainee.' Mary smiles. 'Never mind. We'll go to her car and see if we can catch her; thanks for your help.'

'Was she carrying anything?' Jamie asks.

The woman looks at him. 'I'm sorry, love? Like what?'

Jamie thought of the empty laundry basket. 'I don't know. Something bulky.'

'No,' muses the woman slowly. 'She only had her backpack when she bought the batteries.'

'I thought you said she bought cigarettes?' Mary remarks.

The woman's smile widens, exposing gums the colour of bubblegum. 'That's right, dear, but that was the second time.'

'The second time? What are you talking about?' Jamie sounds like he's about to snap.

'Like I said, love, she came in twice. The first time to buy batteries, and the second to get the cigarettes. I suppose she must have forgotten them the first time round.' The woman's eyes suddenly widen. 'Actually, now I come to think of it, the second time, the time for the cigarettes, she had a carrier bag with her.'

'A carrier bag?'

'Tesco.' The woman nods happily. 'Or it might have been Lidl. Definitely a supermarket.'

'She didn't have any food in her room,' Jamie says.

'Books,' the woman says. 'Old books.'

Silence ticks around the shop as Mary stares at her. Finally she says, 'Batteries?'

'Yes, dear.'

I wouldn't fancy getting stuck out here. I've only got a torch, and even that's got flat batteries!

That's what Athene had said to her, that first night in the café.

'I know where she is,' Mary says, turning round and heading for the door.

'What? Where?' Jamie nods at the woman and follows Mary. He almost runs into her as Mary stops and spins back round.

'What?' Jamie says again. 'What is it?'

Mary ignores him, and slowly walks back to the counter. The woman grins at her nervously.

'You said she came back in for cigarettes?'

'That's right; a pack of Lucky Strikes.'

'Lucky strikes,' Mary repeats. Somewhere behind her she hears Jamie draw a sharp breath.

'That's what Bella used to sm–'

'Soft pack. She was very insistent on that.'

I bet she was, thinks Mary, but all she did was nod her thanks and turn back to the door. As she walks towards it she feels disconnected.

'Luckily no one really smokes anymore, so I still had a pack left over from last time.' The voice behind her is light, almost skip-away.

Mary looks at her fingers on the door handle. They are mottled and scarred from cleaning. Red and veiny from life.

She turns back again and studies the old woman. 'Last time?'

'Yes. I got some in then, and there was still one pack left over. How fortunate is that?' She gives them another radioactive blast of her teeth.

'She's been here before? I mean before this last couple of days?'

'Oh, yes! She was here last year. Such a nice girl.'

'Last year?' The disbelief in Jamie's voice is a solid thing. 'Last *year*!'

'On holiday,' the woman confirms, nodding. 'She was here for about a week in the summer. She'd rented a caravan. She didn't have that multicoloured hair then; it was much shorter. In fact she mainly wore a Parka, because of all the rain.'

'She was here last summer?' Jamie asks, looking like he's been punched. 'In this village?'

'Yes. Goodness how it rained; do you remember? I thought the beck was going to burst its banks! I distinctly recall because she asked me about the house.'

Even though the woman is still smiling, her eyes are not smiling, Mary realises. Her eyes glitter like a child's stolen marble. Hard and old and unforgiving.

'The house?'

'Blea Fell. Where the fire was. She wanted to know how to find it. I remember because it had been so long since I'd even heard of the place being mentioned.'

'Wait a minute,' Jamie says, his voice laced with confusion. Confusion and, Mary can hear, fear. 'She'd been here before? Last year?'

'That's what I said.' The woman smirks at him like he's an idiot. 'Actually, it was quite odd.'

'What was?' Mary feels the trickle of earth she's felt since Athene arrived. 'What was odd?'

'I remember asking her why she wanted to know. Why she wanted to go there. She just smiled at me and tapped her book.'

'*Wuthering Heights*?' Mary whispers.

The woman shakes her head. 'No, love, it was a diary. One of those old ones with proper paper, like artists or writers used to have.'

An image of Bella writing in her diary flashes across Mary's mind. All the diaries she wrote, year after year, pouring out her secret stories. Enough to fill a laundry bag.

'Why was it so odd? Did she say why she wanted to go there?'

'She said she wanted to find a snow globe.'

56

BELLA'S LAST DAY: THE WINTER FAIR

'Four quid, love!' the attendant was shouting down at her, a careless smile on his battered face, his legs apart, supporting the swing and sway of his body on the uneven surface of the Waltzer. He had a roll-up cigarette tucked behind his ear. A fighter's ear – cartilage bruised and broken – but his eyes were kind and smiling, and he didn't ask why she was all alone in the middle of the curved chair. She handed over the coins, and he pulled down the bar. He was about to walk away when he paused and turned back to look at her. He stared for a long beat, his gaze slightly out of focus, like there was something in the air between them.

For one moment Bella thought he was going to ask if she was pregnant; tell her she couldn't ride in her condition. Then he leant in and asked her if she wanted to be spun. He had a smile playing round his lips, flitting and shimmering on his face. She smiled and nodded.

The ride slowly filled up, but no one joined her. She could see Trent and Mouse, at the stall with the metal buzzer, where a hoop had to be threaded along a wire without letting its side touch in order to win a prize. Trent was playing, but Mouse was not paying attention; she was looking around the fair, searching. Searching for her, Bella realised.

The ride started with a bang and a shudder, disappearing Mouse and Trent out of view with a jolt. As it picked up speed, the car rocked from side to side. Bella watched as the roustabout walked between the cars, giving them little spins to add to the momentum, until some were turning full circles, pushing their squealing occupants hard against the leather backrest. Bella closed her eyes, letting the movement send her somewhere else. When she opened them again the operator was standing in front of her, the smile still on his face.

'Sure?' he mouthed, holding his hands up, ready to spin. Bella smiled and nodded. The boy smiled back, put a hand to his lips, and blew her a butterfly kiss.

'Hold tight!'

Then he sauntered round to the rear of her car and grabbed the rail behind the backrest. He waited for an upturn on the carousel, then spun her into the downturn, causing her to grab hold of the safety rail to prevent herself from slamming against the side.

'Faster!' she screamed, laughing. The roustabout laughed with her and spun her again. And again. Spin and spin again until the world was more of a blur than her thoughts could keep up with. Until everything was made up of sound, and shape, and colour, and it all resided in the moment. No past and no future. No parents and no baby. No sister. Just the velocity of spinning to nowhere.

This is what it feels like to crash, she thought.

Then she opened her eyes and looked at the wild boy with the rose smile.

Thank you, she mouthed.

57

OUTSIDE THE VILLAGE SHOP

'Mouse.'

Jamie and Mary pull up short when they hear the voice behind them. Mary feels Jamie tighten beside her, climb inside himself like a runaway hiding in a storm drain. Slowly, she turns around and looks at the man behind her.

'Hello, Trent.'

Trent is leaning against his car, shaking a Marlboro out of a pack and removing it with his mouth.

'Still got your quest for cancer, then,' she says, pointing at his cigarette with her jutting chin. She hides behind the quipping. Even though she knew Trent was coming, she wasn't prepared for it. Wasn't prepared to actually see him in the flesh.

'We should have died with Bella that night, Mouse, I'm just trying to play catch-up.'

Mouse's voice trips in her throat, blocking it. The brutality of his statement has taken her breath away. There is no mellowing with time. Seemingly no distance between the man before her and the teenager weeping in the snow over the wrecked body of his girlfriend. She looks at him in horror. He smiles back at her.

And then the sinking sun catches his face, and Mary realises that what she mistook for brutality is baked-in guilt. The lines on his face are not only prison-deep, but train-tracks of sadness made a decade ago. That when he said they should have died he wasn't being flippant, he was being truthful. With the sun shifted, she can see in his eyes, a haunted house, sadness deep within them.

It was still current for him, she realises. The present is merely a continuation of the past, with no reflection and no closure. She guesses he must not be long out of prison. What was it? Driving under the influence? Breaking and entering? Two sentences of manslaughter? Added to what he had done to Jamie the previous summer?

'I did die that night, Trent,' Mary says softly. 'Or at least any part of me that meant anything.'

Before Trent can answer, Jamie leans forward. 'Why are you here?' he spits.

Mary looks at him. There is an old anger in his face that she suspects has been buried for decades.

'Why the fuck have you come back, Trent? What do you know about the girl?'

Trent looks at him quizzically, as if trying to work out what he means.

'The girl? What girl? I'm here, like I told Mouse, because of the email. Because of the picture of the night... well, the night Bella died.'

Trent is smaller, Mary realises, which strikes her as odd. One would have thought that life would have filled him out. But maybe, she thinks, he's had all the life he could when he was younger.

Like her.

'The night you killed her, you mean!' Jamie was practically shouting, his hands clenched into fists.

He's afraid of him, Mary thinks. *After all these years, he's still afraid of him.*

'Yes, Jamie,' Trent says quietly, his voice slicing up the dusk creeping into the air. 'The night I killed her. I haven't forgotten.'

Except you didn't, Mary thinks. *You didn't kill her; she killed herself.*

Where are we going?

Straight to hell, Mouse.

That was what Bella had said to her, just before spinning the wheel of the car and crashing out of reality.

Mary swallows. 'Why did you burn down Blea Fell, Trent? I never got to ask.'

Both Trent and Jamie turn to stare at her. Trent's eyes are clear, she notices. Spiderwebbed with pain or memory, but clear. He raises his eyebrows.

'You got taken into custody and I never got to see you. And then your identity was withheld because of your age so I never got to visit.'

'You would have visited me?' Trent asks. 'Really?' He smiles and shakes his head slowly. 'I don't think so.'

'Well, you *were* fucking each other.' Jamie's voice is cold. They turn to look at him, and he shrinks under their gaze. 'What?'

'This is so messed up.' Mary stays looking at Jamie. 'Why do you need to be so hurtful?' Her gaze is steady, trying to drill past the scared man to the boy she used to know. Before that night when Bella died; before the night in the pub when Bella left with her dad, and Jamie... Mouse blinks. Before Trent beat him into a new shape at school.

Mary has a flash memory of Jamie handing her the picture he had taken, of her and Bella by the pond. She looks at Trent.

'You were there,' she says.

'I was where?' Trent asks.

'When I was twelve. You and Jamie gave me the picture he had taken.' Mary looks round, then points at the beck. 'Over there. You were Jamie's friend, then. Just before we started at high school.' She gazes at them both, certain she is holding a piece of the jigsaw in her mind. 'What happened to change it?'

Trent looks at her steadily. He licks his lips, and Mary thinks with amazement he might actually be about to tell her, when Jamie says, 'For God's sake! We haven't got time for this!'

'I burnt it down because I promised.' Trent says, answering her first question instead.

'We need to go and find Athene or whatever her name is and get her to tell us why she's doing this!' Jamie's voice is laced with frustration and fear. Mary ignores him.

'Who, Trent? Who would possibly tell you to burn down a house and kill a human being? And even if they did, why the hell would you? You've just spent half your life in prison! Why?'

But instead of answering her, Trent turns to face Jamie.

'What's Athene got to do with this?' he asks.

There is a pause, like the day is taking its breath.

'What do you mean? She's the girl who started this!' Jamie's eyes are wide with suspicion. 'It was her phone you rang just before you came here. It was probably her who sent you the email and the pictures!'

'What are you even talking about?' Trent raises his voice, cutting through Jamie's. 'What girl? What's this got to do with Athene?'

'That's her name,' Mary says quietly. 'That's the name of the girl who came up here and got us together. We think she's with the police. She's gone to Blea Fell. That's why she wanted the batteries.' Mary points at the sky, the light retreating like it had lost the battle. 'For her torch.'

'But that's not possible. Athene is...'

Trent's voice fades, and Mary can see that he is genuinely confused. Confused and sad and frightened.

'Who is Athene, Trent? How do you know her?'

Trent looks at her blankly for a moment, then lets out a long breath. 'We all know her, Mouse. It was her secret name. She'd found it in a book she'd discovered in her room, under the floorboards. Or at least that's what she told me.'

Mary can't speak. She feels like she is dying of sadness inside.

'What book?' Jamie asks. 'Who are you talking about?'

'I'm talking about Bella,' says Trent simply. 'Athene was Bella's secret name for herself. It's a version of Athena.' He looked at both of their shocked faces.

'Athene was Bella.'

58

ATHENE'S PHONE

😈 what's happening?

👻 they found your fakefone. Hooked up with H.

😈 good. I'm at BF. Do they know where to go?

👻 not sure. All looks quite tense.

😈 OK. See what happens. If we need to we can nudge them.

👻 OK. Athene?

😈 yes?

👻 thank you.

😈 xx

59

THE CRAVEN HEAD: 1997

Jamie was so happy. He had spent his life friendless. The nearest he had ever got to companionship was Mouse, but he had never been able to make the break; tell her how he felt. She had been the only one who hadn't ripped him. Who hadn't taunted and belittled and ridiculed him. Not like all the others, but Jamie didn't like to dwell, because thinking about the worst hurt his head, and Jamie's head was a balancing act. The only way he'd managed to survive was to split his mind into boxes, little chests where he could lock things out of sight. He'd found a method of being that allowed him to get up each day and function. He kept his mind in the present, dealing with what was in front of him, and anything that was hurtful, comments or kicks or whatever he put in his boxes, locked away. It helped him to cope.

When he was younger he had wondered: why? Why the other boys and girls didn't like him. Hated him. Even at primary school they had shunned him. He was left alone for hours in the classroom, building his Lego or Meccano. Trying to fill his lonely mind with puzzles and jigsaws. Only Mouse had shown him any compassion.

That's why he loved her.

He would never tell her, of course. He wasn't stupid; he knew she didn't love him. The pictures he'd taken of her and Bella clearly showed who she loved. He didn't mind. It was enough that he loved her. She was like her own box in his head; one he could visit at night. Perfectly harmless. It was just in his head.

Besides, he had Trent now. Trent, who despite being super cool, actually seemed to like him. That's where he was going. To Trent's room. He and his father were moving out of the hotel today, and Jamie wanted to give him a present; a Zippo he had found in the bar while cleaning up. It was one of those old fashioned ones, with the curved edge, like James Dean used. He knew Trent would like it.

Jamie bounded up the stairs and through the fire door onto the second floor. Briskly, he walked down the corridor to room twelve. He hoped he wasn't too late, and they hadn't left already. He and his dad had bought a place at the top of the village. A quiet voice inside of Jamie told him that once Trent had moved then things might change between them.

Jamie walked down the narrow hall and opened the door to number twelve, pulling the lighter out of his pocket.

'Hey, Trent! Guess what I found in the bar downstai–'

Jamie stopped, half in and half out of the doorway, looking at the scene in front of him. All the eagerness he'd felt a moment before ran away; blood through the drain of an autopsy floor.

'I'm sorry,' he stammered. 'I'm sorry I should have knocked. I didn't mean to...'

He tried to look away but he couldn't. It was like looking at the magazines he occasionally found when he cleaned the rooms. He knew what he was looking at was wrong, but he couldn't stop it.

'Get out.' The man's voice was matter of fact. A voice not

used to being disobeyed. Ever. Jamie nodded, looking down and backing out.

'Yes. I should have knocked. I'm really really sorry.'

He wasn't saying sorry to the man. He didn't care about the man, although he knew the man could probably hurt him if he wanted. He was saying sorry to Trent. And to himself. Not sorry that he wasn't strong enough to go in and stop it. But sorry that he'd seen it. That Trent knew he'd seen it.

Because Trent wouldn't forgive him. Because he'd barged in on what Trent didn't want him to see. Didn't want anyone to see. Witnessed the thing that made all of Trent's attitude a lie. As much an armour as anything Jamie wore. Really it should bring them together, but Jamie knew it wouldn't. It would break them apart.

Jamie shut the door gently, and walked woodenly back to his own room, the Zippo forgotten in his pocket. As if on autopilot he made his way through the hotel to his tiny room at the back of the building, thinking of all the things he wouldn't now do. All the shared moments he wouldn't now have. When he had shut the door he looked at the pictures of Bella and Mouse, hung from pegs on a string next to the wardrobe he had converted into a dark room. Of half of Bella and Mouse as the photographs were enlarged. Of only Mouse. Then he took all the images of Trent that he had made in his mind and put them gently in a new box in his head and turned the lock.

60

THE WINTER FAIR

'You don't mean it,' Trent said flatly. He had pulled Mouse into a snicket; a dark narrow tunnel of an alley just off the square. The half-tab of E he had taken was stronger than he thought, and he had an overwhelming desire to kiss her.

'I fucking do,' Mouse hissed. Even though she was pushing him away, the narrowness of the alley meant they were still almost touching. Although Trent wasn't tall, he was taller than her and, in the confined space, she felt vulnerable. Trent was clearly off his face, the smell of booze leaking out of his mouth, and his eyes drug-gleamed and spinning in the reflected light of the fair. 'I don't want you to kiss me. In fact I don't want you to kiss me ever again!'

'Why not?' Trent looked genuinely hurt.

Mouse couldn't believe he could be so stupid. 'Why not? Why not? Because you're my best friend's boyfriend, that's why!'

'Don't get all high and mighty now, Mouse,' Trent said, leaning forward and whispering in her ear, his breath wet from the warmth of his lungs. 'I don't recall you saying that when you were banging my bones.'

'Oh, get yourself a bloody room, you self-centred prick,' she hissed, sliding past him, further into the alley. 'It was never about me. All you wanted to do was have a pedal on the dyke-bike. You were so see-through you were pathetic.'

Trent actually staggered at the vitriol of her words, but Mouse was too wound up with shame to notice. She leaned back against the wall and kicked it with her heel.

'You know, the first time I met you I thought you were special, different from all the other tossers who went to that school. And then when you moved in on Bella I still tried to believe that you were different; that you were everything she thought you were. That you would be her knight in shining armour; be the person that I couldn't seem to be for her, though God knows I tried. I would have run away to the end of the world with her.'

'Then why didn't you!' he spat, lumbering towards her, getting in her space. 'If you're so in love with her why didn't you!'

'Because she didn't want me!' Mouse half screamed. The words seemed to echo around the snicket, bouncing off the hard walls and splintering in the even harder air. Mouse took a deep, shuddering breath. 'Because she didn't want me. And then she didn't need me. She had you.'

The truth of the words, finally spoken out loud, seemed to take the sparks of anger out of them both. Beyond the alley the fair sounded distorted, as if their little bubble was slightly out of sync.

'Do you know why I slept with you, Trent?' Mouse asked suddenly, turning to face the boy. Trent didn't answer.

'Do you know why I let you touch me? Why I let you take me like a trophy even though Bella is my best friend? In fact my only friend?'

'Don't forget creepy-Jamie. He's your friend.'

Mouse batted the words away. In the back of her mind she heard the high, sharp bells of the pinball machine. 'Jamie's not my friend,' she said, hard. 'He was just someone I pitied, and I don't even do that anymore.'

'Why not? What did he do?'

'Shut up. We're not talking about Jamie, we're talking about you. Shall I tell you why I slept with you, even though I think you're poison?'

Mouse was too fired up to see the desperation on Trent's face breaking through the alcohol and drugs. The loneliness.

'Why?' he whispered.

'Because it was the only way I could be with Bella! To touch what she touched. To kiss what she kissed. I thought if I let you take me I could be with her...'

Mouse walked right up to him, her nose almost touching his. 'Through you,' she finished. She nodded sharply and slid past him and out towards the entrance of the alley. Before she left she turned to face him. She was in a dark silhouette with the fair behind her, but he was lit up from the lights and the snow. As Mouse looked at him she could see the glitter in his eyes. She thought it was the glitter of hardness; that he was shut down.

Good, she thought.

'Once Bella shut me out, I was left with nothing. I thought...' She grinned, hardly believing how stupid she'd been. 'I thought that at least if I went with you there'd still be *some* connection to her, however pathetic it was. At least I could pretend that there was still something we shared.'

She stared at Trent a moment longer; at his funfair face and glittering eyes.

'Nothing to say?' she challenged, her eyes stinging. Trent just stayed staring at her, motionless. She waited a beat.

'Thought so.' Mouse took a step back, out onto the street. 'I'm off to find Bella. Maybe see you at the disco if I can't persuade her to come home with me.'

Mouse made a dismissive hiss and turned round, back into

the madness of the fair, barging past a figure retching against the wall. She would find Bella and tell her everything. About her and Trent. About what happened the night Bella left her with Jamie. About every last fucked-up thing that had happened in her life recently.

Back in the alley, Trent stayed staring out at the Mouse-shaped space of emptiness, letting diamonds fall from his eyes. After a long while he used his sleeve to wipe the tears away. He slumped against the wall, the effort of being what he had created exhausting him. The reform school had made his armour even thicker; even harder to penetrate. Which made the quiet place inside him even smaller, even harder to find. He was petrified that soon he would not be able to find it at all.

'And do you know why I go with Bella?' he whispered into the night. 'Do you know why I let her make me and shape me into what she wants?'

He laughed, hiding the sob in the noise, letting it paint the space between the walls of the alley and sink into the dirty snow.

'So I can be nearer to *you*, Mouse. So I can be nearer to you.'

He stayed still for a few moments, breathing deeply, building back his armour so he could face the fair, then walked out of the snicket, not even glancing at the figure throwing up against the wall. When he had turned the corner the figure straightened. Jamie wiped the pretend sick away and watched the space where Trent had turned. He had heard everything. Everything Mouse had called him. Every syllable of revulsion in Trent's voice. The look on Jamie's face was utterly blank as he stared into the night, as if someone had taken an eraser and wiped away all aspects of humanity, leaving only a mannequin in its place. Only a facsimile of a human being.

Jamie picked up his bag and slowly began walking to the pub.

61

CASE 348: ATHENE

DOCTOR STEVEN MARKLEY: FEBRUARY 2000

It has been a difficult few months but 'Athene' is healthy and well, and shows no sign of trauma. We have chosen this name because it was in the book we found with her after the 'accident'. It was quite remarkable that the diary was undamaged. Rather than placing her into a care institution it is my recommendation that we attempt to find a solution through adoption. Given the circumstances of her recent history I have placed her birth identity under a suppression order until she is eighteen. At such time she will be contacted and given the option of finding out about her birth mother. I cannot emphasise how delicate this is, given the press interest in the tragedy. It is my recommendation that she is monitored periodically for any signs of disturbance from her experience. As we discovered with the adoption crisis from Eastern Europe (PTS, FAS, etc.) early life trauma can present years later. It is important, however, to perform the assessment discreetly, for the welfare of all concerned.

S Markley

62

OUTSIDE THE CRAVEN HEAD

Mary watches Jamie emerge from the hotel. He'd taken Trent in so he could dump his stuff off. Mary hadn't wanted to go with them, she needed to think. It was freaking her out to see Trent again after all these years. After she had regained consciousness in hospital it was all over: Trent had already been charged. When she had found out about the fire, and the death of Bella's father she had felt numb. It was like Trent's whole history was being erased. It was just lucky that Martha had been out with her mother, otherwise everyone would have died.

And now Trent was back, and so was Martha. And, in a way, so was Bella.

'Did you know about this book that Bella had? With Athene in it?'

Jamie slings himself down on the back seat, behind Mary. He seems to have recovered his composure somewhat. Or at least put a brave face over his anxiety.

Mary shrugs one shoulder, looking at the door to the hotel, watching for Trent. 'No. I remember she had found a book of

Greek legends when she was young. She'd showed it to me, but I never really paid any attention.'

Athene. The secret name Bella had given herself, according to Trent. Maybe written down in a diary and hidden.

Athene, the warrior goddess.

After a few moments Mary hears Jamie moving in his seat, leaning forward. She can feel his breath on her ear as he talks.

'I think Martha's here to take revenge. I think she found out who she was, found out what happened to her parents and her sister, and has called Trent up for payback.'

The tickling air-pressure of Jamie's voice makes her feel sick.

'I reckon when she came up here last year she found Bella's diaries. That's how come she knows so much. I think Bella wrote down her secret name in her secret book. Makes sense, right?'

'I'd have known. I'd have known if Bella had a secret name. She'd have told me.'

'Are you sure?'

Jamie's mouth is practically in her ear. She can smell cigarettes and secrets and a sweet rotting smell. 'What do you really know about those last months, Mouse?'

And the truth is Mary is not sure. Those last few months, before she died, Bella had withdrawn from her; closed herself off like she was shutting down. It was one of the reasons Mary had slept with Trent; a pathetic, fucked-up attempt to reconnect.

Mary stays staring out of the window. Taking in a deep breath she closes her eyes. She feels so tired that she thinks if she went to sleep she'd never wake up again.

Would that be so bad? a small voice inside her says. *Then at least you'd be with her.*

'I know what you did to me that night,' she says, opening her eyes, her voice even softer than his. 'After Bella left, when you'd given me your drugs.'

There's silence behind her, but it's a biting silence. A waiting silence.

'We've never talked about it, but I've never forgotten. Never forgiven.'

'It was the drugs, Mouse. It made everything all loved-up. I just couldn't help it.' Jamie's voice is soft; soft like it used to be at primary school. 'I didn't mean it.'

'Yes you did, Jamie,' she says.

'I stopped before it... Fucking hell, Mouse, you know I wouldn't...'

'Fuck you, Jamie!' Mary hisses, turning in her seat. 'The last thing I remember was you giving me another pill, and then I woke up on the fucking floor with my clothes–'

'We were both wrecked! It just happened. You were wasted, yeah, but–'

'I was unconscious, Jamie! My clothes were in fucking tatters!'

'It was you who kissed me! And then after that it was all a blur!'

She feels the car rock slightly as he hits the back seat with his fists.

'The fucking drugs, Mouse.'

She closes her eyes.

'I'm sorry,' he whispers.

Two words, but it sounds like the summing up of a whole life. Mary looks at him, scratching at his scar, scrabbling at it like he was trying to scrape it off his face. 'It was just the drugs and the booze and the music and the bloody lights from that damned machine. I got rid of the pinball machine, Mouse.' He looks at her pleadingly, like he had done something to help. 'I took it into the backyard and smashed it into little pieces.'

'Yes, but it wasn't the pinball machine that was broken, Jamie, was it?'

Mary's voice is flat. She thought letting out the shame and pain she had kept in her for so many years would help, but it makes her feel more empty. Less whole.

'It was you. It was you that was broken. You were always so good with your hands, Jamie. Taking your photographs and building your Meccano, but you never used them to fix yourself. And then you used your hands to, to... break me. It might not have been rape but it was abuse. Abuse of power.'

She looks at him a moment longer, then turns back in her seat, searching the front of the hotel for Trent. Behind her is only silence, as her words ricochet around the car, their echoes slowly decaying.

'She was covered with bruises. All over her body. Did you know that?'

Mary's not sure if she's heard correctly. The words don't seem to have any connection. Was he talking about her?

'Bella,' Jamie clarifies, as if Mary had asked him a question. 'She was covered in bruises. And not just bruises; cuts and scratches. I saw them.'

Mary slowly turns back to face Jamie. He looks at her with almost no expression. The disconnect from what had just happened was astonishing. It was as if their previous exchange had not occurred.

'What are you saying to me, Jamie?'

Jamie doesn't answer directly; he seems to be on his own track. Mary swallows dryly. She wants to get out of the car, but there's something about the slackness of Jamie's features that keeps her pinned to her seat. Eventually he continues.

'I was always good at watching. Ever since I was young. I guess it was because I grew up in a pub. Mum and Dad too busy to pay attention to me, but always loads of time to put on a show for strangers.' The bitterness in Jamie's voice is heavy.

'Yes, well I'm sorry for you but–'

Jamie keeps talking, as if Mary had said nothing.

'You were the only person who ever showed me any kindness; who ever even noticed me as a human being, rather than a fucking dog to kick, or a monkey to wind up.'

'What's this got to do with the cuts on Bella, Jamie?' Despite herself, Mary is fascinated. Everything about Jamie seemed to have a slight delay; be microscopically out of time.

'But it was okay. I found things to occupy me; places to run. Building stuff out of Meccano. Making a steam engine. Then photography. That fitted right in. It allowed me to be...' he seems to struggle for the word, '...to be part of everything. But still safe.'

Absolute sadness does not excuse you, Mary thinks, but she doesn't say anything.

'And then the internet came along,' Jamie continues, almost as if he is talking to himself. 'And I could make friends without them knowing who I was. I could... watch in safety.'

Mary suddenly remembers a rumour about Jamie; about why his wife left. Something about him watching videos on the net. Dark stuff, so the village mill had said. Bondage; maybe worse. Mary shudders.

'I'm sorry you were lonely, Jamie,' she speaks quietly and slowly. 'But that doesn't–'

'Oh, I was lonely, all right, but I coped.' Jamie's voice is harsh, like he's thrown up a beach of pebbles. 'Right up until Trent came. Then it all went nuclear.'

Mary looks at him, confused. 'What do you mean?'

'It's my fault, really; I should have knocked. I should have bloody knocked and then none of this would have happened!'

Jamie stares at her with such haunted eyes that Mary feels something inside her roll over and die.

'What are you even talking about, Jamie? What did you see?'

'And then he wouldn't be my friend anymore, you understand? Because I'd seen him weak. Instead, because of that, he had to make it worse for me. Worse than the others, even, because he knew how much it hurt me.'

Jamie's voice becomes softer. Sadder. Colder. 'That's why I took the picture. That's why I gave it to Bella. That's why I showed him.'

Mary looks at him aghast, jigsaw pieces from a twenty-year puzzle beginning to slot into place.

'That's why he beat you? Because you'd shown him a picture? A picture of what?' Mary feels an awful weight pressing down on her.

'Of you and Trent.'

'When?' she whispers.

'When he was leaving your house. After you'd...' Jamie looks down. 'You were at the window, watching him. You were naked.'

'And you sent that to Trent?' Mary feels a horror crawling through her, even though it was from so long ago.

But it's not, a dark voice spider-whispers in her head. *It's not long ago because the eggs have all hatched and Bella is back.*

Jamie nods.

'And to Bella.'

'But why?'

'Because it should have been me!' he hisses.

'And that's why you... took advantage of me?' Mary says incredulously. 'Because you think I should've been sleeping with you?'

Jamie shakes his head. 'No. I told you. It wasn't... We were both...' His voice trails off under Mary's gaze.

When he speaks again the dislocation is back, '...And then it all got fucked up that night and Trent went and killed her. He killed her on that road by driving fucked-up, but I'm to blame. I'm to blame for showing him that picture.'

The starkness of the statement stuns them both.

'And now Martha is here, to take revenge on us,' he finishes.

Jamie looks at her like he is already damned. Before she can say anything the door opens and Trent slides in, shutting the door and starting the engine in one fluid movement.

'Sorry for the delay, had to take a call from my parole officer.' He looks at them both, then clocks the tension. 'What?' he says, smiling slightly. 'What did I miss?'

Mary feels the urge to slap him. She is incandescent. 'You knew? You knew about the photo? That Bella had found out about us? You knew and you never thought to tell me?'

Trent stops smiling and slowly turns to Jamie, staring at him with such intensity that Mary is amazed he doesn't burn a hole. 'Nasty scar,' he says after a moment. He says it quietly, his voice almost pleasant. Jamie looks away and licks his lips.

Mary continues. 'She was my friend, Trent! Have you any idea what it was like, being around her? The guilt and the pain and the fucking shame of it! And now I find out that she knew all along! What were you thinking?'

Trent stares at Jamie a moment more, then looks at Mary. The pain in his eyes is there, but so is anger. 'I was thinking of us, Mouse!'

Mary blinks. 'What?'

Trent rubs his hand across his face.

'It doesn't matter. You think this Athene is Martha, yes? You said you knew where she went?'

So many secrets, Mary thinks, looking at him.

Hi, my name is Trent.

The first thing he'd said to her, next to the bridge.

Before he became Heathcliff.

Before Bella tried to kill them.

I wish she'd succeeded, Mary thinks bitterly. *Then at least everything could stop.*

She nods.

'Where is she? At your house? At the police? Why did she need the batteries?' Jamie's voice has lost the dislocation, but regained the fear.

'What batteries?' Trent asks.

'No, she's not gone to my house,' Mary says. 'And she's not gone to the police.'

I'm living in a fucked-up version of Wuthering Heights, she thinks, putting her seat belt on. 'She needs the batteries for her torch.'

'Why does she need a torch?'

'Because where she's gone there isn't any electricity, and it's getting dark.' Mary turns and looks at Trent. 'Come on, it's time to end this. Drive.'

'Where to?' Trent says.

Mary looks out of the window, wishing she had twenty years back so she could put things right.

'On to the moor. To Blea Fell. That's where Martha's gone. To the start.'

63

BELLA'S LAST DAY: THE CRAVEN HEAD DISCO

'Three, two, one, midnight! Happy new year!'

The shitty mobile DJ's voice, distorted with bad amplification and lager, called in the new year, and the shitty barroom drunks gave a shitty barroom cheer.

Mouse felt lost in the crowd.

The whole night had been a disaster. She so wanted to tell Bella about her and Trent; say sorry. Say that given the choice it would be her, not Trent. Always her. Always and forever, until they were old or dead. She had searched for her in the noise and the lights, through the fair. She thought she saw her on the Waltzer, spinning and laughing with the rousta who rode the ride like he owned it, but then Trent had pushed her into that alley; opened up her heart with the sharp blade of her guilt and made her bleed it out in front of him. Later, when she found Bella, the moment had gone; lost in the gutter with the litter and the empty drug wraps and the broken bottles.

'And a special song has been requested for a special girl, to say "I'm sorry"!'

The DJ's voice was beyond cringe, but no one seemed to notice. Mouse dragged on her cigarette, avoiding eye contact with any of the drugged-up, pissed men who were trying to get her attention. It was clear that the record was going to be a slow dance. A grope dance. Mouse could see Trent arguing with Jamie, his finger jabbing into his chest like it was a knife. *Unfinished business*, she thought, letting her eyes linger for a moment, before passing on, looking for her friend.

And then the song began, with the deep note of the bass, and everything clicked into place. Julee Cruise's 'Falling' began, and it was like the world stopped. Mouse looked round, and there was Bella, in the middle of the dance floor, head bowed. Mouse stood up and walked towards her, the drunken crowd fading away. All that was in her mind was: *She forgives me. She forgives me. She forgives me.*

As she stepped onto the micro dance floor, sticky from ash and snakebite, Bella looked up, and Mouse's breath caught in her throat. She was the most beautiful person she had ever seen; not because of something skin-deep, but because of something soul-deep. Bella saw her from the very beginning, when no one else did. She saved her and loved her and carried her and protected her. And then Mouse betrayed her, and everything broke.

But the smile on Bella's face said a different story. It said that she loves her, and forgives her, and will be hers forever.

As the vocals start, Mouse entered Bella's embrace, and they danced away their pain into forever.

She didn't see Trent watching them like the world was ending. She didn't see Jamie leave the pub, tears dropping from his eyes like acid.

She didn't see anything, just felt Bella's heart, hammering against her breast like it wanted to be free.

64

B ROAD TO BLEA FELL: TRENT'S CAR

Trent drives the car along the narrow road, the light dying in the sky. The car is clean, the engine smooth as he navigates the small road. Mary thinks it must be a rental. It doesn't have the feel of an owned thing. She glances a sideways look at him. She can see that his skin is finely lined, with the invisible grime of institutional living stamped on his posture and features. He looks tired, not like he hadn't slept, but like he'd only fitfully lived. She tries to imagine what his life has been like; locked up as a child, then finally released into the world he had never experienced as an adult.

'Were you given a new identity?' she asks, looking at him. She watches as his mouth spasms in what she guesses is a smile; he doesn't take his eyes off the road. She shudders; she is actually amazed he is driving at all, after what had happened.

'What, like in all the detective films?' He laughs softly.

His laugh is nice, not like it was towards the end, that winter. She wonders if prison was a release for him, rather than an incarceration.

She nods.

'Because Martha was,' Mary says slowly. 'After what

happened to Bella, and her parents. When she went into care, she was given a different name to protect her.'

'Protect her?'

'You *had* murdered her sister and her father,' sneers Jamie from the back seat.

Mary's breath catches again at Jamie's brutality.

'Manslaughter,' corrects Trent after a broken heartbeat. 'Not murder.'

'Manslaughter, then. And arson. Let's not forget that.' Jamie's anger seems out of place, his language overly violent. Mary remembers what he was saying just before Trent got into the car. About him being a lost friend. *You must have been completely broken when he rejected you*, she thinks sadly.

'Protect her from her past,' she answers. 'From journalists or whatever. I wonder if she was even told who her real parents were? What happened to her when she was a baby.'

'I imagine not,' Trent says, turning off the B road onto the tiny unmarked lane that led to the track that ended at Blea Fell. 'Or at least not until she was eighteen. When she became an adult I should think she would have been given access to all her records.'

'Which would have explained coming up here!' Jamie says. 'And if she is really training to be a police officer, then that would be how she found your address, Trent. And how she got hold of the photographs.'

The logic of it was undeniable.

'And Bella would have written about James Dean in her diaries,' Mary says. 'About ripping the corners off the cigarette packs.'

'What, like Bella used to do?' Trent glances at her.

She nods.

'She had so many diaries. She wrote her whole life down in

them. If Martha got hold of them then I guess she'd have reason to hate us.'

Don't trust her.

'Bloody hell.' Trent flicks the indicator stick to leave the road and drive onto the stone track to Blea Fell. 'But where would she know where to look?'

There was a constant noise of clicks and pings as sharp stones and pebbles got kicked off the track by the tyres and onto the underside of the car.

'I saw them once,' Jamie says quietly.

'What, the diaries? When. Where?' Mary turns in her seat and looks at him.

'In her house,' Jamie says uncomfortably. 'I was on the moor birdwatching.'

Mary remembers the photo of her by the pond, taken by Jamie with a telephoto lens.

'You were *spying* on her?'

Jamie shrugs. 'Whatever. The point is that she had all these diaries. Her parents and Martha were out somewhere and Bella was sat on the sofa writing in her diary, with all the others around her. She looked really angry.'

'Maybe because she could feel your pervy eyes on her,' Trent mutters, but he doesn't look away from the track. In the fading light the edge is blurring, and there is a steep drop on one side.

'No, she was really upset about something. Anyhow, when she'd finished writing she gathered up all the books and took them somewhere. Hid them somewhere secret, I think. I reckon when Martha came looking for her past she found the diaries, and that told her all about Bella. That's how she knows to do what she's done. That's how she knows how to press our buttons.'

'I don't remember being asked about the diaries when I was interviewed by the police,' Trent says slowly.

'See! That's because they never found them!'

'But why would it matter if they had?' Mary says. 'All they'd have found would be teenage angst and hormonal drama.'

'Are you sure about that?' Jamie says. Something in his voice makes Mary turn round, but Jamie is not looking at her, he is staring at Trent.

'What do you mean?'

'When I was watching from the moor I saw her in the bathroom. Her body was covered in cuts.'

'You were watching her in her bathroom,' Trent says flatly. 'You really are a piece of work, Jamie.'

'What cuts?' Mary asks, ignoring the disgust in Trent's voice. 'Like she'd been in a fight or something?'

Jamie shrugs non-committally, his eyes never leaving Trent's back.

'With herself maybe. Some of them looked like self-harm. They were old, and all over her arms.'

Mary thinks of her friend, who always wore long sleeves, and never showed her skin apart from her extremities. She nods. Towards the end she'd suspected. Had even seen the burns once or twice; but had never pushed. A deep well of shame opens up inside of her. She is brought out of herself by Jamie, who is still talking.

'But not all of them. Some of the cuts, they were on her back. There was no way she could have done those herself; and they looked fresh. Fresh and raw and really fucking nasty.'

The car's engine takes on a deeper note as it climbs the track towards the top of the hill. When it clears the rise, they will be able to see Blea Fell.

Mary realises with a start that the last time she had been in a car with Trent was the night Bella had died, climbing up this same hill after the disco.

'When was this?' asks Trent, cutting across her thoughts.

For a second, she thinks he is asking her about what she is thinking; about the fair and the disco and the drive home in the snow. About when Bella grabbed the wheel and spun them out of their life into a nightmare. Spun herself out of life altogether, leaving Trent to take the blame.

But Trent wasn't talking to her, he was asking Jamie.

'It looked like someone had hurt her. Cut her or scratched her. She had bruises too. And she was hacking at her hair. Maybe she wrote it out in one of her diaries. Maybe that's why she was so angry. And maybe Martha has all those diaries; maybe they were hidden in the laundry bag.'

'When was this?' Trent repeats, just as the car reaches the summit. Jamie smiles nastily.

'Just after you'd come back from reform school, Trent.'

'Oh my God,' Mary whispers, but not at the implications of what Jamie is saying, huge as they were. She is looking out of the window, down the track at the ruin of Blea Fell. The light has left the day completely, leaving the stars shining bright in the blue-black sky; pins of pain on the velvet of the night.

Trent takes his foot off the accelerator, allowing the car to roll to a stop. 'Jesus,' he mutters.

In front of them, lighting up the wreckage of Blea Fell, Bella's ghost forest is on fire.

Each of the strange gnarled trees is burning. From the distance, the twisted branches look like arms stretching out of the flames, reaching into the sky.

Trent turns off the engine and steps out of the car.

A beat later, Mary reaches for the handle, her eyes never leaving the burning trees as she pushes the door open. There is no noise; no sound of cracking or the heat whoosh of burning wood; they are too far away. The flames cast jittery shadows of the trees on the wall of the derelict house.

'It's like they're dancing,' Mary says. 'The shadows. It makes it like the trees are dancing.'

'What do you mean?' Jamie's voice is hoarse, like some of the flames had licked up the hill and snaked down his throat. 'Martha must have set fire to them all. Covered them in petrol or something.'

But Mary isn't listening. She isn't even Mary anymore; she is Mouse. Mouse in her heart and Mouse in her head, walking down the path to confront the figure in the room at the top of the stone steps.

To say sorry.

65

BLEA FELL HOUSE

The strange stunted trees crackle and snap as they burn, with a high whine as the sap boils off. The burning juniper smells slightly sweet, hanging in the air like popcorn at a fair. They are burning so ferociously that there is a sharp heat against Mouse's cheek as she reaches the house and turns down the side, heading for the door at the back.

'Hang on, wait for us! She might be dangerous!' Trent shouts, but Mouse barely hears him. All she can hear is the past, heading towards her like a runaway train. She can feel the pressure of it, the push of it against her heart. As she reaches the corner of the building and turns, the light from the burning trees disappears, and for a moment she is blind, the night sky only blackness above her. She blinks to reboot her sight, and the back door comes into focus, swinging gently on one hinge in the slight breeze.

Not thinking, Mouse strides to it and walks into Blea Fell, no hesitation in her step. She doesn't know if Jamie is right; that Martha came up here last summer and somehow found all of Bella's diaries. Whether Bella had written about the betrayal of Mouse and Trent; had written about how she would revenge herself by killing them all in a final act of madness. And that having found them, Martha was now seeking her own revenge for the death of her sister. It sounded too far-fetched. Too extreme.

Mouse looks through the door into the kitchen. There are candles on the refectory table. Big church candles and small tea lights. Mouse looks wide-eyed. There must be dozens of them.

She steps through the doorway and into the house, looking around the ghost of the kitchen in awe. Her first estimation was low; there must have been a hundred candles lit, stuck and guttering to every surface. Not just the old refectory table, but in the hearth, and in the square that used to house the wooden playpen, and along the window settle.

And on the stone steps that led to Bella's room. Some of the candles are new, whilst others were burnt half down.

Mouse looks up at the ceiling.

Are you up there, Bella? she thinks. *Was heaven too dull?*

Mouse feels like she is in a trance, separated from the real world. She takes a step towards the stone steps

'Bloody hell,' Jamie says, crashing in through the door and looking round. 'It's like a fucking horror film in here!' He takes in all the candles, plus the metal canisters of petrol that are stacked against the wall, presumably used to ignite the trees outside.

'She's definitely taking the *Wuthering Heights* vibe to extremes,' Trent agrees, following in behind him. 'Bella would be proud. Where's Martha, then?'

Before anybody can answer him there is a thump above them, the noise reverberating through the ceiling, sending dust and dry moss motes down, sparkling in the candlelight. They look up, but most of the wood is still intact. Whatever banged from upstairs did not collapse the structure.

'You didn't do a very good job of burning the house down,

did you?' Jamie whispers. Mouse sees he is clutching a piece of wood that must have splintered off the door, holding it like a baseball bat.

'What?' he says, looking embarrassed. 'Those burning trees were freaking me out. I thought she might have gone all Regan on us.'

'I wasn't trying to burn the house down,' Trent says.

'You know; from *The Exorcist*.' Jamie looks up nervously.

'What?' Mouse says, looking away from Jamie and glaring at Trent. 'But that's what you did! When the ambulance came, you fucked off and left us! Bella dead and me unconscious. Left us to set fire to...' she glances round, '...here.'

'Burning the house down was a by-product. And, in point of fact, impossible, as most of the bloody thing's stone.'

'But you said...' She looks at him in confusion, then raises her hands, as if she can divine the truth out of him. 'You went to jail for it! You killed her father!'

Before Trent can answer, music begins playing from above them. The first notes of Japan's 'Ghosts' float down and Mouse lets out a gasp. It was the opening track on Bella's suicide tape; the music mix she had got Mouse to put together. The mix she played in the car on their last drive.

They all recognise it. Even Jamie, who although not in the car, had watched them leave, his face red and swollen from crying.

'Bella,' Mouse whispers, looking above her with a feeling she can't identify at first. It's only after a moment, she realises what it is: release. After all these years of guilt and loss and loneliness. It is release.

She walks across the room and climbs the stone stairs.

After a moment's hesitation, the two men slowly follow her.

66

BELLA'S LAST DAY

'I showed Bella the photo,' Jamie half shouted the words, the ambient noise in the disco ramped up as midnight approached.

Trent was distracted; not really listening. He'd just come out of the toilet, his brain frozen by coke, and was looking for Mouse and Bella. He wanted to be with them when the bells came. Not to kiss them, or pose, or any of the things he normally hid behind; but just to... be with them. He was fairly certain he was going to end his act tonight. What Mouse had said to him in the alley had... clarified him. On one level it was a massive relief. He needed a new way to live.

'What?' he said, scanning the crowds, searching for their shapes.

'The photo. Of you and Mouse. I showed it to Bella.'

'Okay! We're coming up to the top of the clock, folks! If you want to find someone to make face-babies with, now's the time!'

The DJ sounded thrilled with himself but Trent wasn't listening. What Jamie had said finally sank in. Trent turned to look at him. The boy was grinning, the scar a livid mix of alternating colours in the disco lights.

'You *what*?' Trent shouted, disbelieving. The noise of revelry was so loud that nobody gave them a second glance. The drug-buzz in his head was making it hard to think, but a knot had formed in his stomach that had nothing to do with the coke.

'I showed Bella the picture of you and Mouse. A few days ago.'

Trent looked at Jamie, his eyes wild, not believing what he was hearing. 'You did *what*?'

'That picture; I showed it to Bella. I thought she should know.'

Trent felt his brain scrape against his skull. Around them the crowd started gearing up as the DJ began the countdown; encouraging everybody to grab partners and friends. A drunken sea of linking arms and draping shoulders.

'Why the *fuck* did you do that?'

Jamie leant forward, so that he didn't have to shout, placing his mouth next to Trent's ear. He closed his eyes for a second and breathed in through his nose, consuming the boy's smell. The scent of booze and drugs and cigarettes. Then he whispered in his ear.

'I don't think Mouse wants to fuck you anymore, Trent. I think she knows you're damaged goods.'

Trent recoiled like he'd been stung. Jamie's face looked like cuckoo spit, the skin blank with no expression, but something hiding behind it, eating up whatever was behind the mask.

'What the fuck do you mean?'

'I heard you, Trent. I was outside the alley when she dumped you.'

Trent's face was blank for a moment, then recognition sparked in his eyes. His mouth tightened to a scar.

'That was you? Throwing up on the wall?'

Jamie nodded, smiling.

'And I heard what you said about Bella. That you only went

with her to get close to Mouse. It was *always* Mouse, wasn't it? You were never Heathcliff at all. You were Rochester. Except the mad woman in the attic wasn't your wife.' Jamie smiled, exposing white teeth and blood red gums. 'It was your father.'

Around them the room exploded in cheering as the countdown finished, and people started kissing each other and singing in the new year.

'I'm going to fucking kill you, Jamie! If you've said anything to Mouse about this–'

'Calm down, Daddy's boy, your secret's safe with me. You've got enough explaining to do as it is.' Jamie grinned at the horror on Trent's face. They'd never talked about what happened in the hotel room all those years ago; what Jamie had witnessed. Trent took a step back, rocking on his feet. Jamie's smile widened until the corners of his mouth looked like they were about to split open.

Trent punched his finger into Jamie's chest. 'I never want to see you again, understand? If you fucking...' Spittle flew from his mouth. 'What I did to your face will seem like a scratch. I don't want to see you. I don't want to see you talking to Bella. Or Mouse. Or even fucking looking at them, do you understand?'

Each time he spoke, he pushed his finger into Jamie's chest, knocking him back, emphasising the points. Outside their bubble of hate, Julee Cruise's hypnotic voice slithered out of the speakers like mist as she began singing about not getting hurt this time. Jamie just smiled at Trent.

'Don't worry. You'll never see me again. I'm done with the lot of you. You can go and live out your fucked-up little *ménage a trois* until you drown in your own shit as far as I'm concerned.' And then he leaned forward and stared into Trent's eyes.

'I would have done anything for you; do you know that? But you had to throw me away, just because I saw...'

Before Trent can say anything, Jamie turned away, not letting him see the tears spilling from his eyes, burning down his cheeks and blurring his vision. He stumbled outside into the cold night and took in huge freezing breaths, his whole body shaking, until his heart slowed down and his thoughts settled into the cold familiar train-track of his hurt.

And then he walked round the back of the hotel to his room.

67

BELLA'S ROOM: NOW

The closing synth recedes as Mouse enters Bella's room. Like downstairs, the space is illuminated with candlelight. Shadows dance on the walls and mottled ceiling, blurring perspective.

The girl calling herself Athene is sitting on the floor in the corner of the room. She is wearing the same clothes she had on the day before, when she had walked into Mouse's café like a living coda. It seems impossible that it was only a day ago, but in the flickering flames, with her head bowed, she looks so much like Bella it is as if somebody had set fire to time. The girl is illuminated in varying shades of grey and yellow, as if the light couldn't quite reach her. Books are scattered around her; Bella's diaries, sitting on the floor, spines bent, like dead butterflies. Mouse can see a hole where some of the boards of the wooden floor have been removed, in front of the candle-crammed fireplace.

Bella's secret hideaway, she realises. *Where she kept her thoughts for years and years. The ones she didn't share with me.*

'The game's up, love. We know who you are.' Jamie's voice, harsh and a little too loud, is coming into the space behind her, cracking open the silence. His voice is a direct contrast to the dance of warm light. Mouse isn't sure, but she thinks she sees the girl smile. The mournful guitar bass of Joy Division's 'Decades' begins: Bella's second suicide track.

'Do you? And who's that then, Jamie. Who do you think I am?'

The familiar use of his name, as if he were an old friend, throws him.

'You're Martha.' His voice comes out weak, as if part of it was left behind on its journey from brain to mouth; then adds, unnecessarily, 'Bella's sister. But your name was changed.'

Mouse can definitely see the smile. Trent comes into the room, puffing slightly. When he catches sight of Athene she can actually feel the shock wave coming off him. He hasn't seen the girl before.

'Bella,' she hears him whisper.

'Am I?' says the girl, and Mouse isn't sure if she's answering Jamie or Trent. 'I guess you found my police ID then?'

Jamie nods. 'It was a shit hiding place.'

'And did it say Martha?'

Jamie shrugs.

'Your name would have been changed.'

'Who *are* you then?' Mouse interrupts. The girl turns to look at her. Her eyes are black marbles in the candlelight.

'Or maybe I *am* Martha, but they changed my name because there was no one left to look after me when my house was burnt down.' She glances at Trent, then back to Mouse. '*Don't trust her*; that's what Bella wrote on your picture.' She cocks her head sideways slightly, indicating other pictures, scattered on the floor like playing cards. 'In fact she wrote it on *a lot* of pictures. Why was that, Mouse? You don't mind if I call you Mouse, do you? Why shouldn't she trust you? Did you have something to do with her death?' Athene leans forward slightly. 'What happened in that car, Mouse?'

'This is mad,' Trent says, still staring at Athene. 'You look just like her!'

'Because I slept with him,' Mouse whispers. She can hear Trent take a sharp breath. She stays focused on Athene.

'Who?' Athene says, insisting. 'Who did you sleep with?'

'With Trent.' Tears sting Mouse's eyes as they fall. 'But you already know that, don't you?' She points at the diaries. 'Bella already told you.'

'And is that why you killed her? To get rid of the competition? Is that why she's dead and you two are still alive?'

Mouse looks at her aghast, feeling the slap of her words. 'What? No! I loved her. I thought she loved me. I would never hurt her. What I did with Trent has haunted me my whole adult life.' Mouse wanted to shout it but there was nothing in her, she was wrung out.

'No!' Trent steps forward. 'It wasn't like that! Mouse was in the back of the car! She had nothing to do with it!'

Athene turns and looks at him. Points at a sheet of paper on the floor. 'The police report from that night. You were twice over the legal alcohol limit. A cocktail of drugs in your system. It's a wonder you managed to get behind the wheel, let alone drive.'

Trent looks at the sheet of paper. 'Where did you get that?'

'Didn't Jamie tell you?' Athene says, a look of amazement spread across her face. 'I'm with the police.'

'Bollocks. The police would never act like this,' Jamie scoffs. He is still holding the piece of wood, hanging limply in his hand. He leans on it like a crutch.

Athene looks at him.

'And where did Trent get all those drugs, Jamie? The ones that contributed to him crashing the car?'

Jamie suddenly looks wary. 'What? I–'

Athene points at another piece of paper. 'Drug dealing. Torture porn. Spy cams in the bedrooms of your hotel. The local CID have quite a file on you, Jamie.'

Jamie stares at the sheet on the floor, his face the colour of wet ash in the candlelight.

'But it also turns out you were the go-to man back in the day too. Maybe you're responsible for her death?'

'No! Wait–'

'Maybe if you hadn't stuffed them all full of shit they might not have crashed.'

All that can be heard in the room is the dying music of Joy Division and the guttering sigh of the candle.

Mouse turns and looks at Jamie, disgust peppering her gaze. 'You put spy cams in the rooms?'

'And then posted them online; various spaces on the dark web go bananas for that sort of thing.' Athene's voice is quiet.

'I don't know what you're talking about,' Jamie mutters, but he can't meet anybody's eyes. Trent steps a little away from him, as if he were toxic. Athene stands up, startling them. The motion is fluid, elegant. One second she was on the floor, the next standing, legs apart, leaning forward.

'You know, when I turned eighteen and found out who I was, I was so excited. All my life I'd felt disconnected. Then I was told I had this whole other history! I thought I'd discover a whole past to explore, like walking through the wardrobe and entering Narnia. But what did I find instead?' She pointed down at the diaries. 'Murder and betrayal and a sister who was so twisted out of shape until she was screaming inside.'

'It wasn't like that, Martha,' whispers Mouse.

Athene looks at her, and Mouse is shocked to see pity in her eyes.

'Maybe not, but that's how it ended up, isn't it? With murder and hidden love and abuse.'

Mouse opens her mouth, but no sound comes out.

'And rape.' Athene edges a diary forward with her foot, sliding it across the floor. Mouse stares at it. She feels Trent's grip on her arm, steadying her.

'Rape?' she whispers.

'Bella wrote it down. `He raped me, Mouse.` This is dated two weeks before she died.'

Mouse feels Trent's fingers tightening.

'And this. `Time to run away, Heathcliff. I'm pregnant.`' Athene cocks an eye at Trent. 'Heathcliff. That's you, right?'

Mouse opens her mouth, but nothing comes out. Her voice has been stolen.

'Fucking hell,' Jamie says softly.

'Quite,' Athene says. 'Not only was Bella raped, but she was pregnant with a rape-baby when she was in the crash. If Bella hadn't died, I wouldn't have been surprised if she'd killed herself, the pressure she was under.'

Mouse tries to pull away from Trent, but the grip on her arm is iron.

'She was pregnant?' he says. His voice is full of treacle and knives.

'With your baby,' Athene nods. 'The baby you forced into her. Maybe she told you in the car. Maybe that's why you crashed. To kill her and your baby.'

'This is too much,' Jamie says hoarsely. 'I'm out of here, Martha. Whatever revenge you're doing here I'm not part of it. Yes, I gave them drugs, but I never forced anyone to take them. Pathetically, I thought it would make them like me.'

'Stay where you are, Jamie. At the moment this is just me trying to understand a tragedy. Don't make me turn it official.' Athene's voice is steel.

Jamie tenses, considering leaving anyway, but then seems to deflate, his shoulders dipping. He nods once, slowly.

'I never knew she was pregnant. She never told me.' Trent sighs. He is swaying, but his grip on Mouse's arm is locked.

Athene turns back to look at Trent, her voice hard. 'Why would she? Why would she tell the person who raped her what they'd done? You'd be the last person she'd tell.'

'I didn't rape her.'

Athene snorts.

Trent turns to Mouse, his eyes on fire with grief.

'Let go of me!' she hisses. She doesn't want to be near him, doesn't want to be touched by him.

'It wasn't me! Remember when we slept together? Remember I told you I wasn't father material?'

Mouse struggles to break herself from his grasp, nausea uncurling itself from her stomach, but he just pulls her harder, his face only inches from hers.

'I could see in your eyes that you thought it was a shitty thing to say; that you thought I was being a bastard, but it wasn't that. I couldn't tell you. I felt so ashamed and I couldn't handle anything. All I could do was make some smart comment, and leave.'

She stares at him, seeing the desolation in his eyes, in the frame of him, like he is clothes on the wrong hanger.

'What are you saying to me?' she half shouts, half whispers.

'It was because I *can't* have children, Mouse! That's why I'm not father material! My *dad*–' he spat the word out, 'beat me so badly when I was young he damaged me! Kicked me so hard he fucked up my balls; did something to me inside that meant my sperm was dead. I can't have children, Mouse. Bella's baby wasn't mine!'

Mouse stops struggling, seeing the truth in Trent's eyes. She shakes her head in confusion.

'But she wrote...'

'She wrote she'd been raped, yes, but it wasn't me. And she never told me she was pregnant.'

He wipes his face with his hand, smearing snot and tears across his waxy skin. Then he looks at Athene.

'When I was young, my dad used to... make me do things.'

Mouse looks at him. The pain and sorrow that must have always been living just beneath the surface, but she had never seen. She shakes her head, feeling a well open up; how she'd failed both Trent and Bella. Trent watches her, and shrugs, perhaps thinking she doesn't believe him.

'Ask Jamie. He saw it once. Came into my room and saw my dad...'

'I didn't mean to...' Jamie whispers, in shadows at the back of the room.

Trent turns to face Athene. 'I never raped her. I was a shit boyfriend, and I cheated on her with Mouse, but I never raped your sister.'

Athene stares at him a long beat, then sighs. 'I believe you.'

Trent nods. 'Thank you. I loved Bella. She was beautiful and messed up, and I couldn't be who she wanted me to be while she was alive and I'm sorrier than you can ever know.'

'I know you are. She wrote about you all the time in her diaries. She loved you, even though she knew you were in love with Mouse.'

Trent stares at her, saying nothing.

'*What?*' Mouse whispers.

'She knew?' Trent's face is a patchwork of sorrow.

Athene nods. 'She tried to shape you, and you tried to be Heathcliff for her, but she knew it was an act. She knew you were just like her. That's why she asked you.'

Trent blinks.

'Just like her?' Mouse looks from Athene to Trent. 'What the fuck does that mean?'

Trent looks at Mouse. 'It means I didn't rape Bella, Mouse.' He sighs and swallows, like he's swallowing a bag of hurt. 'But I know who did.'

The room seems to suck itself in, the air becoming hard to find. Mouse looks at Trent, then at Jamie. Jamie shakes his head, back and forth, his eyes never leaving Mouse's.

'I didn't,' he whispers. 'I never touched her. I just photographed...'

'Not Jamie,' says Trent. 'Her father. Bella's father raped her. She told me the night she died.'

68

BELLA'S LAST DAY: JUST BEFORE THE CRASH

'I've got something I need to tell you.'

Bella's arm was wrapped around Trent, and she was leaning into him, whispering in his ear. Mouse was semi-conscious in the back and Bella turned the music low. He was only half listening, his altercation with Jamie still playing in his head. Between the conversation, the drugs and Bella shrouding him like girl-mist, it was hard to negotiate the road. The car was slipping and sliding like it had a will of its own. He should really slow down, but he was too fired up. He thought he'd shut Jamie down with the beating, but all it had done was open him up. Trent risked a glance in the mirror at Mouse. She had her eyes closed and a half bottle of gin in her hand. Bella's tape was playing on the stereo, and she seemed to be lost in the music, a small smile playing on her lips. He wondered what she was thinking about.

'I don't want you to say anything, I just need you to listen,' whispered Bella in his ear.

He'd seen Mouse dancing with Bella in the bar, dancing like they were the only people in the world. He felt sick inside as he drove. Was Bella playing with him? Jamie had said he'd given the picture to her, so Bella must know about him and Mouse. Or at least must know that they slept together. She wouldn't know about what he really felt, of course. What he'd felt ever since the first day he'd seen Mouse, watching the water in the beck like it knew a secret. He'd always hidden that. Not even Mouse knew that. Trent smiled. It was good that she'd closed him down; told him where to go. He was nothing but bad news on burnt paper. Damaged goods. Broken bottles.

'I want you to know that I'm sorry.'

Bella finally penetrated his thoughts. He started to ask her what she meant, but she put her hand over his mouth. Not hard, but gently, her finger across his lips, like he was a child. She pushed gently, parting them and slipping her finger inside, rubbing it over his gums. The action reignited the speed that he spread there himself before they left, and he felt his head disconnecting as the drug took hold. He concentrated on keeping the car in the middle of the road. It had begun to snow again. Bella's voice in his ear was barely above the sound in his own head, slow and cold, seeping its way into him.

'I'm sorry for what happened to you. I'm sorry for what he made you do. What he made you feel.'

Trent felt an iciness fill him. Involuntarily, he clenched his teeth, breaking the skin on Bella's finger. She didn't cry out as he tasted her blood, only continued calmly whispering in his ear.

'Jamie told me. He told me when he gave me the picture, but I already knew. I knew the first time I saw you.'

Trent tried to push her finger out of his mouth with his tongue. She had his arm trapped around her, pinned to the back of the seat with the push of her body, and he was too wasted to take his other arm off the wheel and push her away. He felt a rush of shame as an image of his father flashed across his mind; shame about what he and Mouse had done behind her back, and hatred for Jamie for telling her his secret.

'I already knew because I recognised the shadow that clung to you. I recognised it because I'm the same. It happened to me, too, Trent. That's why I chose you.'

Trent's eyes widened. He tried to turn but Bella's grip on his mouth was too tight, keeping him staring straight ahead.

'What are you–?' he began, but then stopped as Bella spoke, ticking out the truth in word-bombs.

'My father started abusing me before I could even walk, Trent. He used to make me hold his cock while he tickled me. Like it was a game. Like it was fun. Before I knew that what he was doing was wrong.' She kissed his ear. 'Except I always knew it was wrong; deep down. We do, don't we? And as I got older and he told me about secrets it was like a little wall built around my heart.'

Trent stared straight ahead. The snow coming down seemed to twist into a curving tunnel. If only he could concentrate on that, he thought, he might be able to stop the high whine inside his head. Bella's voice continued, snaking down through his ear and wrapping itself around his heart, squeezing it.

'And when people started noticing, we moved here, and for the first time my door had a lock on it, and I had the twisted trees that could survive anything. My ghost forest. I saw the trees and knew I was like them. That no matter what, I would survive. And then I met Mouse.'

'Bella, I–'

She put her bleeding finger on his lip again.

'Shh. Let me finish. I think I was in love with Mouse from the very first day. And no matter how much I tried to push her away, I tried to pull her into me as well. I did what I could; never had her over for sleepovers. Never left her alone with him. Tried to make her hate me and leave, even, but none of it worked. We were stuck with each other. And then you came.'

The song ended, and the opening guitar throb of The Clash began.

'From the first time I saw you I knew you were the one. I knew you'd understand. Even though I couldn't tell you I knew that deep down you would know. Because you're the same. I knew you'd understand about the hiding. About the touching. About the hate and blame and having to let the pressure out by any way you can.'

The tears that fell from Trent's eyes, blurring the road, were so heavy and hard and tight they felt like they cut him as they came out. How could he not have noticed? How could he not have cared enough to see what was happening to her?

Because he was so busy covering up, he realised. Building his own armour, making sure nobody ever got close or looked too carefully.

'Knew I was the one for what?' was all he managed to say.

'To burn down my house,' she whispered, stroking his cheek.

Trent's hands felt like putty; he could barely grip the steering wheel, let alone drive in a straight line.

'My father used to make me do things to him, but now he does things to me. He raped me, Trent. He raped me so deep and so hard that all I want to do is die. And even though he's not here in this car with us he's still raping me because I can't turn it off. In here.' She stroked Trent's head while Joe Strummer sang about how if a person was so bad they shouldn't exist.

'Every time I close my eyes I feel his hands, scraping on my skin like it's the wrapper on a sweet. Even when they're open I think I can see him, just out of view. I see his hungry eyes ripping me. Tearing at me strip by strip. I left Mouse that night in the bar and he finally ate my soul, Trent. I can't do it anymore. I'm going to leave. Tonight. With Mouse. We're old enough now that they can't make us come back. I want you to drive us far away.'

She leant in and kissed the side of his mouth, his cheek, then put her lips back up to his ear.

'And then I want you to come back and burn down Blea Fell. Once we're safe I'm going to phone the police and tell them what he did; get them arrested so the house will be deserted.'

'How? Why will they believe–'

Controlling the car was like trying to steer slush.

'I left evidence. Martha…' Bella stopped speaking, as if her tongue had run away. 'Martha needs to be taken somewhere safe,' she finally finished.

'But what about your mum? Where will she go?'

'My mum?' Bella's voice was a mixture of wonder and sadness: silk floating down a river of warm oil. 'She *knew*, Trent. She knew and didn't do anything. I'll tell you where my mum can go. Where they can both go.'

Mouse mumbled something from the back. Bella turned round and smiled at her, hoping her love could be seen through the pain and the drugs and the enormity of what was about to happen. She grinned, cranked the speaker back up, and said where her mum could go, repeating the words Joe Strummer had just spoken. 'Straight to hell.'

She smiled at Mouse, then turned back, and everything went wrong. Everything sped up and slowed down at the same time and it all went where The Clash said it would.

Straight to hell…

69

BELLA'S ROOM

'When I lost control she grabbed the wheel; tried to get us back on the road. Between everything I'd put inside me; all the drink and drugs, plus what she'd just told me, I think I must have phased out.'

Trent looks between Mouse and Jamie, his eyes dark pools, begging them to understand.

'But it was no good; the road was too icy. She spun the wheel but nothing happened; we just kept going, sliding off the road and... you know the rest.'

He turns away from Mouse's stare, unable to meet her eyes. Instead he faces Athene.

'I'm so sorry, Martha. It was my fault. I should have protected her. I should have known...' His voice breaks. 'I should have been a better person. I can understand why you want revenge but it shouldn't be over her death. That was just a stupid accident.'

'But on the plus side you did what she asked.' Athene's voice is light, but her eyes are neutron stars; heavier than heavy. 'You burned down Blea Fell, like she wanted. You killed our father. You revenged her.'

Trent nods, heavy and slow.

'It didn't bring her back, though, did it?'

That truth hangs in the air. The last notes of The Clash fade out.

'At least we all finally know,' Jamie says quietly. 'Maybe now it can be buried, yeah?'

Jamie's talking to Athene, but he's looking at Trent.

Mouse thinks she can see the boy in him. 'I can't believe I never knew.' Mouse's voice is quiet, guttering like the candles.

'You couldn't. None of us could; she was too good,' said Trent, still looking at Athene, but talking to Mouse.

'What do you mean?'

'She was too good at being Bella. Your Bella. My Bella. Compartmentalising herself so she could survive. Hiding within herself.'

'But why *didn't* she tell? I would have run away with her! I wanted to! I was going to! Before that last night. I always wanted to run away with her, and then on that dance floor she finally asked me. I couldn't have been happier.' Mary sniffs hard, sucking back snot and tears. 'I was so happy I thought I'd die from it.' She catches her breath, realising what she has said.

'Why didn't she tell me?' she finishes softly. 'Why didn't she tell anyone?'

The music has ended, and the only sound was the crackle of the candles. Mouse wonders what will happen now. Now that Martha knew the truth. There really wasn't anything left to revenge, was there?

'*You* didn't, though, did you, Mouse? You didn't tell anyone.'

The words are spoken softly; calmly. Mouse turns slowly around and looks at Athene. The girl is staring at her, her head tilted to one side, like she's trying to work out a crossword clue.

'What do you mean?'

'When Jamie raped you. You didn't tell anyone, did you? Not even Bella.'

The silence that follows her words seems to be driven by a truck, slamming into the room and filling up the space.

'Hang on a minute. It wasn't rape! We were both fucked-up on drugs!' Jamie says, but there's a slight pleading edge to his voice, like it's slipped on a cliff path.

'What?' Trent's voice barely makes it out of his body.

'If you say so, Jamie. I guess only you and Mouse know for sure.' Athene looks away from Jamie and at Mouse.

'That night, when Bella got raped by her father, it was the night she'd spent with you in the bar. Playing pinball. She wrote it down in her diary. She wrote that at least she didn't let you in the car. At least you were safe.' Athene's eyes burn into Mouse. '*Were* you safe? Were you really safe, or were you so connected to my sister that what happened to her happened to you as well?'

Mouse opens her mouth but no sound comes out.

'This is all bollocks. I never raped Mouse. I never raped anyone! I'm sorry your sister got fucked-up by her parents, and I'm sorry you've had a shit life.' Jamie waves the stick he is holding around, taking in the room. 'And I'm sorry Trent burned this place down, killing your dad and pre-revenging you so you don't get the chance to do it yourself, but it's over, yeah?' He looks at her, pity stamped on his face. 'It's all history now. What's the point of dragging it back up in this way?'

Athene looks at Jamie with such sad eyes that Mouse wonders what sort of life she must have had, living in care homes then finding out her past was a horror story.

'When did you get the diaries? When you came up last year?' Mouse asks.

'What makes you think I came up last year?' Athene says, a half smile on her face.

'The shopkeeper said she'd seen you.' Jamie gives a little laugh. 'Said she'd even got the special cigarettes in for you; the ones Bella used to smoke.'

'They were hidden under the floorboards, there, weren't they? The diaries.' Mouse points at the gap by the old fireplace, where the hidey-hole could clearly be seen. Athene reaches down and picks up a book.

'Dad has begun hurting Martha. The whole nightmare is happening again. It won't be long until he's sticking things inside her, like he did to me. I don't think I'm strong enough to stop it.'

Jamie, Mouse and Trent look at the girl calling herself Athene. Mouse feels sick. Athene has modulated her voice, flattening it, and making it a little huskier. Making it more like Bella's.

'What...?' Mouse begins.

'It was written in the diary. Her last diary; the one she had on her.' Athene points at the book on her lap, the pages open. She looks down and begins to read: '*Today I found a cigarette burn on Thing's back. It was so awful. That's how it began with me. Hurting then healing. Blurring the difference. I need to end it. I don't think I can face seeing it happen to someone else. I think I always knew this day would come. That's why I called her Thing. I didn't want her to be a real girl. Because real girls end up broken.*'

Mouse can't speak. All she can do is breathe; little sips of air to try to stop her heart exploding.

Athene lets the book drop, then turns to Trent. 'What happened? What happened when you found my father? Obviously it's not in the diaries. What happened when you came here, after the crash?'

Trent looks at the girl a long moment, and nods. 'Yes. I guess I owe you that.'

70

JUST AFTER THE CRASH

Trent screamed into the night. In the distance he could hear the ambulance, but the noise was behind him, lost in the snowstorm.

When Mouse had blacked out, arm stretched toward the still body of Bella, Trent had run. At first he didn't know what he was doing; just knew he needed to get away from the wailing sirens; from the two girls slowly being covered by snow like broken statues in the road. He ran desperately, blindly, anywhere except at the crash. Finally he looked around him, recognising where he was. He knew he was not far from Bella's house, that if he cut across the moor it was only a mile to Blea Fell. He began to run again.

'Bella!' His scream was whipped away by the wind, broken into a thousand lost promises by the icy splinters of snow that seemed to be cutting into him like knives. Not that it mattered; he barely even felt them. All that mattered was that he stay conscious long enough to stagger across the moor to Blea Fell and confront Bella's father.

Bella.

Trent let out another soul-wrenching sob and dragged his

battered body across the moor. Even though he was half blind from the wind and the snow; even though one of his legs was busted and there was a gash in his head where the blood was frozen; he knew he would reach it. Blea Fell. Where Bella had been twisted and bent by her father so much that she had broken. And now she was dead, driven away by strangers to some morgue while her father slept soundly in his bed.

No way. Wasn't going to happen. Because Trent was going to burn his fucking house down.

'Bella!' he screamed again, howling into the storm. Behind him was a trail of blood, weaving this way and that, but always heading in the right direction.

Because even half-blind and fully-fucked, Trent could find his way to Bella's house. The amount of times they'd Cathy and Heathcliff'd it on the moor; chasing each other across the rough land. Trent would have found the house in a coma. And when he got there he was going to torch it. He was going to find her father, smash his bloody brains in, and set fire to the house, like Bella had asked him.

Because it was the least he could do. Because it was all he could do.

He couldn't bring her back, but he could finish what she'd asked him to do. *Would* finish.

He let out a yelp as he tumbled into a dip in the ground, hidden by the snow. As he fell, he screamed, pain exploding down his leg, scouring away the cold. He rolled over and over, losing all sense of anything apart from the agony, until he was stopped suddenly as he banged against something hard. His breath shot out of him in a plume of white pain. Nausea washed over him, and he wondered if he had smashed his head against a rock.

After a few moments, when the sickness faded, he peered up through the biting snow. In the blur of his vision, dark bony hands seemed to reach out for him, spindly fingers crooked and pointing. He blinked the snow away and jammed his frozen hand into his mouth. As his sight cleared he realised where he was, and let out a cruel laugh; hawking up a glob of blood and viscous matter as he did so.

It wasn't a spectre from the underworld, it was one of Bella's ghost trees. He was lying at the foot of one of the juniper trees.

Grunting, he hauled himself to his feet, swaying slightly. He reached his hand out to the tree to steady himself. On the trunk he saw Bella and Mouse's names carved into the bark, like some kind of message for him.

Gritting his teeth, he pushed himself away from the tree and headed for the house.

71

BELLA'S ROOM

Trent slides down to the floor, his back against the mildewed wall. The next track on Bella's death-mix has begun playing softly; Placebo's 'Every you and every me'. Bella's third choice. He reaches into his jacket and pulls out a soft pack of Luckys.

'Their car was gone from in front of the house. I looked in the garage, but that was empty too. I thought there was nobody home. I guessed the police must have called. The hospital or whatever.' He looks at each of them in turn. 'But what was there was a can of petrol, sat in the corner of the garage. You remember how Bella's dad used to keep a can for the generator, cos the electric was always going off?'

'It still does,' Mouse says.

He nods. 'It seemed like a sign to me. I picked it up and took it into the house. Started splashing it all over.' He looks at Athene. 'I thought there was nobody there.'

'But there was.'

Trent takes in a long, shaky sigh. 'Yes. Your dad had locked himself in the study. He must have heard me ranting when I broke in. Talking about him and Bella. Psyching myself up to torch the place.

'Once I knew he was there it only made me madder. Half with him and what he'd done to Bella, half with me and what I'd failed to do for her. I tried breaking the study door down. Kicked it with my boots and smashed it with my fists. I was screaming at him. Bleeding and crying and blaming, but the door didn't budge. After a while I just...' Trent shrugs and pulls out a Zippo from his pocket. To Mouse it looks exactly like the Zippo Athene has. The same Zippo Bella had. '...I ran out of steam. I just sat down in the chair by the fire and lit a cigarette.'

As if to illustrate the memory, Trent snaps up the lid of the Zippo, the metal spinning candlelight off it the colour of butter.

'And then I smoked my cigarette, all the time telling your father what I was going to do with him; how I was going to pay him back for all the things he did to your sister.'

Trent stares at Athene, his eyes containing all the flames in the room.

'And when I'd finished my smoke I placed it on the arm of the chair, upright to let it burn itself out.'

Trent places his cigarette carefully on the wooden floor, the filter on the ground with the tube containing the tobacco pointing up like a roman candle.

'And then I light another. And I smoke it and place it next to the first. Like a cigarette clock. I think that I'll just sit there and wait him out. At some point he'll come out of the room and I'll beat him to a pulp. Then I'll burn the place down. No hurry. So I just sit there, smoking and making my cigarette stopwatch.'

In the silence that follows Mouse suddenly understands; gets what Trent is saying. 'Until you fall asleep.'

Trent nods. 'Passed out. Fell unconscious. Whatever. Do you remember what you said to me, Mouse? That last time? When I was in your room.'

Mouse nods. 'I said that one of these days you were going to burn the house down.'

He dips his head slightly, acknowledging. 'And you were right. When I came to, the place was full of smoke and the police were pulling me out. Apparently when I found out I'd killed him all I did was laugh.'

He shrugs. 'I can't remember.'

'That's why you stayed in prison so long,' Mouse says. 'Because you didn't show any remorse.'

Trent closes his eyes and leans his head back on the wall behind him. Out of the small phone speaker, Brian Molko sang about how there had never been so much at stake. Finally Mouse takes his hand and squeezes it, before looking at Athene.

'So how bloody sad is this? You spend your childhood in a home, then find out who you are, only to discover that your sister was killed in a tragic accident, and your parents were monsters. Then you come here for closure or whatever, and find the diaries, and a whole new shitstorm is opened up, and you think Bella might have been murdered.'

Mouse looks around at the diaries and the candles.

'And maybe you think you can get revenge, but the fact is you're too late. We've already done it for you. Trent sending himself to prison. Me shutting myself down and never leaving, when all I ever wanted was to leave this fucking village and live somewhere with Bella. There's nothing you could possibly do to us that we haven't already done to ourselves.'

Mouse feels Trent squeeze her hand back.

'Can I say something now?' Athene looks at them, still with that half smile playing across her features.

Mouse hitches her breath. 'Sorry, of course.'

'Thank you.' Athene glances at them all in turn, as if to try and work out how everything has fitted together. How everything has come to this one place. Finally she begins to speak.

'Once I found out who I was it was pretty much as you thought. I came up here to try and find out what happened. From the way Bella wrote about you both I didn't think you killed her, but I had to be sure.' She smiles sadly.

'We were so young and fucked-up,' begins Mouse, but Athene puts her hand up to stop her.

'I know. I understand. But as I said, I had to be sure. And now I am. I know neither of you killed her. Not on purpose and not by accident.'

Trent's face creases in confusion.

'What do you mean? I told you she was trying to save us. She didn't crash us on purpose. It wasn't suicide.'

'I know, I'm coming to that, but first we need to correct you on what you got wrong.'

'And what's that?' says Jamie. Mouse had forgotten he was even there.

Athene smiles and spreads her hands wide. 'I'm not Martha.'

Three words. Three words that ring in Mouse's head like a bell from a ghost ship.

'What do you mean? Of course you're Martha! Otherwise how could you–'

'I'm not. I'm sorry but I'm not. My name is Athene.'

Mouse feels the trickle of soil on her neck again. 'But if you're not Martha, who are you?'

'You know who I am.'

Yes, you're Bella, a voice inside her screams, but she knows that can't be true. She shakes her head.

'Do you know that extreme cold can actually help preserve a person's body? Slow down the metabolism?' says the young woman brightly. 'That even as the extremities shut down, the blood rushes to the core areas, protecting and guarding for as long as possible? That even if a person isn't breathing they may still be alive, somewhere deep inside?'

Mouse stares at her in horror, the meaning behind Athene's word sinking in. 'But the injuries...' she begins, but has nowhere to go.

'Wait.' Trent leans forward. 'What do you mean?'

'She was dead,' insists Mouse. 'Half her head was caved in! There was no breath coming out of her mouth!'

'Oh she was dead, all right,' says Athene.

'Then what...' begins Trent, but the look on the girl in front of them silences him.

'Or at least she was when the ambulance arrived. As I said, extreme cold can shut down the extremities, sending all the body's survival capacities to the core areas; protecting the last vestiges of life. The part of the brain known as the amygdala; the vital organs. Even in certain death the body tries to survive.'

'Jesus fucking Christ,' Jamie says.

'He's not here.' Athene smiles at him. 'Jesus Christ. But miracle of miracles, I am.'

'You're her baby. You're Bella's daughter,' Mouse whispers.

72

BELLA'S LAST DAY: THE AMBULANCE

Bella was strapped to the gurney, keeping her as still as possible as the ambulance sped towards the hospital twenty miles away, its sirens screaming across the moor. The paramedics worked hard, but didn't really give her any odds; the damage to her head alone meant she wouldn't be counting buttons any time soon. Still, sometimes the cold slowed down the dying process, lowering the metabolic rate, giving the victim a slim chance. Out of the back windows the second ambulance could be seen, transporting the girl's friend, blue lights scarring across the snow. The police would be searching for the other one, following his blood through the moor, although the weather had turned into full blizzard, making it almost impossible.

'Clear!'

The medic placed the defibrillator pads on the girl's chest and watched the monitor. Her shirt and jacket were bloody ribbons on the ambulance floor where the paramedics had cut them off, looking like streamers at a horror party. The paramedic, Lissy, clenched the corded pads, waiting for the light on the defibrillator unit to turn green. When it did she pulled the triggers, sending a thousand volts into the girl's heart, spasming the muscle, attempting to kick start it back into function. The young body bucked against its straps, then fell back on the gurney.

'It's no go, mate,' said the other medic. 'She's too far gone. And anyway,' he nodded to the damage that had been inflicted on her skull. 'What would be the point?'

Lissy shook her head. She wasn't going to give up just because there was no point. Having no point, in her mind, *was* the point. Otherwise they might as well be judge and jury. One of the things she loved about her job was that she got to help without any of the hindrances of having to decide. All she had to do was turn up and do absolutely everything she could. Others could work out the hard stuff.

'Let's give her our best punt before we write her off. We'll do an intra-c, one more defib and if that doesn't do it call it a wrap. Agreed?'

The other medic nodded. Agreed.

An intracardiac injection, where adrenaline is injected straight into the heart muscle, can sometimes stimulate it back into action, but might also have a price to pay via brain function. Lissy didn't think that would be an issue in this case. Brain function was definitely low on the pecking order of immediate problems. She unlocked the little wall cabinet where the single shot syringe was kept. She brought it up to her face, checking for air bubbles, and removed the plastic cap, exposing the thin needle. Carefully she injected the prone body, sliding the steel deep within her chest, straight to the heart.

Fifteen seconds later they shocked her again. The young body bucked against its ties as the electricity surged through, then lay still. Graveyard still. Morgue still.

Lissy sighed. It had been worth a shot.

'We've got a pulse,' said her colleague unbelievably. 'Fuck a duck but we've got a pulse. Nice one, Igor!'

Lissy felt a surge of energy in her own tired body as she checked the readings on the ECG unit and saw the wavy lines that meant the spark of life was still present.

'Right! The clock is ticking! We need to keep her going until we hit base.'

Lissy stroked the unconscious girl's hair, careful not to snag any of the strands. The hair was matted with blood and what appeared to be engine oil.

She looked at her partner, eyebrows raised. 'Did we get a name?'

'I'm guessing Bella,' he said. 'Her friend kept slipping in and out of consciousness, but she said Bella.'

Lissy nodded and looked down at the girl. She felt a tightening in her head. The broken body they had just shocked couldn't have been more than fifteen. Sixteen, tops.

'Don't worry, Bella, we're taking you to a hospital.'

Lissy picked up the book that came with the girl, flicking through it in case there were any clues as to medical conditions that might be needed to be known.

She looked up when her partner spoke again. He was staring at Bella, a deep frown jigsawing his face.

'You know,' he said slowly, 'I don't think all the damage to her body was done tonight.'

Doctor Ran stared at the images displayed on the illuminated board, deep lines of fatigue giving her forehead the resemblance of a ploughed field. The girl involved in the car crash had multiple injuries and so had been X-rayed for damage, as was routine in any high-impact-related trauma. What was not routine, however, was what the X-rays had revealed.

'Have the police been informed?' she said, her eyes not leaving the illuminated sheets posted up in front of her.

'Yes, doctor.' The nurse shuffled through some papers on his clipboard. 'The room has a constable outside it. Apparently the mother was already on her way with the sister, having been notified when Bella was first admitted, before...' The nurse's voice trailed off.

'Quite,' Ran said.

'They've sent another patrol to the house for the father. The police already here have set up an interview room in the administration block. It was thought better to conduct them here, apparently.'

Ran nodded. In case the girl didn't last the night. In case the mother was needed. It was good that the police were here. It wasn't a situation Ran could deal with on her own. For all she knew the mother was the...

'I'd like to examine the sister. The police won't have anybody available on New Year's Eve. All the police doctors will be in town, dealing with fights.'

Now it was the nurse's turn to nod.

'And no change?' Ran asked.

'No. The girl is breathing with assistance, but no high-brain function detected. The damage done from the accident seems to be beyond repair. As far as diagnosis, it seems that Bella will remain, if she *does* remain, in a permanent vegetative state. Brain dead.'

Ran nodded again, unsurprised. The X-rays showed severe swelling caused by the impact of the brain against the wall of the skull during the accident. That alone would be life threatening, given also the oxygen starvation caused by her heart stopping. They had removed a small portion of her skull to attempt to alleviate the pressure, and syphoned away the excess blood that threatened to drown her from the inside. There was nothing they could do about the six inch rip in her brain where part of the windscreen casing had speared its way in through the soft tissue of her temple deep into her hippocampus. The fact that she was functioning at all was some sort of miracle.

Ran swallowed. 'And the baby? How old is the foetus?'

'No more than sixteen weeks. There's no way the baby will live if we c-section the mother now.'

Ran nodded again. She was beginning to feel like one of those novelty dogs on the dash of old people's cars. She grimaced. 'Normally, of course, it would be up to her parents to make the decision.'

'Whether to cessate intervention,' the nurse said, nodding. 'But given the circumstances, with the police involvement and the baby...'

'That gives us a bit of a moral dilemma then, doesn't it?' Ran said, biting her lip

~

Two weeks later

Bella was not breathing, at least not in the normal sense of the word. The noise the apparatus that squeezed air into her lungs made was too regular to be mistaken for breathing. Too regular and too sad and too mechanical. The girl's skin was waxy. In the hospital bed she looked tiny, like she had been shrunk.

Doctor Ran looked down at her. Even in such a relatively small amount of time, the baby growing inside her had become more noticeable, pushing out against her abdomen under the thin hospital sheet. The scene was somehow creepy, with the sterile room and the tiny pregnant girl with no brain. Ran felt like she was party to some terrible experiment.

'And her father is dead?'

The inspector nodded, staring down in morbid fascination at the girl. 'Killed in a fire by the boyfriend. Apparently the father had locked himself in his study, but the smoke overcame him and he asphyxiated.'

Ran wiped a hand over her tired eyes.

'And the mother?'

'Held under section one of the MHA. It's not clear how much she knew about what was going on, maybe it never will be. She seems to have retreated into herself.'

'What a fucking mess. What about the sister; Martha?'

The inspector nodded.

'Signs of early abuse. Cigarette burns. Cuts. Nothing like Bella, of course, but one can only imagine what would have happened if she hadn't come to our attention by Bella's accident.'

'Plus what was written in the diary, of course.'

'Yes,' said the inspector quietly. 'Plus that.'

They both looked at the girl. If Ran squinted her eyes, she could almost pretend the girl was merely sleeping. Of course, she'd need to squint her ears as well.

'So what happens now?'

'Difficult. Technically the girl has no responsible adult now, so is under the care of the state. We've sought clarification as to whether a termination is legal in this situation. It's my understanding that there is no medical reason why...?' The inspector's words petered out, as if the path they were on had run out and become surrounded by forest.

'No, medically there is no risk to Bella's life in taking the baby to term. Morally, on the other hand...'

Ran found herself on the same path. In the same forest. 'She would just become a human incubator, with no moral agency of her own.'

'She has no chance of recovery?'

'She's dead, inspector. She was dead when she went head first through that windscreen. She was dead when she lay in the snow. She'll be dead when she gives birth to her daughter. She's just...' Ran shrugged hopelessly, '...process now. The end of an equation. Who knows she's here?'

'Almost no one. It was considered... apposite to release a statement saying that the girl involved in the crash was a fatality.'

'Which is technically true.'

'Indeed.'

'What about her friends?'

'Difficult. They are children, and as *in loco* guardians of Bella and her child we have to think what is best for them. It has been decided at present not to inform them of the full facts. They have been told that Bella never regained consciousness after the crash and that she was pronounced brain dead in hospital. The boy is currently on remand awaiting trial for the murder of the father, and possible manslaughter of Bella. The girl is under supervision of her doctor. She appears to have suffered a breakdown. Even if it was considered appropriate to tell her, now would not be the time.'

Ran nodded again. The room fell silent, apart from the hiss and click and gurgling moan of the ventilator.

'So we wait. And the longer we wait the less options we have.'

Five months later

'You're doing really well, Bella! Just a few minutes more!'

The machine that had kept her breathing clicked and ticked, and made its groaning backwards scream, like it was sucking air out of her; not pushing it in.

The five months that Bella had laid in her bed had made her seem more like a painting than a real girl. Her skin had turned from shine to wax and finally to the colour of rain-wet dough; and her hair was like thin string. As her body automatic-piloted its way through the birth, her face made no expression at all.

A full theatre team was present for the delivery, but the atmosphere was strange. None of the normal familial banter was in attendance. Usually the patient was anaesthetised; rendered unconscious while whatever operation was being carried out, so the fact that the patient wasn't answering back or engaging with the team was not unusual. But Bella wasn't only non-commutative, she was absent. There was no spark or consciousness there. She was... nothing. At the centre of all the machines – the ventilator and the monitoring devices and the drip – there was nothing of Bella. Only a black hole where a girl used to be.

And inside her a human being, grown without emotional input or meaning. Doctor Ran, observing from the edge of the room, felt an enormous sadness. She hoped that somewhere deep within Bella there was a spark of consciousness, or feeling. Something for her to understand the enormous gift she was giving. There had been a meeting as to whether a c-section should have been performed. Whether that might be safer for mother and daughter, but Ran had argued against it.

'This is the only thing her body wants to do!' she had said. 'She can't eat or breathe without mechanical assistance. She can't think. She can't look after any of her needs. She can't feel the weight of her baby inside her. But she can give birth!' Ran leaned forward across the table, boring her eyes into the suits that had responsibility for the husk that had once been Bella. 'Let's not take away the only thing her body can do. Her B-contractions have already begun. With the absence of any cerebral anxiety, the chances of the birth being anything but a biological certainty are slim.'

'But surely she needs to be conscious to participate?' said one of the civil servants, perplexed. 'Push, or what have you.'

Ran had smiled. 'Believe it or not, the contractions will happen all by themselves. It might be a slower process, but none the worse for it. Plus there will be a full natal team on hand in case anything goes wrong.'

'But isn't it a bit... freaky. I mean she's brain dead, right?' The court officer looked at her, his brow creased.

Ran nodded.

'So it's like the baby is coming out of a corpse.' The man shuddered. 'A living corpse.'

There was silence in the room. Ran looked out of the window for a moment, collecting her thoughts. On the moor she could see a lone lapwing, tipping against the wind.

'Look, her body wants to give birth. It's the only reason we haven't ceased intervention up to now, yes?' The man had nodded. 'And when the baby *is* born, by whatever method, then all the mechanical aids will be removed, and Bella will be allowed to rest, yes?' Again he nodded.

Ran looked at him, willing him to understand. 'Then let her do this one thing. It is the entire purpose of her existence! Even though she isn't aware on a conscious level, she's aware on a biological level. Over the last five months her body has built itself around her baby. It's a miracle, really. All of her that remains, remains so that she can give birth; produce another human being. Let's not take that away from her, otherwise what is she? Just meat? Just packaging?'

Ran had held her breath, until finally the man had nodded slightly. 'How will the baby be named? If Bella can't and nobody else is left? Will she just be assigned one? Has this happened before?'

Ran looked at him. 'Not this, obviously. This is pretty much unique, as far as I can see. But like this. When the mother has died in childbirth or something. Is there a procedure?'

'As it happens, in this case we already have a name.'

The officer raised his eyebrows, questioning. 'How come?'

'Bella had written it down in her diary. It was one of the reasons we made the original decision to continue the birth, actually. Bella had decided herself not to have a termination. She was going to run away. She had been planning it for some time, apparently. She had just been waiting until she was sixteen, so that she couldn't be forced back.'

'But she wouldn't have been! Once the abuse had been established she would have been removed from–'

'That's the point, though, isn't it? The abuse often *isn't* established. The abuser is very good at covering up their tracks. Controlling their victims. And if, as seems the case, the abuse had been carrying on for a long time, all through childhood, then there are all sorts of psychological difficulties. Abuse wrapped up in love and need.'

Ran wiped a surgical-gloved hand over her eyes, dragging herself back into the present.

'She's coming, Bella! You're doing so well!'

Click. Wheeze. Tick. Beep.

No grunting. No screaming. No crying. Just the machines and the absence of a girl.

Until there was crying; wet and gurgly as one was born and brought out into the world.

'She's here, Bella! You have a beautiful baby girl!'

Ran felt hard tears falling from her eyes as she smiled.

'Hello, baby,' she whispered, as the cord was cut on the infant and she was swaddled and placed on Bella's chest. 'You should be so proud of your mum. She lived long past when she should, just so you could be born.'

73

BELLA'S ROOM

'They kept her going until she came to term, and then she gave birth to me.' Athene stares at the flickering candles, her face a map of the life she has lived. Her marble eyes shine in the yellow glow. 'Even though Bella was for all intents and purposes dead, she still managed to have enough in her for me to live.'

'I don't believe it,' Jamie says, his voice a mix of fascination and disgust. 'They said she was dead.'

'She was, legally speaking. When stem brain function ceases, and the person can only be kept alive through auxiliary means, then that person is legally dead. For the first few months after the accident, Bella was brain dead, but still with some stem function. Then after that... well they kept her going as a kind of biological birth support system.'

'But why didn't we...' Mouse can't take it in. She stares at Athene, seeing Bella melt out of her. She thinks of her friend, alone in a hospital room somewhere, being kept breathing by a machine, her body nothing but a birth-clock.

'Hear about it? You did. Like you said, she was dead. Her father was dead. Her mother was certified. Trent was up for murder and…' Athene pauses for a beat. 'You didn't come out too well in the diaries. Plus you were a child. Your parents were told, of course. What they decided was entirely up to them.'

'My parents knew?' Mouse's brain was whirling. 'And they never told me?'

'I imagine they were protecting you. The guilt you felt for her death would only have increased if you knew the truth.'

Mouse shakes her head, trying to slot in all the new information. 'So you're Bella's daughter? Bella and…'

'Her father, yes,' says Athene simply.

'No wonder you hate us.' Trent's voice is rough with emotion. Athene looks at him, surprised.

'I don't hate you. Without you and Mouse my mother's life would have been unbearable. You both allowed her to pen a narrative that made it…' she shrugs. 'It's all in the diaries.'

'But why this then, coming up here for revenge?'

Athene gives them a big smile that doesn't reach her eyes. In fact it barely reaches her mouth.

'I'd have thought that was obvious. I came up to find out who murdered my mother.'

The silence that fills the room comes in moments, still frames that layer upon each other.

'But I thought you said…' Trent begins before Athene cuts him off.

'What happened to your wife, Jamie?'

'Sorry?' Mouse's head is spinning. 'Louise? What's Jamie's wife got to do with this?'

Athene ignores her. Jamie seems to have become smaller. Stiller. With the attention on him, he looks like a frightened rabbit.

'She left me,' he says softly.

'She did, didn't she?' Athene says. 'And why was that, I wonder?'

Jamie licks his lips and seems to sag a little more, resting heavily on the broken length of wood. 'It just didn't work out.'

'Right. That's probably it. Not because of the things you posted on the web, then? Not because of the torture videos and the rape-porn?'

'What? What videos?' Mouse says. What Athene had said earlier about spy cams whirls in her head. About Jamie being investigated. Mouse stares at him, feeling sick.

Jamie licks his lips again, his eyes skimming, unable to focus on any of them. 'Look, I just liked to watch, okay? I've always liked to watch. It's not a crime.'

'Oh but it is, Jamie! I really am in the police, by the way; joined straight from school. Do you know you can do degrees in policing these days? Not just Criminology, but actual detectiving? Due to my particular circumstances, as you can imagine, I specialised in abuse and the trauma it can cause.'

'I'm not sure how–' Trent began.

'Operation Bayonet. Ring any bells?' Athene looks at him brightly.

'Fuck you,' snarls Jamie. Mouse stares at him, open-mouthed. The violence in his voice seems to cut through the room. 'I don't know what operation you're talking about. Tell it to the others if you like; this has got nothing to do with me. I'm sorry I sold your mum Ecstasy but I'm not responsible for her fuck-up. I'm sorry about what happened with her dad; it must have been awful, but it's got nothing to do with m–'

'It was a Danish police operation to take down Hansa, a dark web marketplace,' Athene continues, as if he hadn't even spoken. 'I say Danish, but it was global, really. Makes sense, right? I mean the web is global so you need global cooperation if you're going to tackle it.'

'Bye.' Jamie turns towards the door and begins walking away.

'That's where we found all the pictures you've been posting.'

Jamie stops, one hand on the handle, the other still clutching the shard of wood. He turns back to stare at Athene, a puzzled look creasing his face. In the candlelight it seems, to Mouse, like his face has become jigsawed; made up of lots of bits that don't quite fit together.

'What pictures?'

Athene smiles at him. 'Do you think just because you used a VPN you were untraceable? You think you're invincible sitting in the dark with your computer?' Athene makes a tutting noise, like a toy train. 'Not these days, I'm afraid. The boys and girls in blue have their own encryption experts.'

'*What* pictures?' Trent repeats the question, echoing Jamie.

Athene stops smiling. 'All of them. All the ones he posted of his guests. From the cameras he'd hidden in the rooms. Of him having sex with them. I imagine he must have shown them the footage and blackmailed them; extorting money to stop him posting them to friends and relatives. Quite a nice little scam.'

'I...' Jamie began, but no other words came out, blocked as if there was a dam in his throat.

'Except he posted them anyway. Shared them with like-minded people online. Traded them.'

'What do you mean?' Mouse whispers.

'I mean like a club that collects people to abuse. They trade pictures and details like trophies.'

'Jesus.' Trent's voice is papered with horror.

'All of which is being investigated by the cyber-crime squad. Horrible, but nothing really to do with me. We only became involved because of the photograph of his wife.'

'His wife? I don't understand. What's his wife got to do with anything?'

Athene looks at Mouse, then at Trent, then finally at Jamie. 'Tell them how your wife died, Jamie.'

The silence seems to stretch, getting tighter and tighter.

Jamie's eyes bore into Athene's, wide like he's drowning and she was the final wave that would take him under. And then he sighs, blinking.

'She died in a crash,' he says finally, a small smile blossoming on his face like a tumour. 'She lost control of her car and skidded off the road.'

'*What?*' Mouse says, a terrible sense of dread creeping over her. 'I thought she–'

But she doesn't get to say any more because Jamie swings the length of wood he had been leaning on into the side of Trent's head with a sickening crunch.

74

BELLA'S ROOM

Mouse watches in horror as the wood connects with Trent's head. One second, Jamie is shaking his head, a small smile playing around his lips, the next he is swinging the splintered piece of wood he had been using as a crutch. Mouse actually felt the air shift as it swung, felt the impact as it connected with Trent's head. Trent had been rising to his feet, but when the wood hit he fell down again as if he was on elastic, and began twitching.

Even as Mouse snaps out of the moment and reacts; reaching out, Jamie turns and kicks her in the stomach. As his boot sinks into her, Mouse doubles over, feeling the pain in her throat as the air explodes out, closely followed by vomit. The violence is stunning in its swiftness. As she bends, clutching her midriff, Jamie brings his knee up, cracking it into her jaw. An electric eel of white pain burrows into her brain, greying out her sight for a beat.

Why? is all she can think, but no answer comes. What comes is Jamie stepping over her and striding towards Athene.

'You fucking bitch; you're just like your mother; just like her little toy friend.'

Toy friend. Deep inside Mouse, she realises he is talking about her. That *she* is the toy friend.

Athene begins to rise, her arm pulled back, but Jamie steps forward and rams his elbow into her face, like he is trying to drive it through her and out the other side. Mouse hears Athene's cheekbone snap as Jamie telegraphs down. The noise isn't like a twig breaking; it's like a chicken carcass being thrown against a wall. Athene falls hard against the wooden boards. Mouse tries to stand; to help, but she can't move. Jamie punches Athene twice in the soft part of her temple, then he straightens, staring down at her. He raises his foot, and for one awful second Mouse thinks he is going to bring his boot down, crushing her head. Instead he takes a deep breath and lowers it again, as if the moment has passed.

The whole thing has taken only a few seconds. He looks down and spits on Athene then walks slowly back to Trent, who lies unconscious on the floor. He reaches down and rummages in the pockets of his jacket, pulling out the car keys. Then he picks up the Zippo that had fallen from Trent's fingers when he had been struck. Weakly, Trent tries to grab his trouser leg.

'Not so fucking nice being on the other side, is it?' Jamie says, standing. Then he turns and looks at Mouse, watching as she dry-heaves pain onto the floor. He smiles. 'This is for you,' mimicking the words Trent had said all those years ago in the school corridor before scarring Jamie.

'No!' Even shouting the single word opens a blossom of pain around her jaw.

Jamie's smile grows wider, then he stamps his foot down, breaking Trent's fingers. Trent lets out a moan, too near unconsciousness to even scream.

Why? mouths Mouse, eyes wide, unable to look away.

When Jamie lifts his boot again, Trent's hand looks like a squashed spider, his fingers pointing in strange, horrible angles.

She still can't speak; all that comes out is a small squeak. Jamie grins at her, his lips pulled back to expose his gums. He puts his hand up to his ear.

'What's that, Mouse?' He looks sideways at her, tilting his head, then raises his hand as if something had just occurred to him. 'You know, that's the same squeaking you made that night, when we were jazzing it up against the pinball machine.' He smiles and glances at Trent, semi-conscious and bleeding on the floor, then at Athene, who looks dazed from the punch, her cheek a broken flower. 'Well, I'd love to stay and chat, but it sounds like I'm completely fucked, so I'm going to do what Trent failed to do. I'm going to burn this shit heap down to the ground.'

Jamie's gaze lingers over her like she's a meal, then he turns and walks out of the room. Just before he crosses the doorway he pauses, turns back slowly and studies them.

'Although when I say fucked…' He walks back into the room and stands over Athene. 'You keep on saying "we", but I don't hear any backup. If this really was a legitimate police operation there'd be a dozen officers here by now.'

Jamie looks around theatrically. 'Hello! Come and arrest me!'

He waits a few moments, then winks. 'It's just you, isn't it? You looked into your mum's death and thought you'd found something. Thought you'd come up here and check it out.' He kneels down in front of Athene. 'What? What did you think you'd found? Something about my wife?'

'What's going on, Jamie?' Mouse asks. 'For fuck's sake! Why did you hit–'

'Shut up.'

Mouse shuts up. Jamie's voice sounds dead and dry and eaten up from the inside. There seems to be nothing left of the Jamie from only a few moments ago. Athene spits blood out onto the floor.

'Died in a car crash,' she mumbled.

Jamie nodded, his mouth turned down in a parody of sadness. 'That's right. It was terribly tragic, but accidents happen. Cars crash.'

'Mechanical failure.' The words come out in short bursts. Mouse thinks maybe a rib is broken. 'Bolt sheared through on the steering column.'

'Really?' Jamie raises his eyebrows. 'It *was* quite an old car. And as I told the police at the time, we weren't very vigilant with the servicing and things. Always very busy with the pub and hotel.'

'Like Trent's car. Like Bella.'

The words are quiet, almost mushy from the swelling that is beginning to misshape Athene's mouth, but they are clear, and break over the room like a wave.

Mouse stares at her. Athene's head is sunk on her chest, with her hair hanging down, covering half her face.

'Yes,' says Jamie happily. 'Just like that.'

Mouse can see Trent trying to get to his feet, but there's something wrong with his co-ordination.

'Wouldn't have found out if you hadn't posted...' Athene hisses in another shallow breath and gobs out another marble of blood, '...on the dark web. Two pictures of the crashes. What you wrote. Made me look back into it. The report noted the sheared bolt in Trent's car, but assumed it was when it crashed.'

Athene bares her teeth. Her gums are covered in blood, black in the low candlelight. Half the candles have already burnt down.

'Not *why* it crashed.'

'What did he write?' Trent's voice sounds like broken spanners. 'About the crash?'

Jamie gave a little laugh that seemed to have got twisted somewhere inside.

'*Spot the difference*. You know, like those pictures in the paper where they look identical but there are subtle changes?' He smiles and reaches out a hand, stroking Athene's face. 'Except the difference here was minimal. They were both fucking bitches and they were both going to go to the police.'

Jamie stands.

'That's why they had to die. The difference was that in Bella's case there was an extra bonus: you were all going to die too.'

75

BEFORE THE BELLS

'Fuck off, Jamie.' Bella looked out into the night, smoking her cigarette. She felt calm and sane for the first time in days. It was as if the Waltzer had spun all the confusion out of her. The self-hatred she had felt about being raped. The guilt she had carried about how she had treated Trent and Mouse: all gone. It was as if a tidal wave had broken, leaving everything washed clean.

'But she cheated on you, Bella. They both did!'

'I don't care.' She blew out a tight vortex of smoke. Mingled with her breath hitting the cold air it was like she was a dragon. She grinned. She *was* a dragon and she was going to skip this shit with the princess *and* the prince. 'In fact I don't even blame them. If I was them I'd probably do the same.'

'But the picture! And what he did to you!'

'He didn't do anything to me I didn't deserve.' Bella took another drag.

'But I saw you! The cuts and the scars!'

Although the night was cold, and the area around the back of the pub was deserted, the temperature seemed to drop to absolute zero as Bella slowly turned to look at the boy.

'What?'

'I saw. When I was on the moor. I was looking for birds,' he finished lamely, seeing the hardness in her eyes.

'You were *spying* on me, Jamie? Like some fucking pervert?'

'No!' He took a step backward, banging up against the metal bin. 'I was looking for birds! I just happened to...' He blinked, then stuck out his lip. 'It doesn't matter. The point is I know, all right? I know he beats you up.'

'You're pathetic, Jamie, you know that?' Bella's eyes were two tunnels of dark road. 'No wonder Trent dumped you as a friend. Creeping around. Taking your pictures. Trying to pull people apart. Well, I don't care, okay? Me and Trent and Mouse are solid. There's nothing you can do that will ever break that.'

Jamie looked like he was about to cry. His face seemed to blur with pain, but then settled, all emotion wiped clear. He slug-licked his lips.

'I fucked her, you know. Your precious Mouse.'

If the air had been absolute zero before, now it had gone quantum-cold. The only heat was the tip of Bella's cigarette, glowing like a fuse.

'Sorry?'

'Miss fucking perfect! I fucked her the night you left with your pissed dad! Me and her fucked like goats!' Jamie smiled when he saw Bella flinch. He flicked a look at the mound of her breasts then leaned in. 'She was so fucking dirty, as well.'

'But she could barely stand up when I left,' said Bella slowly. 'She was going to call a taxi and go home. How could you...?'

Too late, Jamie realised his error. He took a step back. 'Yeah well she came-to after we... had a livener.'

'A livener?' Now it was Bella's turn to step in. Close.

Jamie could see the disbelief etched on her face.

'What did you do, Jamie?' she leaned forward, looking into his eyes. 'Did you give her more drugs? What drugs?'

He tried to take another step back, but he was tight against the bin. 'I didn't! We... I mean it just happened. Between us.'

Something like horror swept across Bella's features. Like horror, but much much worse. Realisation.

'And I left her with you. I left her with you and went with...' An awful smile split her face, scarring across her features. She smiled so hard that her lips went white against her teeth. It was the sort of smile that would normally be made with a knife.

'You fucking bastard, Jamie. I wish Trent had cut your heart out.'

'Bella, I didn't–'

'Save it for the police, you raping fuck,' she spat, cutting him off. 'If I were you I'd go and kill myself now, because by tomorrow I'll have gotten out of Mouse whatever shit you told her happened and made her remember the truth, and then you'll be fucked.'

Bella looked at him hard, nodded, then turned and walked back inside.

Jamie watched her go, feeling empty, as if he'd been spilled. He didn't try to stop her, or persuade her it was different than how she had told it; what would be the point? He'd looked in her eyes. There was no coming back from her expression.

No coming back at all.

Only one choice left.

Jamie took a deep breath, wrapped his arms around himself, and went to see Trent for the last time.

76

BLEA FELL

'You know it's really simple to mess with the steering column. Don't believe all those films about cutting brake lines or any of that bollocks. All you need in those old cars is to take the steering wheel off and open up the connecting bolt on the shaft. A flathead screwdriver and a spanner will do it. Takes about two minutes. Then bang down on the bolt with the screwdriver and...' He shrugged, smiling.

'You killed her,' Trent said, his words gaining strength. 'It wasn't skidding on the ice, it was you.'

'If you do it right, the car will drive fine to begin with, then the steering wheel gets looser and looser as time goes on until...' Jamie smiles. 'Doesn't matter how much you spin it, it just goes round and round.'

'You killed Bella and your wife,' says Athene flatly. A statement, not a question.

Jamie shrugs. 'They were going to the police; what else would I do?'

'And you were trying to kill us.' Mouse's voice is full of loathing.

'Of course I fucking was. Trent had made it clear he never wanted to see me again, and you...' Jamie's smile switches on and off. 'Well, you were probably going to start thinking I was some sort of monster.'

Trent tries to stand. Jamie walks over and brings his boot down on his scrambling leg. The snap is clearly audible just before the scream.

'And now I can finish the job.'

Trent collapses back to the floor, clutching his shattered knee.

'All three of you were in that car, although one of you was *inside* someone who was inside that car so it seems kind of right that you should all be in this room when I burn the place down.'

He stares at Athene, breathing heavily on the floor.

'You know, I really hope it was this room your mum was raped in, cos it would have a nice circular feel about it all.'

He takes his phone out of his pocket and snaps off a photo.

'One for the scrapbook,' he says, grinning, then turns and leaves.

Stop him! Mouse tries to say, but the knee to her jaw had stolen her voice. She staggers upright, turning to the door. She can hear Jamie's shoes echoing on the slate of the steps that lead down to the kitchen.

'Don't worry about him; check on Trent!' Athene, her voice wet and mushy from the punch, has managed to stand. Trent is slowly shaking his head, moaning low in his throat. He isn't standing. Looking at the unnatural angle his lower leg juts out, she doubts he'll ever stand again without help. Not that that matters if they're all dead. She turns to Athene.

'We need to get out of here! Jamie said he was going to burn it down!' She knows the house will not burn outright; too much stone and rain to be susceptible to being razed, but there is a lot of wood; a lot of moss and vegetation that has made Blea Fell their home over the decades. She thinks of the burning ghost forest outside; of the cans of petrol lined up against the wall in the kitchen.

She thinks about thick black smoke enveloping them, of dying without a breath. Of dying by the spark of a Zippo that seems to have been at every turn in her life.

'Now!'

She tries to lift Trent, but he is too heavy, and too uncoordinated. She feels panic rising in her, threatening to swamp her.

'It's all right.' Athene grabs Trent's other arm and wrenches it across her shoulder, taking his weight.

'Here, support his head; that blow might have damaged his neck.' Athene is at her side, helping. Mouse nods, and together they lift Trent to his feet.

'Acid,' Trent mumbles, shaking his head. 'I can smell acid.'

'That's not acid, it's petrol,' hisses Athene, using her body to turn them all to face the door. She is right. Mouse can smell the high note of petrol stripping the hairs in her nose. She feels sick with panic. In her mind she can see Jamie, splashing the liquid out of the metal cans onto the surfaces in the derelict kitchen, up the walls and onto the floor. She can actually hear him clumping around, hear the liquid sloshing in their metal containers. With a new feral urgency, she starts dragging Trent to the doorway.

'It's all right, really,' Athene says.

Mouse looks at her incredulously. 'What? We're about to be burned alive!'

'No. Nothing's going to happen. It's going to be all right,' she repeats, grabbing hold of Mouse's arm; holding her tight. Mouse looks into her eyes; sees the truth there.

'How?' she asks. 'How is it going to be all right?'

Athene smiles, only one side of her face is moving because of her busted cheek. Below them there is a *thunk*, hard and sharp, followed by a scream.

'Because there's something Jamie's forgotten.'

77

It takes several seconds for Mouse to unravel the scene as they stumble into Blea Fell's derelict kitchen from the stairs, Trent leaning heavily on her shoulder.

'The candles should have been a bit of a giveaway.' Athene indicates the pale stubs of glowing light cascaded around the room. As she speaks she leans against the wall. Trent slides down it, unable to stand any longer. Just hobbling down the stairs seems to have sapped the small amount of strength he had. 'I mean, just lighting them all would have taken longer than the time I had after I left you, let alone the fact that half of them were burnt down.'

Jamie is on his knees in the middle of the kitchen, one hand keeping himself up by grasping the mottled refectory table, the other hanging loosely by his side. He isn't looking at them, isn't speaking.

'And then there was the shopkeeper, telling you she'd seen me last year, but with different hair.'

Beside him a petrol can lies on its side, liquid guttering out of it in belches and glugs.

'What the fuck?' whispers Trent, staring at Jamie.

Mouse silently agrees. Sticking out of Jamie's shoulder is a wooden splinter of plank, the length of it at right angles to his body.

Thunk. Scream.

The reason it was held in place was two-fold; the rusty spike that must be attached to it, that protruded from Jamie's back like a wet metal finger, and the girl that was firmly holding the other end.

Thunk. Scream.

'The fact is I *didn't* come up here last year,' Athene says. 'It wasn't me the woman saw.'

The girl must have smashed the homemade club into him. Mouse remembers the piece of wood they'd seen outside, with the big rusty nails in it. She stares at her.

'Martha,' Mouse whispers.

'Yes.' Athene limping forward to stand next to her half-sister. 'Told you he'd forgotten something.'

Some-thing, thinks Mouse, remembering Bella's pet name for Martha. She nods, then gasps when Martha pulls back on the wooden stake, ripping the spike out of Jamie's flesh. It releases with a squishy sound like a boot from a bog. Jamie screams and collapses to the floor, grasping at his shoulder.

'She impaled him with a spike!' Trent says hoarsely, still sat on the dirty floor. 'She could have killed him.'

'I was aiming for his head.' Martha's voice isn't like Athene's; it is more like Trent's. There is a roughness there like a burnt painting.

'You can't kill him, no matter what he's done.' Mouse looks pleadingly at the two girls.

'He murdered Bella and tried to kill both of you,' says Martha, not taking her eyes off Jamie. 'He murdered his wife and posted her car crash on the internet. Why the fuck shouldn't we kill him?'

'But you're a police officer!' Mouse says, staring at Athene. 'Surely you can just arrest him? Now you've got the evidence?'

'What evidence? Jamie's not in any of the photos, and whatever physical evidence there might have been – the cars – was destroyed.'

'But the photos! The dark web address or whatever it is. Surely–'

'I lied,' Athene says flatly, staring down at the bleeding man. Jamie was breathing heavily, but was otherwise still, as if listening intently.

'The two crash pictures found by the dark web police operation; it was a fluke that I was attached to the cataloguing. As a new trainee that's the kind of stuff they get us to do. Filing. Indexing digital evidence. I recognised Trent's car straight away.' Athene smiles harshly. 'Why wouldn't I; I had a picture just like it at home, in the file I was given when I turned eighteen.'

'But how did you find Martha?' Trent asks.

'When you join the force they take a DNA sample, so you can be eliminated at a crime scene.' She shrugs. 'I had a match in the system. Martha had a... difficult upbringing. Foster care. Petty crime. She'd been arrested several times.'

'Meant to find each other,' Martha says softly, turning and looking at her sister. Athene smiles and reaches out a hand. Strokes her shoulder.

'Once we found each other, we decided to find out who had killed Bella.'

'Your mother,' Trent, his voice quiet.

'My mother *and* my sister, as we both had the same father. Martha came up here and discovered the diaries. I continued to dig into the web to see who had posted the pictures.'

'And you found Jamie.'

'Not right away. As I said, it was a lie that we knew who it was. To begin with we thought it might be Trent. Or you. When we found the diaries it all looked a little... complicated. Trent cheating on her put both of you in the frame, with maybe even a suicide into the mix.'

'Be much easier these days.' Martha's voice is laced with sadness amongst the sediment of pain. 'You could just be open and form a three-group.'

'But instead Jamie here tries to kill you all, because he thinks Bella is going to make you remember what happened. That it wasn't drug-drunk sex; it was rape.'

Mouse suddenly brings her hand up to her face.

'What is it?' Trent looks at her.

'The night of the crash. Just before we left the disco. Bella danced with me.'

'I remember,' he says. 'Jamie had just told me he'd spilled about the picture.'

'I always thought, after, that what she whispered was about what she was going to do to us. Crash the car. But it wasn't.' Mouse feels tears spring from the well of memories. 'It was about me, not her.'

'What did she say?' Athene's voice is hungry.

'"I'm so sorry,"' Mouse breathes, feeling fresh tears, but this time of love. 'That's what she said. "I'm so sorry." She was talking about what Jamie did to me. She was thinking about me. Even with all she was carrying, she was thinking about me.'

'She loved you,' Athene says simply.

Mouse nods, then looks at Jamie. He stares at her, and all Mouse sees is the boy who had always stared at her, hurt and broken. She shakes her head.

'We still can't kill him. It would be murder. We'd be as bad as him.'

In the silence that fills the room, Mouse feels her heart settle, perhaps for the first time in twenty years. And then Martha's voice cuts through.

'Oh no, we could never be as bad as him.'

Mouse feels her heart beat. Slow and slow. Surely there can't be more?

'Please, let me go,' Jamie says in a small voice.

'Tell her, 'Thene.'

Athene looks at Martha for a beat, then nods. She turns to Mouse, stretching one hand out slightly, then letting it fall.

'Those photos. Of the crashed cars and the blackmail-sex reels? Well, Jamie was very good. There's not one video with him in it. Not his face anyway. No identifying features. The only faces recognisable are the victims.'

'Hence the blackmail,' Martha adds.

'Look, just let me go. Take me to the police. I'm....' There is a strange, hiccupping, cry in the back of his throat. 'I'm sick. Unwell. I need help.'

'I don't understand. What has this got to...' Mouse looks from one girl to the other, then at Jamie.

'Upstairs, when I said only you and him could know what happened that night, by the pinball machine?' Athene gazes at her.

Mouse nods, cold creeping through her bones like vines.

'I know *you* couldn't, because you were drugged.'

'We both were!' Jamie says. 'We were E'd up out–'

'It wasn't Ecstasy; or at least not *only* Ecstasy. And he,' Athene snapped. She flicked her eyes on the kneeling man like she was flicking acid. 'Didn't seem to be on drugs at all.'

Jamie opened his mouth, but no sound came out.

'How did you know it was by a pinball machine,' Mouse says quietly, staring at Athene.

Martha nods to herself, attention still on Jamie.

'That night, the night he raped you,' Athene says softly. 'He filmed it too. While you were unconscious on Rohypnol or whatever he gave you, he...' Athene moves her hands gently, '... he degraded you and dehumanised you and filmed it all.'

Mouse feels a heat spread over her face, even as it drained from her heart.

'Not real,' whispers Jamie to himself. 'Just acting. Not real.'

'No,' Mouse says, shaking her head.

'It's true. He filmed it all.'

Mouse continues to shake her head, not wanting to believe.

'And later, he posted it all. On the web.'

'It's all there, for anyone who knows how to watch.' Martha's voice is hammer hard.

'He said it just happened. That he woke up and...' Mouse's voice trails off.

'But you never believed it, did you?' Athene stares at her, eyes deep pools of sadness in the candlelight. 'Not really. That's why you hesitated last night. When I said I needed somewhere to stay. Why you gave me your mobile. In case–'

'Anyone who has a computer, or a smartphone. Anyone in his sick little group,' Martha continues, as if Athene hadn't spoken.

Mouse looks from Martha to Athene, then at Jamie. Jamie's eyes are wide with pain and fear. Then Mouse looks at the phone held loosely in Athene's hand.

'Show me,' she says.

'No! I need to go to a hospital! I'm–'

'Show me.'

Athene shakes her head.

'Please. I need to see.'

Athene looks at Mouse for a long second, nods, then taps at her phone.

78

THE CRAVEN HEAD: AFTER CLOSING TIME

'Just need to rest for a minute.'

Mouse's words came out slurred, like somebody had covered them in honey. Jamie watched as she slumped against the pinball machine, letting her head fall against the glass covering the playfield.

'Mouse?'

Jamie gave her a little shake. 'Mouse, are you okay?' He tried again, concern on his face. 'Mouse? Can you hear me?'

No answer.

Slowly the expression slipped off his features until all that was left was a kind of blankness, as if his skin was nothing more than dough. He stared at the back of her head, checking for movement. After a moment, he walked away, back into the main bar, checking to make sure no one was there. He'd gotten rid of the last of the stragglers an hour ago; helped them out and locked the door, but sometimes his dad liked to come down. Not so much these days, but it was still worth checking. He walked behind the bar to the door that led through to the staff staircase and listened. Satisfied, he slid the bolt. Nobody was coming down that way to surprise him. Next he walked to the door that led out into the lobby; he'd secured it earlier, but better to be safe than sorry. Once he was sure, he walked back into the games room. Mouse was still where she was when he left her; a little lower maybe. The lights on the scoreboard flickered and strobed above her. He reached out and dimmed the room light, creating shadows around the unconscious girl.

Jamie smiled, his tongue slipping out between his teeth slightly. He could see the gentle rise and fall of her chest against the glass. Where she had slipped down, her dress skirt had risen slightly.

This was going to be so much fun.

Jamie walked back into the bar and pulled his camcorder from under the counter, switching it on. The machine made the little click and *whirr* sound that meant the tape was in and ready for use. He checked the battery indicator light to make sure there was enough juice. Nodding to himself when he saw the green light, he walked further down the bar to the cupboard that housed the crisps and nut refills. He squatted down, rummaging among the boxes, pulling out the small plastic first aid kit they kept. He opened it and removed the travel tub of Vaseline. Bar work was prone to small cuts and burns; broken bottles and boiling water for glass cleaning, so Vaseline was always a handy product to have.

Jamie took the small tub and the camcorder back to the games room. Mouse was still in the same position, with her upper body lain across the pinball machine like she'd been shot. Jamie wondered if he should put her song on, the one from that TV show? Or maybe the track her and bitch-Bella were always dancing to, like they were a couple of dykes.

No, he thought, shaking his head slightly. The noise might wake somebody up. Either Mouse, or his dad. And he didn't want that to happen, did he? Besides, he could always add a music track later. Jamie looked at Mouse's arms, resting loosely on the machine. He smiled. He put down the camcorder and tin of Vaseline on the little round table next to him, then silently picked it up and positioned it behind and to the side of Mouse. Then he placed a bar stool on the table and put the camera on top. He wished he'd bought his tripod down, but didn't want to risk going up for it. He looked through the viewer and tutted. Quietly, he went around the tables grabbing beer mats. One by one he placed them under the back of the camcorder, tilting it down, until he was satisfied he had the correct angle. Then he switched on the camera and waited a moment, making sure the little REC symbol was flashing in the corner of the tiny screen.

After all, he wouldn't be able to go back for a second take.

Jamie took the lid off the Vaseline and walked up behind Mouse, making sure to keep his face forward. Not that it mattered; he'd positioned the camera on Mouse, lying waist-flat on the pinball; him standing upright behind her would mean his head wouldn't even be in shot. He put down the tin of Vaseline and slowly raised Mouse's dress.

79

BLEA FELL KITCHEN

Mouse watches herself, the attack being parcelled up in seconds of hate by the digital counter displayed in the corner of the shot. She feels numb. She thinks she might throw up as she watches Jamie remove her clothes, and the unscrewing of the tub of Vaseline. She wants to turn off the recording but she can't. She can't seem to stop gripping the phone. It is only when it is gently prised from her fingers that she realises she is crying.

'Jesus fucking Christ, Mouse,' whispers Jamie. 'I'm so sorry.' He tries to stand; to walk over to Mouse, but his legs won't do what he wants. Instead he reaches out an arm towards her, then lets it fall. 'It... just happened.'

'Not your fault, Mouse. No shame involved here from you,' says Athene, her voice seeming so thin as to be shadow skin. She glances at the screen, her face unreadable. 'It goes on for another sixteen minutes.'

'And people can watch...?'

The words die in Mouse's throat.

'Yes, he has it posted on the web, where it's shared around

the dark corners and lapped up by pain-freaks and rape-junkies.' Martha's voice is coffin-thick.

'Sometimes they're threatened or blackmailed into it, and sometimes, like you, they're drugged and have no memory.'

'Those ones are quite sought out, apparently. If the victim doesn't even know they've been raped it gives an extra... frisson. Sleeping beauties, they're called.'

'He also posted pictures of Bella, naked in her bathroom, covered in cuts and bruises.'

'He raped you, Mouse,' Athene says. 'And he posted it online so you can be raped again and again by the gaze of strangers.'

Mouse can barely breathe. She looks at Athene, hoping to see something in there that will help her, but all she sees is pity. Then she looks at Martha. Martha's eyes are burning. Martha's eyes are on fire.

'I want to kill him, Mouse. I want to stop him for ending my sister. Bella was going to run away and be happy with you and Trent. Even what our father did to her couldn't break her. She survived all that and was going to be happy, and Jamie stopped that.'

And, finally, Mouse looks at Jamie.

The first notes of 'Only You' leak out into the candlelit room, and from there into her body, wrapping themselves around her heart.

'Only you, Bella,' she whispers.

Mouse stands.

80

BLEA FELL: THE GHOST FOREST

NINE MONTHS LATER

'You know, I can't believe they didn't die; you'd think after burning like they did it would be game over.'

'No way; these trees will outlast God. Their roots are buried in a prehistoric ocean; a little thing like fire isn't going to even break their stride.'

Athene, Mouse, Trent and Martha stare at the stunted juniper trees. Leaves have returned to the majority of them, and in the spring dew they glitter like they have been draped in pearls.

'Bella would love this,' says Mouse. Even though it's still early the air has a hint of the day's warmth in it.

'What?' Athene asks. 'The four of us here, or *why* we're here?'

'Both.' Trent smiles. The scar on the side of his head where Jamie beat him with the wood club gives him a piratical air. Mouse glances at the stick in his hand. The blow caused more than the rakish scars. The headaches and the discoordination were long term; perhaps the longest. Months of physio meant he was out of the wheelchair, but the stick would be permanent.

Mouse stays within easy reach in case he stumbles. 'She would love both.'

'What time does the solicitor get here?' Martha's face is tight, but not from hate or burden, just from anxiousness. The months of labyrinthine legality to determine ownership of Blea Fell had taken their toll. Now the moment was finally here she was nervous. Athene places a hand on her shoulder.

'Any time now.'

Martha nods slightly. She clutches the remainder of Bella's ashes tight to her. When Athene had turned eighteen she had been given her mother's remains. They have placed a proportion in tiny metal vials and hung them from the juniper trees. In the gentle wind they chime against each other, as if they are on a swaying ship. Mouse hopes Bella's ghost can hear them. Later they are going to scatter the rest in Mouse's garden.

Mouse smiles at Trent.

Not just her garden now.

It has been a long journey, sorting out the legal papers as to Blea Fell's ownership, but finally the deeds are Martha and Athene's. After the papers have been signed, then it will be legal for the demolition crew to begin.

'Are you sure it's what you want?' Trent says. 'You could probably sell it for a fortune.'

The women nod.

'Certain. Bella loved the house, but it became wrapped up in her mind with what was happening there. It's all in the diaries. It's so sad. The very first thing she writes is that her bedroom has a lock on the door. This was when she was eleven.'

'I can't believe I never noticed. I'm so sorry.' Mouse looks at them both, but all she sees is Bella.

'*We* never noticed,' Trent adds.

'She never wanted you to.' Martha's voice is soft, like the

wind across the moor. 'But you know what? Reading the diaries, even after all the awfulness that happened to her, she still lived her life fully.' She looks at Mouse. 'She still fell in love. Still lived on her own terms. Whatever was done to her, it didn't break her. She may not have been able to tell you what was happening to her, but she showed you her love, from the first time she met you, to her very last action in the car.'

'"Only you". That wasn't for Heathcliff here.' Athene grins. 'That was all hers and yours.'

'And you mustn't let Jamie take it from you,' Trent says, reaching out and stroking her hand. She looks into his eyes, hoping to see a spark of Bella in there.

'Ah yes, Jamie. Whatever happened to him?' Martha's words whip away in the wind. In the distance, Mouse thinks she can hear a vehicle; a Land Rover, possibly. The solicitor.

'No one in the village seems to know,' Athene says. 'He disappeared into the night. The police searched his hotel and found some rather worrying things. It seems he was suffering from depression. Seeing me reminded him of Bella and happier days, is the thinking. Apparently his wife died in an automobile accident. His car was found near Whitby, along with a note, blaming himself. As far as I know the case has been closed.'

'That's absolutely tragic,' Trent says, his voice full of concern. All four of them exchange a glance.

A car peaked over the hill and started down the track. A Land Rover, Mouse noted, with satisfaction.

'Poor man; do you think we'll ever find out what happened to him? Where he went?' Martha looks at them, wide-eyed. Mouse looks back, thinking of fire and pinball machines.

'What was that track, Trent? The one by The Clash on the mixtape?'

'"Straight to hell",' he says.

'That's the one,' Mouse says with finality, then starts towards the low wall that separates the field from the house. Answering for them all.

When they reach it they turn back and stare at the forest. All the trees have leaves, with many sporting the silver death chimes.

Mouse looks at one in particular.

From this distance, she can't see the initials she and Bella carved, but she knows that they are there.

Protecting their secret.

Under the names is a new carving: a quote from Bella's diary. Emily Bronte.

'I wish I were a girl again, half savage... and free.'

She watches the death bells for a beat, listening to their chimes, remembering how high her and Bella's hearts had soared together.

'What does the C stand for, by the way?' she says, turning to Athene. 'On your police ID. Jamie said that it had the initial "C".'

Athene smiles. 'Athene's my middle name. I took it when I read Bella's diaries. The C is the name she gave me.'

'So what is it?'

Athene's smile widens, and she looks out over the moor.

'The only thing it could be: Cathy.'

Athene grins and runs to catch up with Martha.

Mouse watches her a moment, then over at the trees, listening to the wind as it dances around and through them.

'Only you, Bella,' she whispers. 'Only ever you.'

Then she turns and helps Trent over the low wall, and hand in hand they walk toward Athene and Martha.

The end

'***The murdered haunt their murderers***'

Cathy. *Wuthering Heights*.

ACKNOWLEDGEMENTS

So many people to thank, so let's crack on.

To the people who read, from the first word to the last drink; thank you. There really is no point if you're not there.

Thanks to Chris, Chrissy, Clive, Elisabeth, Gabriel, Joseph, Lily, Loretta, Noney and Phil.

Thanks to Gary and Rodney for technical advice.

Thanks to Jim and Xach for the music short to Bella's diary.

Thanks to Dominique for all the extra miles.

Thanks to Lula for the final cut.

Thanks to all at Bloodhound, who made the whole process so enjoyable.

Thanks to Emily, without whom Bella would not exist.

Finally, Josephine.

Only you, my love.

S.

Printed in Great Britain
by Amazon